FEAST OF ASHES

FEAST OF ASHES

VICTORIA WILLIAMSON

NEEM TREE
PRESS

Published by Neem Tree Press Limited, 2023
Copyright © Victoria Williamson, 2023

Victoria Williamson asserts her rights under the Copyright, Designs and Patents Act 1988 to be recognised as the author of this work

1 3 5 7 9 10 8 6 4 2

Neem Tree Press Limited
95A Ridgmount Gardens, London, WC1E 7AZ
United Kingdom
info@neemtreepress.com
www.neemtreepress.com

A catalogue record for this book is available from the British Library

ISBN 978-1-911107-87-3 Paperback
ISBN 978-1-911107-88-0 Ebook

Printed and bound in Great Britain

My debut YA novel is for Martin, for being the endless font of inspiration and encouragement I needed when my own motivation batteries were running low.

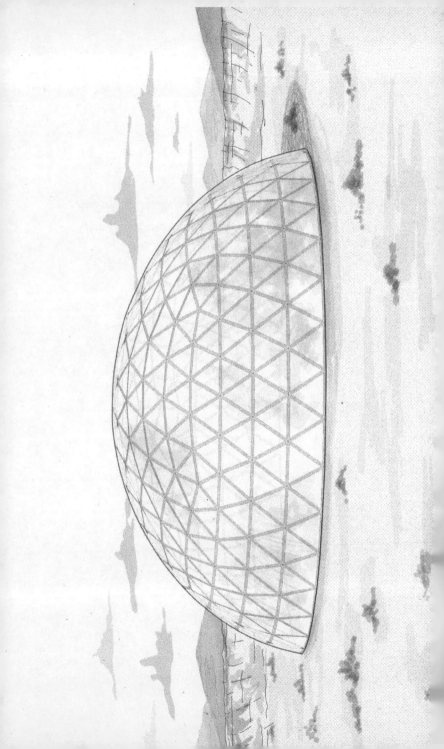

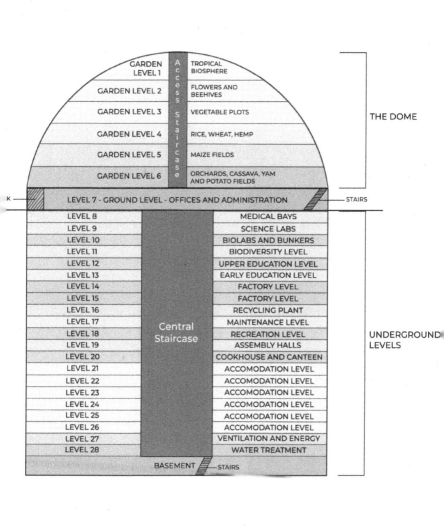

GARDEN LEVEL 1 — TROPICAL BIOSPHERE

GARDEN LEVEL 2 — FLOWERS AND BEEHIVES

GARDEN LEVEL 3 — VEGETABLE PLOTS

GARDEN LEVEL 4 — RICE, WHEAT, HEMP

GARDEN LEVEL 5 — MAIZE FIELDS

GARDEN LEVEL 6 — ORCHARDS, CASSAVA, YAM AND POTATO FIELDS

Access Staircase

THE DOME

K —

LEVEL 7 - GROUND LEVEL - OFFICES AND ADMINISTRATION — STAIRS

LEVEL 8	MEDICAL BAYS
LEVEL 9	SCIENCE LABS
LEVEL 10	BIOLABS AND BUNKERS
LEVEL 11	BIODIVERSITY LEVEL
LEVEL 12	UPPER EDUCATION LEVEL
LEVEL 13	EARLY EDUCATION LEVEL
LEVEL 14	FACTORY LEVEL
LEVEL 15	FACTORY LEVEL
LEVEL 16	RECYCLING PLANT
LEVEL 17	MAINTENANCE LEVEL
LEVEL 18	RECREATION LEVEL
LEVEL 19	ASSEMBLY HALLS
LEVEL 20	COOKHOUSE AND CANTEEN
LEVEL 21	ACCOMODATION LEVEL
LEVEL 22	ACCOMODATION LEVEL
LEVEL 23	ACCOMODATION LEVEL
LEVEL 24	ACCOMODATION LEVEL
LEVEL 25	ACCOMODATION LEVEL
LEVEL 26	ACCOMODATION LEVEL
LEVEL 27	VENTILATION AND ENERGY
LEVEL 28	WATER TREATMENT

Central Staircase

UNDERGROUND LEVELS

BASEMENT — STAIRS

PART 1

THE BEGINNING OF THE END

CHAPTER 1

FIVE DAYS/121 HOURS TO THE END

I'll never forget the date September the third, 2123. How could I? That was the day I killed fourteen thousand, seven hundred and fifty-six people.

But I ought to start at the beginning. The beginning of the end, that is. It all started a week before the official harvest, with an apple in the Gardens of Eden Five. And not just any apple—this was a beauty. Round and red, it hung high in the only apple tree at the edge of the orchard, near the wall of the Dome. It wasn't really a wall of course, just the inside of the sphere sealing us all off from the deadly air of the outside world.

Anyway, the first time I caught sight of it, I decided that apple was mine. It's not as if I hadn't earned it. I worked my backside off on the maintenance crew, and I didn't see why the planters and harvesters should get first pick. It's not like the rest of us didn't work just as hard.

A week before the harvest began, I stood under the tree in Garden Level Six, gazing up at that bright red ball as I fiddled with the water sprinkler sticking up between the roots. It was broken for the fourth time in less than two weeks. I should know, it was me who kept breaking it. I had to have some excuse to go sneaking into the orchard when my duty sheet had "Level Twenty—cookhouse lightbulb replacement" and "Level Nine—science lab nutriscope calibration" scrawled across it.

I scowled at the sheet and stuffed it in the back pocket of my cotton trousers. Foreman Tafari may have lousy handwriting, but he knew how to assign work in a way that kept every level of Eden Five running as smooth as greased gears. If he caught me shirking duty up here, I'd be for it.

I unscrewed the broken sprinkler cap yet again, one eye on my electric spanner, the other on the apple. I'd have to claim it soon, it was almost ready to fall. Today was Sunday, the harvest set for the coming Saturday.

Friday, I decided. On Friday I'd make off with my shiny prize.

I could picture my teeth sinking into the crimson skin with a loud popping crunch, and my mouth watered at the thought of its sweet juice on my tongue. I hadn't had an apple all year, not since the last harvest. I only got that one because I won it in a contest to see which member of the maintenance crew could repair the most circuit boards in sixty minutes. There was only one apple tree in the whole of the Dome's six garden levels—planted from a single seed found in the emergency terra-farming supplies when Eden Five was

4

built over eighty years ago. Unlike the giant crates of papaya, mangoes, guavas and oranges which were put into storage or sent to the cookhouse for turning into preserves, the few apples the tree produced were used as prizes for the end-of-harvest celebrations. The tree was old now and wouldn't bear fruit for much longer. The gardening team had decided to replace it with another mango tree next season. This was my last opportunity to taste an apple ever again—I couldn't leave it to chance.

I fiddled with the sprinkler, stalling for as long as I could so I could gaze up at the tempting apple for a while longer. A week to go until the harvest. It felt like a lifetime.

Everything was planted strictly in season here, the ultraviolet lights on the inside of the Dome timed to mimic night and day. I used to wonder why the huge diamond-shaped panes of glass set in their curved frames weren't see-through, and why we couldn't watch the real sun blazing down on the wilds outside. Then I joined the maintenance crew and learned that the whole outside surface of the Dome was covered in solar panels that soaked up the real sun's rays, converting them to electricity that powered Eden Five's six garden levels and twenty-one underground levels. I guess they probably taught us that in school, but that would have been on one of the many days when I just wasn't listening.

I replaced the sprinkler cap and wiped the grease on the cuff of my shirt. I'd taken my bright yellow maintenance overalls off and hidden them in a service hatch on one of the stairwells. I'd figured out a while back that the dark green cotton of my standard issue shirt and trousers blended in

5

better with the plants whenever I wanted to sneak around the upper levels. It wasn't just that apple I was after, I had another reason—just as secret—to hang around the maize fields during duty hours.

That reason had eyes browner than the earth he worked on with his strong hands, and a smile that flashed brighter than the Dome's solar bulbs. I grinned like an idiot when I thought of him, glad it was still just a secret for now. I wouldn't like him to know how fast my heart pounded when he looked my way. Not yet anyway, not till I'd got myself under control. I was sixteen, not a little kid, and I'd be damned if I was going to let some boy see me go all weak-kneed for one of his smiles.

I was just straightening up when a gruff voice called through the trees, "Adina? Is that you, girl? Get your lazy butt over here right now!"

I groaned inwardly and trudged back through the long rows of fruit trees. I should've known Foreman Tafari would be prowling about the Gardens this close to harvest time. That guy could spot a worker shirking from four levels away. I swear he had x-ray vision. I stepped out of the trees and swung my tool bag onto my shoulder, trying to look busy and nonchalant at the same time. "Problem?" I asked.

"Duty sheet," the big man growled, holding out a grubby hand.

I sighed and reached for the paper stuffed in my back pocket. He barely glanced at it. He didn't need to—he had every maintenance duty he'd ever assigned filed away in that cunning little brain of his. His beady eyes glared down at me, his breath coming out of his nose in angry puffs like a broken air-conditioning unit. "Says here you're assigned to Levels Twenty and Nine today."

"Oh, really?" I leaned over and scanned the page held in his beefy hands, feigning surprise. Despite my suddenly dry mouth, I had to bite my tongue to stop from making a crack about his crappy handwriting. *Just act dumb*, I told myself, *and he might let you get away with it just this once.*

"So?" he demanded. "What you doing on Level Six, girl? What you doing in the *Gardens*?"

He said the word "Gardens" like it had four r's in it. Going by the state of his handwriting, that's probably the way he spelled it too.

I shrugged, trying to look innocent. "Some of the sprinklers in the orchard were bust. Thought I'd repair them before starting my other duties. That is what we're meant to do isn't it—repair things?"

He wasn't buying my innocent act. He leaned down, his stale breath making me gag.

"You think I don't know what you're up to, girl? Think I don't see the way you go sneaking—"

"Is something the matter?" a sharp voice cut in.

I looked up, my heart sinking further. Usually I'd be glad for any rescue I could get when Foreman Tafari went on one of his rants. But Director Eshe was the last person I wanted to see right now. It wasn't just because she was in charge of Eden Five and could have me permanently assigned to fixing the toilet systems' plumbing if she liked. It was worse than that. There was something about the way she looked at me that made me want to shrivel up in shame at the thought of every

7

bad deed I'd ever done. Like she could see right through me to my very soul, and saw only a rotten hole there. I know that sounds crazy, but I felt like I disappointed her deeply in some way, and it drove me mad wondering what it was.

Everything about Director Eshe, from the hair cropped close to her scalp to the carefully pressed blue shirt that stood out against the deep black of her skin, screamed efficiency and neatness. Her eyes rested disapprovingly on my untidy mop of hair for a long moment, and I made a mental note to get my mother to comb it into braids for me. Then she raised an eyebrow at Foreman Tafari. "Well?"

"Girl's shirking duty again." The Foreman waved the duty sheet at me accusingly.

"I wasn't!" I protested, before he could list all my other crimes. "I was fixing the sprinklers in the orchard. Weren't you talking just last week at the workers' assembly about the importance of initiative, Director? That's what I was doing— showing initiative." It wasn't really a lie, I mean, it takes a good bit of ambition and invention to sneak anything out of the Gardens with the planters watching us all the time.

"Initiative's all very well," Director Eshe said, "but it's not much use to us if you don't get your assigned duties done first." She stared right through me again with those keen brown eyes of hers, and I lowered my gaze, shuffling my feet uncomfortably. "Are you sure you're happy on the maintenance crew, Adina? Your teachers all had you marked down as a science team candidate. You've missed a few years of training now, but it's not too late to change your mind."

Urgh, this again.

8

I'd told them a billion times I didn't want to be on their stupid science team playing with numbers and analysing soil samples all day. Most of the kids in Eden Five left school at fourteen to join one of the work crews. They trained as planters in the Gardens, production staff on the Factory Level where our clothes and other necessaries were made, food technicians in the cookhouse, teachers on the Education Levels, and a few made it onto the small medical crew. Given the choice, there was no way I was staying on in school a minute longer than I had to. I'd joined the maintenance crew as a technician the first chance I got. I liked being a techie, fixing things and solving problems, but I had a more important reason for putting up with Foreman Tafari and all his crap. The maintenance crew was the one team that got to wander round all the levels of Eden Five without a pass. Sure, I'd get some funny looks if I was somewhere I shouldn't be and I didn't have a work order written out on my duty sheet. But I'd never had this much freedom to explore Eden Five before, and I wasn't about to give it up to go and sit in some dull lab all day.

I shook my head. Director Eshe could give me all the disappointed looks she wanted, but I wasn't letting her send me back to school.

"Got ideas above her station, this one," Foreman Tafari grumbled. "Thinks she's smarter than the rest of us and doesn't need to do what she's told. Ought to send her outside the Dome to clean the solar panels—that'd sort her out and set her head straight. How about it, girl?" He glowered at me. "Should I put you down for maintenance duty on the *outside*?"

9

I looked up quickly to see if he was joking, but his face was deadly serious.

Outside.

My heart skipped a beat in terror at the thought. Outside the Dome of Eden Five? Outside in the wastelands where once there had been a whole world? Now only the wind whipped the dry dust of the wilds, the air filled with biopoisons that would claw through your body and kill you slowly. I didn't know much about the outside, I just knew it was somewhere I never wanted to go. Some of the other techies on the maintenance crew talked about it sometimes when a solar panel failed and they had to leave the safety of the Dome to fix it. They whispered round the airlock doors as they pulled on their biohazard suits, their faces grim. They didn't say much when they came back in either, but their hushed conversations were filled with words like "scorched earth", "deadlines", and "barren". I knew what those words meant from the few times I did pay attention in school. I didn't need to go and see it for myself.

Director Eshe had just opened her mouth to speak when her communication pad beeped and lit up. She looked down, the lines in her forehead deepening as she read the report. "The water pressure alarm system's gone off in the basement below Level Twenty-Eight again," she muttered. "That's the third time this week. Tafari, get your best team members together—we have to get this sorted before something serious happens. Get back to work, Adina," she told me as she hurried off. "This place relies on everybody pulling their weight. We don't want Eden Five falling down around our ears because you can't be bothered doing the duties assigned to you. And put your work suit back on."

Foreman Tafari glared at me on the way past, looking back over his shoulder and following me with his beady eyes until he reached the greenhouse doors that led to the lower levels. When he was gone, I felt another set of eyes on me.

I turned round.

A group of teenage planters was standing at the edge of a potato field, leaning on their plastic hoes and spades as they watched me getting a public dressing down from the Director and the maintenance crew foreman. The tallest boy in the group said something, and the others burst out laughing. I felt my face grow hot under his gaze, and I cursed my bad luck. Why did *he* have to see that? I thought Otienno worked the Level Three vegetable plots on the Sunday half-day shift. It's not like I didn't have his duty schedule memorised by now.

The others went back to work, but Otienno didn't lower his gaze. He was eighteen, and had the kind of easy confidence that comes from being bigger than all the other boys his age. His brown skin was paler than mine, his eyes dark and deep set. Just looking at the muscles that bulged on his forearms beneath his rolled-up sleeves did strange things to my stomach. I lifted my hand to wave, just before I realised how stupid it would look. My arm froze halfway up, and I stuffed my hand back in my pocket. I turned away quickly, but not before I caught the flash of his amused smile. A low chuckle followed me through the rows of groundnut plants, making me blush harder. I felt about ten years old.

Next time I'll talk to him, I promised myself. *Next time.*

But I promised myself the same thing every time I saw him working away in the Gardens. It would be easy if only he wasn't so damn popular. He always seemed to be surrounded by a group of boys laughing at his jokes or girls smiling whenever he whispered something secret in their ears. But maybe I liked him because he was popular. I often wondered what that would feel like, to have other kids jostling to sit next to me in the cookhouse canteen, or running to be the first to tell me a fresh bit of gossip. It's not like I was a total social reject, like anyone ever went out of their way to avoid me or anything. But apart from fixing things, my other main talent was rubbing people up the wrong way. The way I did things, the way I said things just seemed to annoy people, and they'd roll their eyes and ask why I always had to be so difficult. They didn't ignore me or shun me in the canteen or anything that obvious, but they didn't sit next to me either if there were free seats somewhere else.

I turned out of the groundnut beds, heading for the doors, when the sight of something I'd seen a million times before made me stop short.

The wall of the Dome rose up in front of me, towering high overhead. The five other garden levels above were floored with glass, and through the tangle of soil, roots and vegetable plots, I could just make out the point in the distant ceiling above where the Dome's support beams came together and met the very top of the access stairway that spiralled up through the centre of the Gardens. Each large glass wall panel had a row of three ultraviolet skytube lights set behind its pane. It was midday, so now they were glowing bright blue. If

12

you didn't look too closely through the glass, it was just like the Gardens were surrounded by sunny blue skies. I know that's what it looked like—I'd seen pictures of the real sky in old books when I was little.

But it wasn't the sight of the Dome's skytubes that stopped me. On the corner of one glass panel in front of me, a small round light was blinking red. On, off, on, off it went, a silent warning sign. I dropped my tool kit and pulled out a maintenance request form. This would have to be reported. The red emergency light meant the solar panel on the other side of the glass had failed. I frowned as I scrawled the identification number on the form, already feeling sorry for the poor techie who'd have to suit up and go outside into the wilds to fix it.

"It's all red!" said a voice suddenly from behind me. "Red for danger!"

I didn't need to turn round. I knew exactly who that high-pitched, hovering-on-the-edge-of-a-nervous-breakdown voice belonged to.

"We're not in any danger, Baba," I sighed without looking up from my form. "It's just a warning light letting the techies know we have to fix the solar panel."

"Red for danger, Adina!" the voice quivered. "Red for death! We're all going to die!"

That made me whirl round faster than an air-con fan on its highest setting. "Baba, what the hell are you—"

I didn't finish, I just stared at the old man standing behind me with my mouth open. Baba Weseka was so skinny, his green shirt and trousers hung round his bones like stalks on a withered corn cob. Even though he looked ancient, I knew he couldn't be more than sixty at most. That still made him the oldest person here—life was tough when Eden Five was first built, and it took years for the Gardens to grow enough food for everyone. There were a few members of the first generation born in Eden Five left—grandparents who still did odd jobs in the factory rooms or worked in the cookhouse. We all knew Baba Weseka had been born here, same as them, but some days he'd get so confused, he'd tell everyone he'd been born in the time *before*, when people still lived in the outside world. Those were the days he'd swear blind that the ground of the wilds outside now ran with blood instead of rivers, so you didn't want to go believing anything Baba Weseka said when he was in one of *those* moods.

He was definitely not having one of his good days—I could tell straight off from the way he was staring back at me with eyes wide as overripe peas ready to burst from their pod. It wasn't his crazy eyes that made me shiver, though; I was used to their glazed expression by now. I was even used to his visions of doom and warnings of impending disaster. What I wasn't used to was the sight of the bright red blood that dripped from deep gashes in both his palms.

"Red for danger, Adina," he gasped again, holding his hands before my face so the blood ran down his wrists and dripped to the ground. "Red for death. We're all going to die!"

CHAPTER 2

FIVE DAYS/120 HOURS TO THE END

"Gods, Baba!" I groaned, stuffing the maintenance request form back into my pocket. "What have you gone and done to yourself now?"

"I didn't mean to." Baba Weseka looked down at his bleeding hands in confusion. "I don't know how...don't know..." He gazed around as though searching for something. On the ground, the sharp blade of an electric pruning shear glinted in the artificial sunlight, bright spots of blood drying on the metal teeth.

"You know you're not supposed to touch the planters' equipment, Baba," I told him. "That stuff's dangerous if you don't know how to work it."

"I just wanted to help look after the plants," he whimpered, stroking one of the groundnut seedlings and getting blood all over the leaves. "Why won't they let me help?"

Because you're a one-man walking biohazard, I thought. *And if I don't get your mutated blood off the grass and leaves right away, then we're all in trouble.*

"Hey, it's OK," I said out loud instead, grabbing him by the shoulders and sitting him down on an irrigation pipe before he could go into full-scale meltdown mode on me. "It's just a couple of cuts, we'll get them cleaned up in no time."

I pulled a pair of latex gloves from my toolbox and opened the mini medical kit all the techies carried around in case of emergencies. It was meant for dealing with minor accidents like burns and electric shocks, but I was pretty sure Baba Weseka bleeding his contaminated blood all over the garden levels was a bigger emergency than anything the techies had to deal with on a regular basis.

"Keep your hands still so I can bandage them, Baba," I said, trying to stem the flow of blood with a layer of gauze before he could get any more on the ground or on the plants. "You know it's not safe for you to bleed on anything."

"I was just trying to help," the old man said sadly, looking up at me with those milky brown eyes of his that always seemed to be focused on a different version of reality than the rest of us could see.

"I know you want to help, but you're not allowed in the Gardens, and you're not supposed to walk around without your gloves on," I reminded him for the billionth time. "It's dangerous."

"The gloves make my hands itch," he whined, just the way my little sister did when she had to put her safety gear on for the emergency drill in the bunkers. "Will you make the danger go away, Adina?" he asked, pointing at the warning light that was still blinking on and off.

You're the danger I'm talking about, you numbskull, I sighed to myself. "It's OK, Baba," I said aloud, "I'll make sure it gets fixed."

"Don't go outside!" The old man's eyes went wide again at the thought, the whites of his cataracts shimmering red in the warning light's glow. "Not safe! The wilds are full of Nomalies."

"Baba, there's no such thing as a Nomaly," I told him as I wrapped more gauze around his hands. I tried to sound reassuring, but it just came out exasperated. Baba Weseka had been telling us stories of monsters in the wilds since we were kids, but now that I was old enough to know better, his far-fetched tales just irritated me.

He'd always been odd, ever since I could remember. There was a good reason for that, though.

When Baba Weseka was a young man, he'd somehow managed to get outside.

Our teachers used to tell us the story at the start of every school term as a warning. He'd gone "stir crazy," telling everyone he needed to feel the real sun on his face and the wind at his back. He'd been sent to the medical rooms for observation, but somehow, he'd managed to sneak out and get into the Dome's airlock. He'd been smart back then, people said, before he lost his mind. He'd figured out how to engage the release mechanism, even though he'd been a planter and hadn't had any maintenance training. Before the techies could reach him, he was outside and running for freedom—without a biohazard suit, without a biofilter, without anything to protect him from the biopoisons in the wilds.

Our teachers said it took the rescue crew nearly ten hours to find him and bring him back to Eden Five. By then, it was too late. Even ten minutes would've been too late. The biopoisons were on his skin, in his bloodstream, in his brain. They'd worked their way right down to his DNA, twisting it, mutating it in ways the scientists and medics just couldn't wrap their heads around. They kept him in quarantine for nearly six months, our teachers said, doing test after test while the workers all screamed their heads off about the contamination risks. Half the workers had been in favour of keeping him quarantined for the rest of his life, assuming he survived the contamination. The rest all wanted to throw him straight back out into the wilds. By the time the medical team released him, declaring him safe as long as he wore gloves at all times and didn't let his body fluids come into contact with anything living, no one wanted to get within six feet of him.

That's when he started talking about Nomalies.

I'm not sure anyone really believes he's seen monsters out in the wilds, but all the same, his stories of spider creatures scuttling through the dust all around the protective Dome of Eden Five have kept more than just me awake at night. Director Eshe herself says his stories are all nonsense. But if she's wrong and there really is something scary living out there, then I for one do not want to know about it.

His weird stories and poisoned blood weren't the only things that made Baba Weseka a social outcast after he was released from quarantine. It didn't help that after his "escape," as he called it, he could barely string a sentence together that didn't sound crazy, and he suffered from fits that left him foaming at the mouth and rolling on the floor. When that happened, everyone just stood back and watched from a safe distance until the biohazard team came to clean him up. The workers also had him to thank for the warnings we got at every weekly assembly about the dangers that awaited anyone daft enough to try a "great escape" like him. No wonder the old people his age shunned him, and parents shut their doors tight at night when he shuffled through the corridors of the accommodation levels looking for someone to talk to.

If I was smart, I wouldn't go near him either. But somehow, I couldn't help feeling sorry for him. Either that, or I was way dumber than I thought I was.

"It's no good, the cuts are too deep," I said, pulling the ends of the bandages into a rough knot to keep the gauze strips tight. "Come with me to the medical bay, Baba, they'll get your hands stitched up there."

"Not there, no!" Baba Weseka shook his bald head, his eyes wide. His hair had all fallen out after he'd been in the wilds, and his light brown skin had a strange yellow tinge that made it look like melted wax under the strip lights. "They'll lock me up and I'll never get out again."

"No, they won't." I rolled my eyes impatiently as I scooped up the clumps of soil where his blood had landed and dumped them into the small biohazard pots I kept in my tool kit for emergency spillages. I stripped off some of the leaves from the plants he'd touched, then put a couple of yellow marker flags down for the clean-up crew. It was their job to deal with the contamination site now. "Come on, Baba, don't make a fuss," I coaxed. "I've got work to do and I'll be in trouble if you make me late."

That did the trick. There was no way he'd do anything that would get me punished. We weren't exactly friends, Baba Weseka and me. But I looked out for him all the same, yelling at the little kids when they laughed at him, and stopping the other teenagers from stealing his food in the canteen when the overseer wasn't looking. I don't know why I did it. I guess it bugged me that he got picked on just because he wasn't the same as everyone else. I was so tired of the sameness of Eden Five—the grey steel of the endless staircases, the monotony of the daily work schedule, the dull glow of the underground strip lighting and the sickly green gobs of plastic that every piece of furniture and equipment was made of. Everything in Eden Five got spat out of the 3D printers and manufacturing pods from the same patterns and moulds. Every single thing on every level was the same size, shape and colour, from our regulation shirts right down to the underpants we wore.

Maybe I looked out for Baba Weseka because he was the only thing in Eden Five that was different.

I led him through the plantain plots by the arm, shoving a biohazard report form at one of the planters as I passed and telling her, "There's been a spillage in sector 6J, get the clean-up crew here right way. I've marked the spot."

The planter took one look at Baba Weseka and his bandaged hands and ran off with her hair standing on end. I knew I could count on her paranoia to have the clean-up crew mopping up the contamination in the Gardens within minutes.

"Wait!" Baba Weseka stopped suddenly, gazing around again as though he suddenly remembered what he'd been looking for earlier. "Where is she?"

I didn't need to ask who "she" was, and I couldn't help groaning out loud either. "Baba, you didn't bring your dog up here too, did you? You're supposed to keep her locked in your homeroom. You know she's not allowed anywhere near the Gardens."

Technically she wasn't allowed, full stop. There were other animals besides dogs in Eden Five, but they were all kept underground on the Biodiversity Level. "Slaughterhouse Level" my little sister called it, wrinkling her nose when it was mentioned. It was a fair point—most of the animals were destined for the cookhouse. Baba Weseka's dog had been bred as one of the test animals about ten years ago in the medical lab where he had to go each week for regular blood tests. Baba Weseka had decided that they were soulmates, and he'd howled so much when she was scheduled for medical experimentation that the doctors had given up and let him keep her.

"Anyango?" I called, peering through the heavy clusters of ripe plantain. There was a shuffling noise, and then I saw a pair of yellow paws poking out from behind a tree trunk. The rest of the dog stayed put, though, her suspicious eyes disappearing again when she caught sight of me.

"She's a good dog," Baba grinned. "Good dog."

No, she's not, she's a sixty-pound bundle of biohazard that's going to get me confined to my quarters every evening for the next month if I don't get her out of the garden levels before anyone else sees her, I thought.

"Anyango, come here." I clicked my fingers at the dog who was whining behind the tree. She poked her skinny muzzle out from under a plantain cluster, sniffed in my direction, then shuffled back till her paws were the only thing visible once more.

"Anyango!" I tried again. The dog looked back out at me, squinting at the sound of her name, which Baba said meant "friend" in one of the old languages. I wasn't sure he was right about that. It was probably something else he'd just made up—I knew the name wasn't from Swahili, as we still learned that in school, even though we mostly just used English now. Anyango was Baba Weseka's only real friend, but she didn't seem to like the sound of her name much. She was a bit like my little sister, Alitash, that way. Not that my little sister's a dog, I mean she doesn't like getting called by her full name either. People always call her Tash. I guess the dog was used to only getting called Anyango when she was in trouble.

"Yango?" I tried.

The dog shuffled forward on her belly this time, her tongue lolling dumbly over her slack jaw. Gods, she was stupid.

"She's a good dog, good dog." Baba Weseka smiled at her, bending down to pat her while I strung a length of cable from my toolbox round her neck to act as a lead. I didn't want her wandering off again on my watch. If the clean-up crew knew she'd been up here along with Baba Weseka and his contaminated blood, there would be hell to pay, and this time Director Eshe might insist the vets get rid of her for good.

22

A few years back, Baba Weseka had got confused after one of his fits and brought Yango into the canteen with him. Everyone went nuts about the contamination hazard. Director Eshe finally put her foot down and said the dog had to go back where she belonged. On her orders, the vets had come to the canteen and taken the dog down to the cages on Level Eleven, locking her up with the other animals. Baba Weseka hadn't argued, hadn't tried to reason with them or complain. He just sat down and cried. He sobbed and sobbed for three days straight, curled up in a little ball under one of the canteen tables and putting everyone off their food until Director Eshe gave up and let his dog go. Nobody tried to take Yango from him after that.

"Come on, you stupid mutt," I grumbled, pulling on the lead. Yango grinned up at me, and I had to fight the urge to kick the ugly, smelly thing that lay on her back all submissive and whining, trying to get me to rub her scabby belly. "I said move!"

Yango gave a loud yelp and did as she was told.

I headed for the greenhouse doors, somehow managing to clomp down four flights of stairs with a heavy toolbox, a whimpering dog, and Baba Weseka in tow. It wasn't an easy job, and I was pretty sure I deserved a medal by the time I'd tied Yango up to the stair rail outside the medical bay and dumped Baba Weseka down on a free examination bed. The medic on duty threw me a disgusted look when she saw who I'd brought in. It was clear she thought I deserved a year's worth of punishment duty for my trouble.

"Gods, Adina, what's he doing in here?" she snapped, staring in disgust at the man on the bed like he was a walking

23

disease or something. I couldn't remember the girl's name, but I did remember she'd been a couple of year's above me in school and had been a real cow back then too. Just my luck to get the trainee medic instead of a qualified doctor.

"He's cut his hands," I said, showing her the hasty bandage job I'd done. Blood was starting to seep through the gauze. She was going to have to get stitching quickly if she didn't want her nice clean medical room turning into another contamination site.

"Oh, great." The trainee medic pulled on a double layer of gloves and wrapped Baba Weseka's hands in protective biohazard bags right up to his elbows, pulling them so tight that he whimpered and looked at me in confusion.

"Aren't you going to stitch them up?" I demanded. "He needs the wounds cleaned."

"It's too dangerous for me to tackle," the girl growled at me, backing off from Baba Weseka and dropping her contaminated gloves down a waste chute. "I'm going to call in one of the doctors to do it. They're all busy just now—wait here while I go find one, and make sure *he* doesn't go anywhere." She threw one more disgusted look at Baba Weseka over her shoulder and practically ran for the inner rooms.

I glared at the door she'd disappeared through and wished her a silent death involving a tank of biohazard waste and a whole colony of flesh-eating bugs.

It's not that I didn't get that Baba Weseka and his blood were a contamination risk, I mean, I was still wearing my gloves and the first thing I was going to do when I got back to my homeroom was take a shower just in case. I wasn't about to take any chances around him either. But Gods, why did everyone have to act like just breathing too close to him was going to instantly turn them into mutants or something?

"Hang in there, Baba," I said, giving his arm a reassuring squeeze. "We'll get you fixed up in just a minute."

But when I looked down at him, I knew straight away that it was going to take a lot longer than that. Baba Weseka's face had turned even more yellow than usual, and his whole body was trembling. I knew exactly what the warning signs meant.

I grabbed his feet and swung his legs up onto the bed before he keeled over, snatching a towel from the medical trolley and laying it under his chin to catch the foam that was already flecking his lips. I lifted the bed's side rails just in time. In another three seconds he was fitting, his whole body jerking and his eyes rolling in their sockets. It lasted so long I thought he was going to break his bones before it was over, but finally his eyes snapped shut and his body went limp, drool running down his chin into the waiting towel. He lay so still that for a minute I thought he was dead.

"Help!" I yelled, trying to call the medic back in. I had a sneaky suspicion she was hiding behind the door and just watching from a safe distance, but then suddenly Baba Weseka grabbed my wrist and I had to turn my attention back to him.

"Fire!" he gasped, blinking at me in terror. "It's burning, Adina!"

"Burning? Are you too hot? Here, take your shirt off." I eased the green shirt from his thin body, careful not to disturb the biohazard bags around his arms. "Is that better?" I put my gloved hand to his forehead, but his skin was so cold he might've been sweating ice.

"No, not just me, all of us are burning," Baba Weseka croaked. "The fire, it eats us all up, then the Nomalies rise from the dust. They're coming, Adina, the fire and the Nomalies and nothing can stop them!"

"Ssh, it's OK," I tried to reassure him, pushing him back down on the bed and stroking his forehead. "Nothing is going to hurt us; it was just a bad dream. There's no such thing as Nomalies, Baba."

"I've seen them, Adina!" he gasped, trying to sit back up. "I've seen them with my own eyes!"

I didn't know what to say to that, but luckily I didn't have to say anything at all because at that moment two doctors wearing biohazard suits came running in with syringes, suturing kits, and piles of bandages and took over.

"Have you come into contact with him?" one of them snapped at me through a facemask.

"No, I've been wearing gloves." I held up my hands to show him.

"Drop them down the waste chute and get back to work. We'll deal with this."

I didn't want to leave Baba with them and their rough hands, but there was nothing more I could do for him now. Besides, Foreman Tafari was bound to be lurking about somewhere nearby just waiting to catch me shirking again.

"I've got to go, Baba. Look, I'm taking your homeroom keycard so I can drop Yango off for you, OK?" I told him, fishing around in the pocket of his shirt for the thin square of plastic that unlocked his quarters. "I'll come back and check on you later."

I dropped my gloves into the medical waste chute and gave him a reassuring smile as I headed for the exit. Baba Weseka didn't smile back. His eyes were wide and he was looking at me in sheer terror as the doctors pushed a needle full of sedative into his arm.

"Adina!" he called as I opened the door.

"What is it, Baba?" I turned back to look at him.

"It starts with an apple and ends in ashes."

"What?" I had no idea what that was supposed to mean.

But Baba Weseka's eyes closed, and he lay back on the bed with a long sigh. I left the doctors to it and went to untie Yango from the stair rail. When I got there, I found Yango had company. A ten-year-old girl was sitting on the stairway stroking the dog's ears. Hearing my footsteps clanging on the metal walkway, she turned and looked up at me guiltily. I recognised that sharp face and frizzy black hair right away. They followed me around Eden Five like I was the sun and she was a planet caught in my gravity field. I was so sick of the sight of her I could scream. One of these days I was going to punch her grubby little face and knock her right out of orbit.

I scowled back at her, and she jumped up and ran off down the stairway before I could get any closer, her footsteps echoing away to nothing as she headed for the schoolhouse level. She was skipping class again. I'd report that too and enjoy it far more than trekking down to the maintenance rooms to report the bust solar panel I'd seen in the Gardens. It'd serve her right for always following me around like an unwanted

27

shadow. Who the hell did she think she was anyway, my sister or something? I only had one real sister, and that was Tash.

I pulled out another report form from my toolbox, a blue behaviour one this time. I couldn't help grinning in satisfaction as I wrote the kid's name across the top.

Chiku deserved to be punished.

CHAPTER 3

FOUR DAYS/89 HOURS TO THE END

Even when I was working instead of shirking, I had a hard time keeping my mind on the job. I had so many wild schemes, so many clever plans, so much I wanted to *do*. Four days before I ended our world, my head was a million miles away.

"Adina, are you actually listening to me?" Dejen asked. He scooted across the lab bench, brushing my repair parts into a pile and getting in my light. I pushed his head to one side and continued fixing the microscope.

"Yes. History lecture, blah-blah. Sciencey stuff, blah-blah. Old times before the collapse, blah-blah. It's fascinating. I'd *love* to hear more."

Dejen tried hard not to smile, but the corners of his mouth turned up despite his frown. I liked it when he smiled. He had such dark skin his teeth stood out like chips of polished glass. Dejen was only a year older than me, but you wouldn't

29

have known it from his serious face. He had old eyes, full of learning and knowledge. I only wished he'd keep the stuff he learned to himself sometimes.

"I don't get you," he shook his head. "How come you're never interested in the world the way it was before the Gardens were built?"

"What's the use of asking questions no one knows the answers to?" I asked, peering at the microscope's tiny screws and selecting an electric driver. "The whole world's gone. We're never getting it back. It's all just wilds out there now."

"But—"

"Why go reading books about a world that doesn't exist anymore? Why watch videpods full of stuff we'll never get to see with our own eyes? Does it make you happy, Dejen, huh? Seeing all the nice things we'll never have?"

"You're totally missing the point. Don't you ever wonder how it all got like this?"

I set down my screwdriver and began to recite. "'Due to environmental changes, the world's ecosystems began to mutate. By the mid twenty-first century, biopoisons in the plant and wildlife food chains had altered the landscapes and caused the continents to become uninhabitable. Gardens of Eden were built around the world to preserve human life and protect natural biodiversity—'" I ran out of breath before I got to the end and gave up. "See? I did pay attention in school occasionally."

"But is that what you actually believe? You think that's the way it happened here in Africa?" Dejen had a way of looking at me so intently it made everything else I was doing seem trivial. It was like his questions just had to be answered or his head would burst, his itching brain exploding all over the lab. It was pretty irritating, especially when what I was doing was repairing his damn microscope for him.

Africa.

I rolled the word round in my head, tasting it on the tip of my tongue. It had an earthy feel to it, a strange tang that sent shivers down my spine. It made me feel the way I did once as a kid, hanging upside down by my knees from the stairway rails as a dare. The deep drop below me, down, down through the centre of the spiral staircase all the way to the basement made me dizzy and tingly all at the same time. I hadn't been afraid of accidentally falling, I'd been afraid I'd give in to that thrilling urge to let myself go. That's how I felt when I heard the name "Africa." I knew from school lessons that's where we were, that there were other equally barren continents way out past the wilds, beyond wide oceans with even stranger names. It made my head hurt at the size of it all, the size of the world's wastelands. I didn't say that out loud, though. I just said, "What do you mean? Of course that's the way it happened."

"But it's all so vague!" Dejen protested. "'Due to environmental changes'—what does that even mean?"

"How should I know?" I shrugged. "I'm a techie, not a scientist. And if you want this microscope fixed before dinnertime, you'd better let me get on with it and stop asking so many dumb questions."

Dejen sighed again, a deep sound of frustration that echoed round the empty lab room. He went back to his soil

31

sample analysis, muttering to himself as he clinked test tubes and measuring beakers together. I felt sorry for him. He was probably the smartest guy in the whole of Eden Five, and here he was stuck in a dingy lab, asking questions that would never be answered. There was nobody left alive who knew the answers.

Dejen and I had been best friends our whole lives. He'd started school a year before me, but they'd fast-tracked him through so many classes that he joined the science team when he was only fourteen, instead of sixteen like the other scientists. He'd been so excited, telling me he'd learn all about the outside world in the labs. But now, after three whole years of basic biology work, he still wasn't any closer to answering any of the questions about Eden Five that whizzed round his head day and night. It must just eat him up.

I'd stopped asking questions a long time ago. I mean, why bother? It's not like the adults knew any more about the world outside than we did. Maybe Director Eshe had some answers, but I wasn't about to go knocking on her office door to find out.

"I just wish I knew what was out there," Dejen said almost to himself as he played with his test tubes and pipettes. "I wish I could go and see for myself."

"See what, Dejen?" I asked. "There's nothing out there. Not unless you believe in Baba Weseka's Nomalies…?"

He looked up and gave me a sideways grin when he saw I was teasing him. "How's he doing anyway? Baba Weseka, I mean. You seem to spend more time around him than just about anyone else."

"Yeah, that's not saying much seeing as no one else will go anywhere near him," I muttered. I always got defensive whenever anyone mentioned me looking out for Baba Weseka, like they assumed him and his craziness were all my responsibility. And it was some responsibility, let me tell you. There were times when Baba's mind wandered so badly he'd sit in the canteen at midnight in his pyjamas waiting for lunch to be served, or turn up at the weekly assembly with cuts and bruises after forgetting how to open a tin of dried food with a can opener. A few months back I found him wandering around the basement crying to himself. He'd soiled his trousers because he'd forgotten where the sanitation units on each level were, and kept going down the stairways looking for them until he hit the dead end of the basement. No one would help him or show him the right way. They all just kept their distance and whispered about him and his contaminated body fluids behind their hands. It made me mad how cruel they could be to him.

"I didn't say it was a bad thing, Adi," Dejen smiled. "It's nice you take care of him."

"Stop making me sound like a better person than I really am," I said, giving him a playful elbow in the ribs to hide my embarrassment. "We both know I'm a selfish cow at times."

"I didn't say you were a saint either," Dejen laughed, straightening the test tubes I'd knocked over. Then he looked up at me seriously again with those intense eyes of his. "Did Baba say anything yesterday? When he was having a fit, I mean?"

"Not much." I shrugged, fiddling with my screwdriver and hoping Dejen wasn't going to give me the third degree over what I'd heard in the medical bay. I didn't want to talk about what Baba Weseka had said about danger and fire and death. It creeped me out just thinking about it, so I said instead, "It was just the usual crazy stuff about Nomalies in the wilds. He's convinced they're real. What d'you think, Dejen? You think there's any truth to his stories, or is he just nuts like everyone says?"

Dejen frowned like he wasn't sure what to think. He was such a geek he acted like every question was a science puzzle, and he hated having to come up with an answer when he had no real data to go on. "I don't know, Adi, I mean—spider creatures living in the wilds when there's nothing else out there? It's a bit far-fetched. If they were real, then how come no one else has seen them? The techies have to go outside to fix the solar panels—if there was anything living out there, then they would have seen them, wouldn't they?"

Dejen meant to be reassuring, but his words just made me feel worse. Yeah, the crews all came back inside after their repair sessions on the Dome telling the rest of us there was nothing to see, but that's not the story we heard in the techies' break room during the night shift. After they'd had a couple of drinks, the ones who'd been outside let their guard down and things slipped out. Sightings. Strange shapes on the horizon. Movement in the restless dust. Too many legs attached to awkward bodies that crawled and scuttled and shifted out of view before anyone could get a real fix on them.

It made me shiver when I remembered their stories.

"You OK?" Dejen asked, seeing me go quiet all of a sudden.

"Yeah, just wondering if I'm ever going to get this damn microscope fixed," I said, grabbing my screwdriver again and attacking the microscope like it had got itself broken on purpose just to get on my nerves.

We worked in silence for a while, both absorbed in our own tasks. This was why I got on so well with Dejen. It wasn't just that we could talk, even if his stupid questions did sometimes drive me crazy. It was that we didn't have to talk, not if we didn't want to. We could just be there in the same room, doing different things, without it being awkward. The only other person I could just be myself around was my sister, Tash.

"Do you ever wonder," Dejen started suddenly, breaking the silence just as I was beginning to enjoy it, "What the words 'Amonston Corporation' mean?"

"What?" Gods, could the guy get any more random?

"I was just thinking—"

"There's a surprise. Couldn't do it silently, could you?"

"No, listen, Adi. They're everywhere, and no one seems to know what they mean." He held up an old beaker with a small stamp on the base that read "Amonston Corporation" in white letters. I looked down at my electric screwdriver. It was one of the very oldest ones. The experienced techies nabbed all the best stuff, leaving the equipment on its last legs for the newest recruits. The same words were stamped along the screwdriver's handle, half rubbed away with use. I'd seen it there loads of times, but like most things around Eden Five I couldn't explain, I hadn't paid it much attention.

"It's probably the people who built Eden Five. A sort of signature, you know, like the pyramid builders carved on the

35

tombs when they were finished." I looked up eagerly, hoping he'd be impressed I remembered something from my school history lessons. But Dejen was frowning at the stamp on the beaker like he hadn't heard me. He did that sometimes, asked a question then went off into his own little puzzle-solving trance without listening to the answer. It bugged the hell out of me.

I did some thinking of my own as I finished off the microscope, trying to remember all the places I'd seen the "Amonston Corporation" stamp.

The biohazard suits hanging outside the airlock.

The water pipes in the plumbing system.

The syringes in the medical rooms.

The handles of the old spades in the Gardens' tool sheds. Hmm...the handles of the spades the planters used. The handles gripped by strong hands that swung from broad shoulders. A slow smile below dark eyes, a rough layer of stubble shadowing a square jaw...

This time when Dejen started talking, it was me who wasn't listening. He had to shake my arm to get my attention. "Adina? Didn't you hear the dinner bell?"

"The dinner what...? Oh, right."

Otienno's dark eyes faded back into my dreams, and I started shoving my tools back into my bag.

"You coming down to the canteen?" Dejen asked. "I've got some pudding credits left, and I hear they're doing sponge cake tonight. Fancy it?"

I did fancy it, but not tonight. Tonight was special. I shook my head. "My mother's cooking dinner tonight. She and my father both have the evening shift off for once, so we're eating together." It was a rare occurrence, and I'd been looking forward to it all week.

"That's nice. So have things…improved between them, then?" Dejen asked tentatively. He knew better than to ask about my parents, it always put me in a bad mood. I shrugged and scowled down at the lab bench. I clattered my tools as I stuffed them in my bag, hoping he'd shut up. He didn't.

"What about Chiku, is she invited? She is your sister, after all."

Gods, he was really sticking both feet in it today.

"That ugly little beast isn't my sister, understand?" I growled, getting right up in Dejen's face. He was taller than me by a head, so I had to stand on tiptoe. "Tash is my sister. The only sister I've got. So stop talking about Chiku like she's got anything to do with me and my family, OK?"

"OK, Adi, sorry, I just thought…"

Urgh, I hated him calling me Adi when he'd just pissed me off. I wanted to be mad at him, not reminded that he was my best friend and the only one who had a pet name for me. I shouldered my bag and stomped out, letting the door of the lab slam shut behind me.

"Have a good dinner!" I heard him call down the stairway after me.

He could be such a pain.

CHAPTER 4

FOUR DAYS/88 HOURS TO THE END

By the time I walked fifteen levels down to my own accommodation floor, past the biolabs, the "Slaughterhouse Level," the factory rooms, and the busy cookhouse canteen, I wasn't mad anymore. The red-hot fury that fizzed through me every time I heard Chiku's name had cooled. Now my stomach had started to knot, and cold, jittery shivers were running down my spine. I was nervous. Nervous of dinner with my own family. How dumb can you get? But I wanted it to be perfect. I *longed* for it to be perfect, the way it was before Chiku...

No. I wasn't going to think like that. Now we had Tash to make up for that mistake. It was going to be perfect. My parents weren't going to fight, they were going to look at each other across the dinner table the way they used to when I was little, their eyes all misty and full of secret smiles.

The minute I swiped my keycard in the entry slot and opened my homeroom door, I knew it wasn't going to be quite so easy. The air in the cramped room had an anxious edge to it, full of nervous anticipation and disinfected surfaces. My mother fussed over the small electric cooker in the corner, her face tense. The tang of burnt chicken wafted ominously from the pots bubbling on the hob. I wished she'd waited for me to help with the meal. My mother always burned food when she was stressed. My father hated burnt food.

"Set the table, Adina," my mother said without turning round. "He'll be back soon." She didn't need to tell me who "he" was.

Tash was sitting at the small table set between the cooker and the bunkbeds. She looked up and smiled when I walked in, but her eyes were uneasy. She watched the food preparations warily, her fingers playing with the edges of her homework notepad. She knew something was wrong, something she couldn't fix. How could she? She was only six.

I tapped her nose playfully and flashed her a reassuring grin. I was going to make this evening perfect, I vowed, or die in the attempt. I helped Tash finish the homework questions on her pad, then pulled out the set of plastic plates and cups from the cupboard by the cooker. They weren't fancy, but they were all we had.

"You should've waited for me, I could've done the cooking," I said quietly to my mother. I meant it to sound soothing, like I was reassuring her she didn't have to do everything on her own and she had me to help. Instead, it came out like an accusation.

"You weren't back," my mother snapped, stirring a mound of over-cooked vegetables that were slowly turning to sludge at the bottom of the pot. "If I can't rely on you, then I have to do things myself." She thumped a pan of congealing maize meal down on the electric ring and heaved a tired sigh. She was having a bad day. I turned away, hurt.

I fiddled with the knives and forks, a mixture of righteous anger and guilt stinging my eyes. I worked hard on the maintenance team, but not nearly as hard as I could. I shirked duties and skipped assignments to go off exploring, coming home late to find behaviour reports filed against me. I wasted my canteen credits on puddings and treats, and then had to borrow from my mother and little sister to get lunch at the end of the month. I forgot to bring home supplies, my mother's handwritten reminder notes next to the cooker piling up into little paper mountains. I wasn't nearly as much help to my family as I wanted to be. I was too selfish.

I went to my tool bag and pulled out the secret bundle I'd carried home. Tash leaned over my shoulder, watching me unwrap the plastic and take out two little yellow balls the size of tangerines. "What are those?" she asked, wrinkling her nose like she always did when she didn't understand something. "They smell."

"They're candles," I told her, "made out of beeswax." I didn't tell her they cost me half my canteen credits for the month—my mother would've been horrified. But I'd seen a picture in one of Dejen's books of a dinner party in the old times, with a table all laid out with flowers and lacy white napkins. In the faded photo, tall red sticks of wax cast a romantic glow over plates filled with tender cuts of meat and fresh vegetables. It looked so special. That's what I wanted for this evening.

I set the candles down on the table and unwrapped the second bundle. It looked like a pile of withered leaves, but inside I'd hidden the small bunch of flowers I took from the Gardens earlier that day. I had to sneak them past the planters and the scientists doing sap analysis up on Level Two, but I wasn't worried about them catching me. I could handle another behaviour report. I wasn't even scared of being seen by Otienno. I mean, it's not like it would've done my reputation any harm if he knew I had the guts to go stealing from the Gardens in the middle of a work shift, would it? No, it was Director Eshe and her disapproving eyes I'd been worried about running into with my shirt sleeves stuffed with stolen flowers. I didn't want her looking at me in that awful, disappointed way again.

I filled a plastic cup with water from the sink and put the three pink roses inside, setting them on the table between the candles. It didn't look quite the way I'd hoped. In my head, our small homeroom would be instantly transformed into a fairy-tale castle. Instead, the yellow candles looked sickly and deformed, the droopy flowers already half wilted and brown around the edges. The ugly green plastic of the table and chairs didn't help. Everything looked so stark beneath the ultraviolet strip lights. Maybe once I lit the candles it would start to look more romantic.

My mother was sighing louder now, the smell of burned food almost overpowering. Tash had gone very quiet, her lips quivering. She sat on my bed beneath her own bunk, clutching her rag doll and gazing at the door expectantly. I found myself staring at the door too, willing my father's footsteps to sound on the metal landing of the stairway before the food was all turned to ashes in my mother's angry pots. By the time I finally heard his keycard in the lock, I knew there'd be no salvaging the food. How the evening went now would depend entirely on what mood he was in. I held my breath and watched to see what he would do.

I'd once thought my father was as big as a bear, with arms that could lift me right above his head and swing me round while I screeched with laughter. But that was when I was little. That was before Chiku. Now the man who opened the door seemed shrunk to half the size I remembered, his arms lean and wiry instead of thick and powerful. His short hair was grizzled round the edges, deep frown lines crossing his brow. His dark brown eyes were changeable: sometimes they flashed with laughter, other times they seem to turn inward, becoming brooding and resentful. As he stepped into our homeroom, he took the whole scene in at a glance.

The smoke rising from the hissing pots.

My mother's tired, strained face.

The table set with half-dead flowers.

His daughters watching him with wary, distrustful eyes.

He grunted and threw himself down in one of the plastic chairs, rubbing a hand wearily across his face.

It was Tash, the youngest and smartest of us all, who seemed to know instinctively what to do. She clambered off the bunk and went over to our father, pulling shyly at his trouser leg. "Dolly's got a sore tummy," she said, holding the ragdoll up for inspection. She always did that when she wanted attention or reassurance. She gave you her doll and told you there was something wrong with it. It was Tash who had the sore belly. The poor kid's insides were probably twisted into knots with the tension in the room. Our father seemed to sense this, and he lifted Tash up onto his knee, patting the doll's stomach as Tash snuggled into his neck.

I let out a long, silent breath. It was going to be OK.

I helped my mother spoon the blackened food onto the plates, setting them on the table with a glance at my father. He didn't comment on the state of the food, he just picked up his fork and waited for the rest of us to sit down. I grabbed an electric spark gun out of my tool bag and lit the candles, eager to change the mood in the room. The flames flared angrily, guttering and spitting in the centre of the table.

"What are those things meant to be?" My father frowned at them. "It's against the rules to have naked flames outside the lab rooms. You know that, Adina."

"They're candles," I protested. "And it's not like they're going to start a fire when we're all sitting round staring at them, are they?" The smoky balls of smelly wax were starting to sting my eyes, but I wasn't ready to admit defeat just yet. "They don't look right with the overhead lights on—wait." I jumped up and turned the switch on the wall, dimming the strip lights to a faint electric hum. The room was plunged into darkness, the candles giving off only a feeble orange glow.

"Turn the lights back on," my mother sighed. "We can't see what we're eating."

"But it's *romantic*," I wailed, disappointed they weren't creating the effect I'd been seeing in my head. I'd pestered one of the beekeepers on Level Two every day for a whole week to get hold of the wax, then traded half my lunch credits for the month to get a factory worker to process it for me.

"Open the door at least, Adina," my father said. "Let a bit of the landing light in."

I knew he was more interested in letting out the stench of burnt food and cooking smoke without starting an argument with my mother than playing along with my dinner party fantasy, but I took it as a small sign of support anyway. Most of the other families on our accommodation level had their doors shut, or were eating up in the canteen four levels above, so there wasn't too much noise to disturb our meal despite the open door. With the extra light from the landing outside glinting off the plastic plates and softening the edges around the unappetising food, our homeroom actually looked quite cosy.

We ate in silence for a while, the dismal click of plastic knives and forks sounding too loud in the half-light. I racked my brain to think of something to say, something that would have us all laughing and reminiscing about happier times. Something that would make us all feel more at ease with each other. But my mind had gone blank, the carefully worded little speeches I'd practised in my head all deserting me.

Again, it was our clever little Tash who managed to break through the adult awkwardness filling the room. "I got full marks again on my maths test today," she announced suddenly, her eyes darting round each of us for approval. "Teacher says I can move up a class after the harvest."

My mother set down her fork and beamed at her. She worked as one of the teachers on the Early Education Level, and having a daughter fast-track at such a young age would be something to brag about to the other workers. I'd given her little enough to be proud of with all the times I skipped school and refused to do assignments.

"Good girl." Our father patted Tash on the head. "Keep it up and you'll be a teacher yourself soon, just like your mother. Maybe you can start helping her with some of her classes."

Our mother smiled at the half-compliment. We all knew Tash was smart enough to make the science team, but it made her happy to think her youngest daughter might choose to follow in her footsteps. "Tash was teaching before she could walk," she reminded us. "Do you remember that time a few years back when she rounded up all the children on this level and marched them back to our homeroom to teach them their ABC's? I was only out of the room five minutes, and when I came back I could barely make it through the door for crying toddlers and dolls lined up on the chairs."

I laughed. I remembered that day only too well. Tash didn't have a boardpad to write on for everyone to see, so she improvised using the inside of the door, a paintbrush, and a bowl of watery tomato sauce. It had taken me hours of scrubbing to get all the sticky patches off the floor.

Our father smiled too now, a real smile that lit up his face and smoothed out all the worry lines. I felt a warm glow spread from my stomach all the way down to the tips of my fingers. This is what I had wanted. This was the way our family dinners were supposed to be.

But suddenly our father's smile vanished. He stared at the open door, his eyes darkening to a frown. I turned to look.

A ten-year-old girl with raggy hair and a permanently runny nose was standing in the doorway, looking in on our happy scene with greedy, envious eyes. She stepped back at the sudden attention.

"What do you want?" I demanded.

Chiku shrugged, rubbing her nose on the sleeve of her creased shirt. Gods, I hated it when she did that, it was disgusting. "Wanted to see if Tash was coming out to play," she mumbled through a faceful of snot and sleeve.

"Alitash is having her dinner," my mother said in a high, strained voice. "Go and play somewhere else for now."

My father was gripping his knife and fork too tightly, the vein in his forehead pulsing. Chiku stepped back further, but hovered just outside on the landing, kicking at the stairway rails.

Clunk. Clunk. Clunk. Clunk.

The noise echoed through our strangely quiet homeroom. My mother looked down at her plate, pushing her food around restlessly, her lips pulled back in a thin tight line. Tash looked from one silent parent to the other, sensing the tension but not understanding. "Can I go and play?" she whispered to me. "I'm done. I don't like this chicken, it tastes funny."

"You're not done," I snapped. "Eat your food."

Clunk. Clunk. Clunk. Clunk.

There was a long pause. I gritted my teeth and waited. Then the idle thumping sound started again.

Clunk. Clunk. Clunk. Clunk.

I leapt to my feet and rushed outside, closing the door behind me. I grabbed Chiku by her scrawny neck and squeezed hard.

"Ow!" she whined, trying to twist away. "You're hurting me! Let go!"

"I'll hurt you worse if you don't leave my family alone," I growled, pushing her towards the stairs.

"I just wanted to play with Tash." Chiku kept squirming in my grip, getting snot smeared on the cuff of my shirt. That just made me angrier.

"She doesn't like you!" I told her, shaking her hard. "Nobody likes you. You're not wanted here. Go and play with the other children nobody wants and leave my little sister alone."

I pushed her down the stairs, letting her go before she'd found her balance. She stumbled, scraping her knees on the edge of a metal step. She screwed up her face, snot streaming from her nose with the effort not to cry. "She's my sister too," she sniffed.

"No, she's not!" I snarled. "You don't have any sisters. Stay away from my family or I'll throw you off the stairs and let you fall to the basement and split your ugly head open. Don't think I won't. I'll tell everyone it was an accident and they'll believe me."

Chiku looked at me for a long moment, her teary eyes resentful. She decided I was serious. I watched her limp down two full levels before I was sure she wasn't coming back. Then I took a long calming breath and headed for our homeroom to see if I could salvage the dinner.

By the time I got back, I knew it was too late. The strip lights were back on, the room lit up starkly in their harsh glare. The candles had been blown out. They sat smoking on the table, the foul-smelling wax oozing down the sides like fat yellow tears. The plates were piled by the sink, my mother scraping the remains of the meal into the recycling unit. The blackened food had hardly been touched, shrivelled chicken breast plopping down into the biohazard bags. I felt my throat tighten. That food must've cost my mother a fortune in credit.

My father was clattering around in the little sanitation unit, changing out of the overalls he wore to work on his factory level. He emerged moments later, looking flushed and irritable. "I'm stepping over to Faraji's for a little while," he said, barely glancing in my mother's direction. "Don't wait up."

He was gone before I could urge him to stay. I hated it when he went to his friend's homeroom. It was always full of factory workers drinking and smoking illegal tobacco leaves they grew in their kitchens and sanitation units. My father would come back in the early hours of the morning, stumbling and bleary eyed. I stared at the roses wilting on the plastic table. I'd been so stupid. I'd thought a few half-dead flowers and a couple of stinking candles could fix everything that Chiku had done to our family.

I snatched the candles and the roses up and threw them in the trash, slamming the lid down with such force the whole sink unit shook. I should never have looked in Dejen's stupid book. Didn't I tell him looking at nice things we couldn't have would just make us unhappy? I'd been right. My chest was heaving with the effort not to cry, my eyes stinging with unwanted tears. Then I felt my mother's hand on my shoulder, squeezing it lightly. She understood how I felt. She always understood. "Come and sit down, Adina," she said softly. "It's time I did something with that hair of yours."

I let her lead me to one of the plastic chairs, all the fight going out of me. Her warm hands set to work on my wiry hair, gently tugging the wayward clumps into order and combing them out into rows. Very quietly, her breath on my scalp, she began to gather the short strands into tight braids.

Tash lay on my bed, watching her work. She was still clutching her ragdoll, her face tight with worry. I held out my arms, and she came running to sit in my lap, her puffs of hair tickling my face. I'd done her hair myself, tying off small sections with brightly coloured bands to form little pompoms across her head. One band had snapped, the strands of hair coming loose. I took another comb from my mother's sanitation bag, teasing the pompom back into place as Tash nuzzled my cheek.

I imagined what we must look like to the passing neighbours, the three of us sitting there combing each other's hair. Anyone looking in through the door my father had left half open would think we were such a happy family. But we were broken. I knew it deep down in my gut. It was all Chiku's fault, and I made her pay for it every opportunity I got.

Like the time Chiku wanted me to do her hair. She'd seen the way I did Tash's hair, all nicely braided up with colourful bands. We'd sit out on the landing some evenings, me tying Tash's hair up while she read to me from her school books.

Out of the corner of my eye, I would see Chiku's snotty little face peering down from the top of the steps, watching us. Sometimes I'd chase her away, but other times I just didn't want to give her the attention she came looking for.

One day Chiku had made the mistake of asking me to do her ratty hair for her. She'd brought a comb with half its teeth missing, and a little sliver of mirror. She knew she wouldn't be allowed into our homeroom to play with our nicely washed sanitation things. I'd sat her down on the stairs, pretending I was going to do braids. I told her I'd need to shave the ends of her hair to get it to the right length for braiding. Then I'd taken a flat razor and cut everything off, one matted piece at a time, right down to her scalp. She just sat there like one of those dumb little test mice in the medical lab the whole time, thinking I was making her pretty. I'll never forget the look in her eyes when I picked up the mirror and showed her. Chiku had squalled like a baby when she'd seen what I'd done. I could still see her ugly little face now, all gasping and puffy.

Serves her right, I thought, listening to my mother's sad, tired breathing above me and feeling Tash trembling in my arms. *After what she did to my family, Chiku deserves everything she gets.*

CHAPTER 5

THREE DAYS/70 HOURS
TO THE END

I wanted last night to be perfect. Today I just wanted to stay alive.

I stared at the assignment scrawled across my duty sheet, gulping down the rising panic. "Level Seven—solar panel maintenance" it said. Level Seven was ground level, the lowest floor of the Dome. But there were no solar panels inside the Dome. Just to make it clear what I was assigned to do, Foreman Tafari had added "OUTSIDE" in big bold letters at the bottom of the sheet.

This was it. I'd broken the rules one too many times. He was finally making good on his threats. I was being sent into the wilds outside the Dome.

I waited beside the airlock for the head technician, my heart pounding in my chest. If I'd thought for a minute I'd be the one fixing it, I wouldn't have been so quick to report the broken solar panel. I'd never been out before—only a handful of the more experienced techies had. I hopped from foot to foot with nerves as I waited for Makena to report for duty, Baba Weseka's stories of Nomalies spinning round my head.

There's no such thing as monsters in the wilds, I told myself, feeling less and less sure as the minutes ticked away.

Along one wall of the long corridor leading to the airlock was a glass-panelled storage cabinet. Inside, a row of biohazard suits of various sizes hung on wire frames. The thin, pale brown material had the unpleasant texture of withered flesh, and I couldn't help thinking they looked like a row of dead techies who'd been skinned alive and strung up to dry.

Maybe the Nomalies got them, said the voice in my head that just wouldn't shut up.

"Oh, you're here already, Adina. Great. Ready for your first trip into the wilds?"

Makena Chang, the head techie, came clomping down the corridor, all calm efficiency and easy smiles. She looked like she was going for a stroll through the flower gardens on Level Two, not out into the toxic ruins under the real sky. I tried to smile back, but my grin wasn't real like hers. That wasn't the only difference between us. Her skin was much lighter than mine, her eyes a different shape. There were small groups of workers in Eden Five who were descended from people who weren't local when the Gardens of Eden were built, and Makena was one of them. Some of them said their ancestors were from Asia, but most weren't sure. It was too long ago, and the first generation who came to Eden Five had been too busy trying to survive to hand down any stories about the past.

Makena had been outside more times than anyone, and she'd even personalised the biosuit she always wore. She swiped her keycard in the wall lock and opened the glass doors, pulling out the suit that had little birds painted on the back and sleeves. She looked me up and down, sizing me up, then pulled out another of the leathery brown suits.

"This should fit you."

"Do I have to wear it?" I groaned, shrinking from the blubbery feel of the suit material. I couldn't get the image of flayed techie out of my head.

"Your choice," Makena shrugged. "You either wear the suit, or I fit you with a biofilter." She pointed to the triangular devices that sat on a shelf in the cabinet. The metal filters were the shape of flattened pebbles, small enough to fit snugly in the palm of my hand. They looked harmless enough, but I knew wearing one would hurt. Three sharp needles fixed them to the base of the neck between the collarbones, the tiny cleansing mechanism removing the airborne toxins from the wearer's blood as soon as they were breathed in. On the underside next to the skin was a UV patch with super-strong, slow-release chemicals to protect against sun damage. I'd heard one tiny filter could protect you for thirty whole days out in the wilds. Fortunately, it wouldn't take us more than an hour to fix the solar panel. I hoped.

"Come on, Adina, make up your mind, we haven't got all day. I need to get down to the basement to look at the water system pressure again after this—there's something seriously up with it." Makena held the suit in one hand, tossing a biofilter up and down in the other. "Remember, if you wear the filter you'll still have to have a decontamination shower when you come back in. Can't have any biopests hitching a ride in your hair and messing up the DNA of our precious plants."

My stomach turned at the thought of getting into one of those dead flesh suits and shutting myself inside a cramped helmet. But I really didn't fancy climbing round the Dome with needles sticking into my neck then blasting half my skin off in a chemical shower either. I remembered one of the techies had used a filter for a long repair job on the outside a few months back. He'd stunk of disinfectant for a whole week after. I took the suit from Makena and started pulling it on.

While I struggled with the strangely heavy material, Makena slipped her own suit on with practised ease and started going through the repair drill. "You've got your radio on the right side of the helmet—you already know how to work one of those. The oxygen generator's the big box on the left—it's already calibrated, so don't fiddle with it once you're out there. Basically, your helmet's the most important piece of equipment you've got, it's the thing that'll keep you alive once we leave the airlock, so if you *do* lose your footing and fall off the Dome, try not to land on your head, OK?"

"I'll try to remember that," I muttered with one arm stuck at an awkward angle behind my back in the rubbery suit. Makena flashed me a grin that said she was only kidding, coming to my rescue and straightening me out. As soon as she clamped my helmet in place, I wanted to tear it off again. The soft hiss of oxygen by my ear was spooky, unnaturally loud in the claustrophobic bubble. I knew it was stupid—it was

54

the same chemically manufactured air that gushed from the environmental control pipes inside Eden Five. But somehow in the confines of the helmet it seemed more artificial, and I found myself drawing great gulps of it down, terrified I wasn't getting enough oxygen.

"Slowly," Makena's voice crackled in the other ear when she pressed her radio button. "Take deep, slow breaths or you'll make yourself lightheaded. You'll get used to it in a minute."

"Foreman Tafari must really hate me," I panted. "He's been threatening to send me out for weeks. Didn't think he'd actually do it, though."

"This isn't punishment, Adina," Makena chuckled in my ear speaker. "You're not here for rule breaking, you're here because you're one of the best young techies we've got. The solar panels are getting old, they need constant maintenance, and that means I need all the techies on the team learning how to go out and fix them. Ready?" She stepped up to the airlock and swiped her keycard.

I nodded. "Let's get it over with."

The huge airlock wheel spun automatically, the door opening to reveal the small compartment beyond. Makena pulled one of the specially prepared toolboxes from the storage case, handing me another. I followed her into the airlock, my legs feeling weak and wobbly inside the biosuit. She swiped her keycard again and the door swung shut. I fought the urge to lunge for the wheel and open it again, but then there was a rush of air as the vacuum seal kicked in, and it was too late. A haze of gas clouded my helmet's visor for a long moment. When it cleared, the red light above the main door blinked green. A loud scraping of metal on metal sent jarring vibrations through my helmet, and before I knew it, the door to the wilds was wide open before me.

Makena marched straight out without a moment's hesitation. But I couldn't be that brave. Not the first time. I stood at the threshold, half blinded by the glaring sun beating down on the wastelands. My eyes slowly adjusted behind my visor, and I started to make out colours and shapes. Well, I say colours, but it was really just *colour*. Everything was a strange yellow-brown, somewhere between dead sand and sickly soil. Even the sky was brown, I couldn't make out a horizon.

When I took my first shaky steps out of the airlock and into the barren landscape, I realised I was looking at everything wrong. Eden Five was built at the bottom of an ancient lake, long dried up. In the distance on all sides, the banks of the lake rose up gently, forming small hills around the Dome that cut off my view of the wilds beyond. When I stepped away from the safety of the towering Dome and looked straight up, I nearly fell backwards in surprise.

The sky wasn't yellow-brown after all. That was the tops of the hills I saw from the airlock. The sky was blue. Bright, bright blue, so pure it made my throat tighten and my eyes ache. It sounds crazy to say a colour could make you want to cry, but the sky was so beautiful I could barely breathe for looking at it.

The real sky.

The *African* sky.

I only realised I was crying when my nose started to run. I put my hand up to wipe it, my gloved fingers banging off the plastiglass and jarring me back to reality. I was outside in the wilds in a biosuit, the thin layer of manufactured material all that stood between me and the air that would kill me. I couldn't feel the wind that swirled round the basin of the lake, but I could see the puffs of dry dirt it caught up, sending them spinning in little clouds over the cracked ground. I couldn't see the biotoxins filling the air either, but I knew they were there. Just one lungful would be enough to poison my bloodstream, tearing at the delicate strands of my DNA and mutating my body in horrible ways. I shuddered, suddenly cold despite my suit's thermal regulators.

"You OK down there?" Makena called. She was already climbing up one of the maintenance ladders that criss-crossed the huge Dome.

"Yeah. Just coming."

I turned and headed up the ladder after her, clutching my tool kit tightly in one hand and clinging to the rungs with the other. The Dome was huge. It had to be, I suppose—it held the Office Level and all six of Eden Five's garden levels stacked one on top of the other all the way up to the high roof. Solar panels were clamped across its entire surface, shimmering black in the blazing sun. I tried not to look at the sun. It wasn't just because it hurt my eyes. There was something about its fierce, cruel intensity that frightened me.

We stopped one level up, by the solar panel that had failed on Level Six.

"This is the one." Makena checked her infopad. Only the heads of the workgroups got the precious infopads that doubled as communication devices. The rest of us had to make do with recycled paper. We set our toolboxes down on the narrow maintenance walkway that ringed the Dome and unscrewed the panel's protective lid. I looked over Makena's shoulder as she peered inside, checking the photovoltaic modules for damage. "Just a couple of bust fuses, nothing serious. You OK to fix it on your own?"

"Sure," I nodded. I'd been fixing solar-panel parts inside the workshop since I joined the maintenance team. There was nothing to it. "Where are you going?" My heart lurched in terror at the thought of her going back inside and leaving me out here all on my own. Instead Makena pointed up.

"A panel on Level One was reported this morning. Think it might need one of the modules replaced, so I'll handle it myself. Just give me a call if you need help down here, alright?"

She gave my helmet a friendly pat and swung back onto the ladder, climbing up towards the top of the Dome. I watched her for a while, her suit turning black against the blue of the sky as she shrunk to a tiny figure in the distance. Then I went back to the panel and got on with my work, stripping fuses and replacing them with new electronic parts from the toolbox. The sooner I got this finished, the sooner I could get back inside the safety of Eden Five.

I was nearly done, when suddenly the hairs on the back of my neck stood on end. It was a strange feeling, a cold, shuddery wave that tingled down my spine and settled deep in my stomach like I was sickening for something. I checked the suit's thermal settings, but they hadn't budged. I was stalling for time. I knew what was making me feel so uneasy. I just didn't have the courage to turn and look.

Something was watching me. I knew it as surely as I knew when Otienno's eyes were on me in the Gardens, or when Chiku was peering out at me from the dark corners of the stairways. But this was different. The feel of these eyes was different, less…human.

I took a deep breath and turned around too quickly, grabbing onto the rail to stop myself from falling off the maintenance walkway and toppling to the ground. I stared out across the wastelands stretching up to the small hills around the dry lake.

Nothing. There was nothing there.

But I'd felt it, those eyes boring into the back of my helmet, trying to see all the way through into my head.

Nomalies, Baba Weseka had said. *There are Nomalies in the wilds.*

I wasn't quite sure what a Nomaly was, but I knew it was something bad. I stared at the wastelands, straining my eyes against the sun's glare and leaning as hard as I dared against the rail. Then I saw it. The flash of a black shape moving between two mounds of earth. No, not moving—*scuttling*. Through the clouds of dust, I thought I saw spiderlike legs curled close to a bloated body. Something bulbous sat on top of a stalk-like neck. It might have been a head.

I'd thumped the radio button on my helmet before I even knew my hand was moving. "Makena?" I could hear my voice shaking.

"What's the matter?" the head techie answered immediately.

"Makena, I think there's something out there."

"Out where?"

"Out *there*. In the wilds. I saw…" I peered at the spot where I thought I'd seen something scuttling. The dust clouds swirled restlessly over the still earth. Nothing else moved. "I saw something." But my voice was uncertain now.

There was silence for a moment, then a loud laugh crackled down the radio link. "Seeing Nomalies are you? Don't worry, every techie sees things their first time out."

"You mean Nomalies are *real*?" I gasped. My stomach flipped at the thought.

"Of course not!" Makena laughed harder. "I mean you've all been listening to Baba Weseka and his crazy stories. You kids all come out and see exactly what you think you'll see. Once you've been out a few times, you'll realise that it's just the wind stirring up dust clouds into strange shapes, nothing more than that."

But I wasn't so sure. I hadn't come out expecting to see Nomalies, not really. And I certainly hadn't been expecting to see something so monstrous, so *insect*-like. I didn't have that kind of imagination.

"So…there's nothing out here?" I asked. Gods, I sounded like Tash looking for reassurance. Any minute now I'd be climbing up to show Makena a doll and tell her it had funny things going on in its stomach.

"There's nothing out there, Adina, just the empty wilds. Hang in there, kid, I'm nearly finished. I'll be down in a few minutes."

I sat down on the maintenance walkway, my legs swinging out over the edge beneath the handrail. I'd seen something. I was sure of it. At least, I thought I was. I stared at the spot between the two earth mounds until my eyes hurt, then I looked away at the small hills beyond.

For the first time, looking out over that barren landscape beneath the stunning sky, I wondered how it had got this way. We were taught all about ecosystems in school biology lessons. The future of Eden Five depended on us keeping the delicate balance between plants, insects and birds just right. Our lives depended on rearing healthy animals and plants. We were taught in history class that it all went wrong over eighty years ago. The balance was lost. The world's ecosystems collapsed. Many people died. So *many* people. Gardens of Eden were built on every continent to house the survivors and provide a protected, pure environment to preserve the remaining plant and animal species. But Dejen was right. We'd never been taught *why* it happened. No wonder it bugged him.

"Makena?" I pressed the radio button again. "Why did the environment suddenly collapse in the old times? Why did they have to build Edens?"

Makena chuckled again. "I thought you couldn't wait to get out of school? Didn't you go to the classes on ecosystem failure?"

"Yes, I did, I don't mean…" I bit my lip, trying to phrase the question right. "I mean, what set it all off? What did the people in the old times do wrong?"

"I don't know, but it wasn't sudden," Makena told me. "The environmental changes didn't happen all at once. There was enough time to build the Gardens of Eden to protect the survivors."

"Oh. And everywhere's like this? Every part of the whole world's just wilds and wastelands?"

"Yes, everything's dead."

"How do we know?"

There was radio silence again. I could almost see Makena blinking.

"Sorry, what do you mean?" she asked after a pause.

"I mean, how do we know *everywhere* is like this?"

"It's in the history books."

"No, I mean how do we know *now*? Maybe some places weren't as bad as others. Isn't there any way to communicate with the other Edens to find out?" The thought sent a sudden thrill down my spine. What if the world wasn't all like this? What if there was some corner of the Earth left that was green like our Gardens, only with a real sky above it instead of an artificial one made of ultraviolet lights?

"It's a nice thought, Adina, but apart from the communications system inside Eden Five, we've only got basic shortwave radio. Director Eshe is the only one authorised to use it. She can reach some of the other Edens in Africa, but that's as far as it goes."

"But how did they talk to people on other continents in the old days?"

"They had communication systems in space. 'Satellites,' I think they called them. They'd all be broken and abandoned now."

"But couldn't we fix them up again? Talk to the people in the other Gardens?"

"Don't be daft! Our suits and biofilters wouldn't last long enough for us to trek the hundreds of miles across to Eden Four, never mind get us to another continent. How would we get all the way into space? We just don't have the equipment, not anymore." Makena was starting to sound a little frustrated. I guess that's what comes of being a techie and knowing your skills are a century out of date. "Anyway," she sighed, "what would be the point? Every Eden's probably the same inside, they wouldn't have anything new to tell us."

What would be the point? It was the same thing I said to Dejen all the time when he asked questions about the world. I'd never realised how irritating it sounded until now. We were all so used to not knowing the answers we'd just accepted the huge gap in our history. I swung my legs harder, banging my feet off the bottom of the walkway as I thought. There was something else that was bugging me, and it was all Dejen's fault.

"Makena?"

"Gods, Adina, do you want me to get this job done today or not?"

"Just one last question. What's the Amonston Corporation?"

"What? Oh, you mean the labels over everything? I don't really know. Must be the people who built this place, I suppose."

"Did they build every Eden?"

"How should I know? Look, I'm coming down now. I need my free hand for the ladder, so don't radio me unless it's an emergency, OK?"

"OK."

I gathered up my toolbox and headed for the end of the walkway. Then I stopped. Why hadn't I noticed it before? On the corner of every solar panel, stamped in small white lettering, were the words "Amonston Corporation—Feeding the World." There was a symbol too, a large "A" in the shape of a star sitting in a "C" that looked like a crescent moon. I smiled. We were right, it must have been the Amonston Corporation who built Eden Five. And if they were feeding the world, they must've built all the other Edens as well. They must've been good people who really cared about the future of humanity, not like the others who messed the whole world up.

By the time Makena joined me back on the ground I was feeling elated. I'd just survived my first trip out into the wilds. I couldn't wait to tell Dejen. But when we stepped into the airlock, I looked back out at the barren lake bed one last time.

I wish I hadn't.

Just before the main door swung shut, I saw a black blur dart out from behind the earth mounds and come scuttling towards us. I caught a glimpse of a tangle of legs—or maybe it was arms—and a horrible, deformed head bobbing about on the end of a spindly neck. The door clanged shut before it could reach us, the decontamination sequence kicking in. Clouds of disinfectant filled the airlock, hosing down our suits and killing any trace of biopoisons clinging to us from the outside.

There's no such thing as Nomalies, I told myself, balling my hands into fists inside the rubbery gloves of my suit. *It was just the wind stirring up the dust.*

When the purifying gases cleared and the green light blinked on, I glanced over at Makena. She was already stepping back into the corridor and pulling off her suit, whistling to herself at a job well done. She hadn't seen a thing. Maybe there hadn't been anything to see after all.

"You OK?" she asked, seeing me gazing back at the airlock doors, a puzzled frown on my face.

"Yeah. Fine. It's just…a lot to take in, you know?"

Makena nodded. "Your first walk in the wilds is pretty special. I remember my first time out—couldn't sleep for a week after. All I could think about was getting out again to stand under that blue sky."

I stayed silent as I tugged my suit off and hung it back up in the storage case. I had a feeling I wouldn't be sleeping for a week either, but it certainly wasn't because I wanted to go back outside. Makena was already checking my duty schedule on her infopad by the time I was done. "Says here you're assigned to fix the faulty wiring in the air filters down on Level Twenty-Eight. That's a pretty important job, Adina—those conduits are filled with pure oxygen. The smallest spark could start a bonfire down in the basement. You'd better get on to it right away."

"Will do," I nodded, picking up my tool bag.

I had no intention of trekking all the way down to Level Twenty-Eight just to go fiddling with a bunch of wires some dumb techie had put in wrong.

I had better things to do.

CHAPTER 6

THREE DAYS/68 HOURS TO THE END

I hurried down the spiral stairway circling round to the science laboratories two levels below. Wandering through the labyrinth of corridors between the lab rooms, I peered through the plastiglass set in the doors. In each science unit, biologists bent over workbenches and microscopes, peering at cell samples and recording the chemical compositions of natural fertilisers for the Gardens. Their research kept Eden Five's ecosystem thriving, maintaining the perfect balance between plant and animal life. It was an important job.

At the end of a quiet corridor, I found what I was looking for. A single scientist sat alone in an empty lab room, utterly absorbed in his research. Dejen liked to work by himself.

I slid my keycard into the doorlock, grinning at the little green light that flashed. I loved being a techie—my maintenance keycard could open almost any door in Eden

Five. Only the lead scientists and heads of the workgroups had higher clearance. And Director Eshe, of course.

I rushed into the silent room, breathless with excitement, boots clomping over the sterile tiles. "Guess where I've been today?" I panted.

"Outside fixing the solar panels," Dejen said without even looking up from his microscope.

"How did you know?" I demanded. "I didn't tell anyone."

"Would you come barging in here just to tell me you'd spent the morning fixing the toilets?" Dejen looked up with a smile, one eyebrow raised.

Gods, it was annoying how he always knew *everything*.

"How did it go?" he asked.

I opened my mouth, then closed it again, unsure how to answer. I sat down on one of the high stools and scratched my wrists where the rubbery suit gloves had squeezed tight against my skin. Dejen waited patiently, not hurrying me for an answer.

"It was...kind of weird." I said at last. "Everything was dead. But the sky was so blue! I mean real blue, *living* blue, not like the inside of the Dome." I stopped, frustrated that I couldn't find the words to describe what I'd seen.

"Go on," Dejen encouraged, "what else?"

"I saw something out there, Dejen, I'm sure of it." He was the only person I could tell, the only one who would believe me.

"Something?" He put down his cell slides and pushed the microscope away, turning to face me properly now. "What kind of something?"

"It was moving—it looked alive. There were legs, and a head, and it came towards the airlock like it wanted to get *inside*." When I said it out loud, it sounded insane. But Dejen didn't look at me like I was mad. He just frowned at me with those thoughtful brown eyes of his, the gears turning in his brain with an almost audible click.

"Are you saying you saw a *Nomaly*?" he asked.

"Crazy, huh?"

"Just a bit," he agreed, but I knew he wasn't doubting me.

I couldn't help laughing at myself. Somehow just being believed made me feel like it was OK to admit I might have been mistaken. "It was probably just a dust cloud. The head techie says everyone sees things their first time out."

"Perhaps. You should take a camera next time, though, just in case."

"Then you think maybe there might actually be something out there?"

I was surprised. Dejen was usually the first to roll his eyes when Baba Weseka started ranting about Nomalies and disaster. "You said the other day that the idea of anything living out there was far-fetched, that you didn't believe in the stories."

"I don't believe other people's stories, Adi," Dejen said seriously, "but if you say you saw something out there, then I believe you. Besides," he added quickly before I could make a joke to hide my embarrassment at the compliment, "I don't think everything's as simple as we've been taught in our history classes. There's more to it—more to the environmental failure and the wilds. More to the Gardens."

"How do you know?"

"When I got back to my homeroom last night, my parents were arguing. I heard them yelling halfway down the corridor."

I sat up, interested now. Dejen's parents were usually so close, working together, eating together in the canteen, even finishing each other's sentences when they got excited about a new piece of biological research. I'd watch them sometimes during the weekly Sunday-night workers' meeting in the assembly hall, sitting holding hands in the back row and whispering together like teenagers. I wished my parents were like that. "What were they arguing about?"

"Something about secrets and Director Eshe keeping the truth from us. My father's always going on about how it isn't right she keeps videpods from the old times locked up in her office and won't let anyone look at them unless they fill in a request form in triplicate. I mean, how can we request to watch something if we don't even know what's on the videpods in the first place?"

"You think she's hiding something?" I frowned. What could there possibly be to hide? The world's ecosystems collapsed, the Gardens were built, and some people survived. Simple. End of story. "What do you think it is?"

"I don't know." Dejen toyed with the edges of the book that lay open beside his microscope. "But I think it has something to do with the Amonston Corporation. My mother was telling my father not to do anything stupid. She said something about too much information causing riots in Eden Two. She seemed to think my father was going to go breaking into Director Eshe's office to steal the videpods or something."

I smiled at the idea. It was ridiculous. Dejen's father was the head of the science team, and he followed Eden Five's strict rules even more closely than Dejen did himself.

"Oh!" I suddenly remembered. "I saw the name 'Amonston Corporation' all over the solar panels outside. It said they were 'Feeding the World.' They must've built the Gardens, huh? I bet they were pretty great people."

"Maybe…" Dejen said slowly. He had a habit of disagreeing with his eyes instead of his words. I wish he'd just come right out and say what he was thinking instead of always leaving me to guess. I couldn't be bothered playing his little guessing game this time. I looked at the colourful book on the workbench and changed the subject.

"Looks like Director Eshe doesn't keep *everything* about the old times locked up. What's your book about?"

Dejen lifted the flap of the cover. It said "Wildlife of the Great Rift Valley" in big red letters. Underneath was a picture of a vast green landscape filled with blue lakes. "I've been putting in requests to Director Eshe for months for this one. Here," he slid it across the workbench, "have a look."

I hesitated. I'd said I wasn't going to look at Dejen's books anymore, that they'd just make me wish for all the things that were long gone. But I couldn't help myself. I flicked through the pages, mesmerised. There were green mountains towering over tree-studded plains, and wide-open grasslands that stretched to the horizon. Strange animals crouched at water holes filled with flocks of exotic birds. Great grey

70

beasts wallowed in the mud, their heads half visible above the water line. The colours of the world were dizzying—the deep yellow pelts of the horned animals that looked like giant goats, the bold black and white stripes of the horse-like creatures, and the bright pink feathers of long-legged wading birds. I'd never seen anything like it in all my life. "Where is this?" I gasped.

"Here," Dejen said quietly. "Right outside Eden Five."

"Seriously?" I couldn't believe the barren wasteland I'd seen just a short time ago was the same place as the green valley in the book. I didn't want to believe it. It was too sad. I slammed the book shut. "I have to get back to work," I muttered.

Dejen seemed to know how I felt. He took the book back, touching it almost lovingly as he placed it in a drawer. The lunch bell went, but we both ignored it. Somehow those beautiful pictures had taken our appetite away.

"Maybe the wildlife was saved." Dejen tried to sound encouraging. "My father says there were Sanctuaries built off the coast that had biodiversity levels holding all the animals from the old times—you know, a bit like Noah's Ark from Sunday lessons on the old books?"

"Maybe." I shrugged. "But it's not like we'll ever get to see them." I knew what he was talking about, as I'd sneaked a peek at the old contraband maps Dejen's father kept stashed in his homeroom. The nearest Sanctuary to us was Sanctuary Seven, built out at sea south-east from Eden Five. There was little chance anyone could make it there in thirty days before their biofilter gave out.

71

"You got more assignments this afternoon?" Dejen asked, trying to get me to stop scowling at the floor. He always got fidgety and restless when I was unhappy.

"Some stupid job down in Level Twenty-Eight fixing the wiring. It can wait—I've got something more important to do."

"Something against the rules?" Dejen's brows creased into a disapproving frown. "You're not going to go hanging around the Gardens again drooling over that dumb planter are you? I've told you a million times, Adi—Otienno's bad news. I heard the other day that he—"

"Drop it, Dejen, it's none of your business." I picked up my tool bag and headed for the corridor before I could hear another lecture about what a waste of space Otienno was. Dejen was never going to understand what I saw in him, but I was pretty sure every other girl in Eden Five felt exactly the same way about Otienno as I did, so Dejen's opinion on the subject didn't count.

I was so excited about my secret plan that I couldn't help poking my head back round the door and grinning at him before I walked off. "It's none of your business, but I'll tell you all about it tomorrow anyway, OK?"

I could never keep secrets from Dejen for long.

But I didn't know then that he had a secret plan of his own, a dark, dangerous secret that would unravel our whole history and change our world forever.

I'm glad I didn't know then.

I might've tried to stop him.

CHAPTER 7

TWO DAYS/48 HOURS TO THE END

Fixing the wiring in the air filters on Level Twenty-Eight wasn't the only job I'd been shirking. Over the last few weeks, there were a number of small assignments I'd skipped, signing them off on my duty sheet and pretending they were taken care of. I had a good reason, of course, but it had nothing to do with that juicy apple hanging in the orchard waiting for me. No, this time it was all about Tash. The poor kid had a hard time of it, what with the cold war my parents had been fighting her whole short life and everything. I wanted something special for her, something to show her how much she was loved. The only thing was, it was totally against the rules.

"Is it done?"

I leaned across the assembly line in the main factory room and whispered in the ear of one of the teenage workers. He glanced over at the workgroup head prowling between the conveyor belts at the far side of the room. Then he nodded quickly, his voice low when he whispered back, "It's done. Wait five minutes. I'll go and get your share."

The worker set down the plastic parts of the recycling unit he'd been assembling and disappeared off behind the banks of 3D printers. I opened the casing of one of the printing engines, fiddling with the wires while I waited, trying to pretend I was busy.

The giant 3D printing machines were the powerhouses that kept Eden Five supplied with everything we needed to live our everyday lives. Day after day, they spat out plastic tables, chairs, garden tools, kitchen equipment, pipes, wire casings and plastiglass test tubes and beakers for the labs. They printed the equipment layer by layer from the templates stored in the computer terminals, the factory workers assembling the parts according to the request orders submitted by each of the other workgroups.

The plastic in Eden Five was all re-used again and again, the huge recycling plant on Level Sixteen breaking old equipment down into its component chemicals and feeding the compounds back to the 3D printers in thick pipes to be made into something new. In the smaller factory rooms we had a food processing plant, a fabric workshop and a paper mill. We just didn't have the minerals and metals needed to mass-make the chips and circuit boards for the electronic infopads, radio units and maintenance tools. The few metals we did have were carefully rationed—the scientists got any new electronic equipment that was commissioned, the 3D printers and computers used up the remainder, while the maintenance crew had to fight over the scraps. Mostly families had to make do with writing on recycled paper and melting down old household furniture if we wanted anything new made. And that was only if we saved up enough work credits to pay for the processing.

I'd often wondered why the 3D templates stored on the computers were so limited. I mean, technically you could print anything you wanted with one of those things if you had the base coding for the original and enough raw materials for the job, right? As a kid looking through books from the old times, I'd dreamed of building an aeroplane on the factory levels and flying away from the confines of Eden Five to find somewhere new, somewhere green, with gardens you didn't need a pass or a maintenance assignment to wander round. Then I grew up and found out about templates and base coding.

And that was when my dream died.

The computers were only programmed with a small number of designs—garden tools, household furniture, and maintenance equipment mostly. The computer technicians knew how to service the computers, how to keep them running and the printers going, but they had no idea how to write new programmes to print new designs. There were no handbooks, and the few times the technicians had tried to alter the codes, the computers had frozen for whole days at a time. It was almost as though the computers had started running some kind of defence program to keep workers from making any changes. That soon put an end to all experimenting with them. I stopped dreaming of leaving Eden Five after that. This is all I had—an entire planet of possibilities shrunk down to a world of twenty-eight artificially maintained levels.

Gods, it sucked.

Whoever built Eden Five had left us with plenty of crappy plastic to play with, but no *real* materials. We had hardly any of the conducting minerals and metals needed to build new electronic equipment, just enough to fix the wiring in the support systems now and again and keep the computers and solar panels running. And just enough 3D printer templates to keep our daily lives in Eden Five ticking along as they always had since the Gardens were first built, not enough for us to develop independent science equipment of our own. It was as though the builders of Eden Five didn't *want* us advancing, didn't want us reaching out with radios and vehicles and biofilters that lasted more than thirty days. It made me mad just thinking about it.

I drummed my fingers impatiently on the printer lid, feeling conspicuous in my yellow worksuit. The labourers on the factory levels all wore brown, and I stood out like a chemical spill on a newly washed floor. I just hoped no one would ask to see my duty sheet before I could collect what I came here for.

Over the hum of the printers, I caught the sound of a familiar voice. I turned to see my father standing close by on the assembly line, the sleeves of his brown worksuit rolled up as he fitted plastic parts together with practised hands. I was just about to take a chance and go and say hello, when I saw he wasn't working alone. A petite woman with a cute button nose and round hips was working next to him, giggling when he bent down and whispered something only she could hear. I felt a sick lurch in my stomach, a churning that was halfway between fear and jealousy on my mother's behalf. This was how it had all started more than ten years ago, when I was just old enough to know that something had gone wrong.

When I was little, my mother had been engrossed in her teaching work, staying late on the education levels to tutor the slower students and prepare lessons. My father had felt neglected, left alone in our homeroom at night looking after a little kid when he'd rather be drinking with his friends. There had been long, heated arguments in the small hours of the morning, when I lay curled in my bunk with the blankets pulled up over my head. Then my father had started staying late at work too—earning extra credits, he'd said. But when one of the young female factory workers turned up at our homeroom door with a swollen belly and a mouthful of accusations, it was too late to fix things.

They've been broken ever since.

But Chiku's mother had been a long time ago, and she'd died of an infection just after Chiku was born. My father wouldn't make that mistake again. He *couldn't* make that mistake again—it would rip what was left of our family life to pieces.

I glared at the back of the pretty woman's head, willing her to have a dreadful accident and spontaneously melt into a puddle of goo. She didn't. Damn.

"Here," said a voice in my ear. I looked round. The worker was back, handing me a small flat rectangle wrapped up in waxy paper. Through the thick wrapper, I could smell the

77

heavy scent of cocoa beans and dark sugar. *Chocolate*. Tash would go nuts.

"Did you dismantle the equipment?" I asked, quickly stuffing the bar into my tool bag.

"We finished the batch this morning and took the processor apart. It's all in storage," the boy nodded.

That was a relief. If our illegal little processing plant at the back of the recycling sheds had been discovered we'd all face a disciplinary hearing. I'd have got the worst punishment—after all, it was my idea. I sort of blamed Dejen though, even though he'd had nothing to do with it. It was all the fault of his damn books.

I'd seen an article about a cocoa farm in one of the dusty journals from the old times. It had been enough to get me thinking. We had cocoa plants in the Gardens, of course, but they were mainly used for flavourings in the cookhouse. I wanted *bars* of chocolate. Thick, sugary bars like the ones in the article, chunks of brown magic that melted in the mouth. Tash had a sweet tooth, she was never out of the canteen the evenings they made hot chocolate with milk and honey.

The idea had come to me a few months ago. A neighbour's kid had come back from the canteen one night with a steaming mug of the stuff. Tash had gone all wide-eyed, twining round my leg and asking if she could borrow my canteen card to get some. The younger kids had a strict sugar allowance to make sure they didn't binge on the unhealthy snacks. Tash never asked for anything, and the one time she did, I couldn't give it to her. I'd traded my canteen card credits that week for a couple of illegal cigarettes. I thought if Otienno saw me smoking round the back of the tool stores where the planter kids all gathered at breaktime, he'd come and talk to me. I knew he smoked—I'd seen him pass round cigarettes and light up when the workgroup head wasn't looking. But instead of looking sharp like him, I'd nearly choked on the damn things, setting the fire alarms and sprinklers off in the Dome.

Anyway, Tash's sad eyes when I said she couldn't have any hot chocolate made me feel like crap. I knew I'd have to make it up to her or I'd never forgive myself. I gathered a few other kids who were willing to make things on the fly, and we hatched a plan. The two factory workers in the group set up a mini-processing machine, the planter pinched a batch of cocoa beans from the Gardens, and the cookhouse assistant stole the other ingredients we needed from the kitchens. I had the hardest job—powering the operation. I had to run an electricity cable off the main power grid without it being detected, which took some doing, believe me. Makena's got every last ounce of juice in Eden Five accounted for, and it wasn't easy shirking off work to set it up with Foreman Tafari always on my case. But we'd done it. Yesterday we started processing the beans. That was what I'd been doing instead of fixing the air filters down on Level Twenty-Eight. If I'd only known then what an important job it was, I'd never have skipped the assignment for a bar of damned chocolate.

My father looked up from his work as I left, our eyes meeting across the crowded factory floor. I couldn't read his expression.

Was it guilt at being caught laughing with the cute young woman?

Was it a defiant "go and tell your mother if you dare?"

Was it a worried frown?

All I could make out was his short nod of recognition, then he went back to his work. That kind of pissed me off. I felt like I'd been dismissed like a stranger. But then again, he was working—what did I expect? Did I think he was going to come running across the room to pick me up and hug me like he did when I was little? He didn't even do that for Tash.

The bell rang for the first lunch sitting, and I headed down to the canteen. I wanted to show Dejen my chocolate bar. Even though he didn't approve of me breaking the rules, he always gave me credit for inventing stuff and being creative. Somehow I needed that little shot of praise from him every now and again—it was like a drug I couldn't quite do without.

I guess it made up for my father's indifference. Almost.

CHAPTER 8

TWO DAYS/47 HOURS TO THE END

The canteen next to the cookhouse was crowded, the lines shuffling forward slowly towards the service hatches. The cookhouse assistants in their orange suits ladled out the food the workers selected into plastic trays, keying the credit price into card machines and waiting till a valid card was swiped before handing the food over. There was always someone who'd maxed out their canteen credit card and couldn't pay. Arguments at mealtimes were part of the routine.

I was hanging at the back of the queue, scanning the busy canteen for Dejen, when a loud ripple of laughter made me turn to look at the doors. Baba Weseka stood in the entrance, blinking in confusion. He'd clearly just woken up after a nap. Hearing the lunch bell, he'd pulled his green shirt on backwards, then stuffed his unlaced boots on the wrong feet and stumbled up the stairs to the canteen. He'd forgotten to lock Yango up again, and she was wrapping herself round his baggy trouser legs, whining in fear at the crowds. It seemed like after his fit in the medical bay a few days ago Baba Weseka was even more muddled than usual. He kept turning round and round, tripping over the dumb dog while he tried to get his bearings. Any minute now she was going to piss on the floor, I just knew it.

I groaned inwardly, willing someone to go and rescue the confused old man. They didn't. Everyone just sat and laughed. As long as he and his contaminated blood and craziness were on the other side of the room, he was a figure of fun rather than a threat. To make matters worse, just then Yango sat on his boots and peed right down his leg. That made the workers roar with laughter. I could see the cookhouse overseer storming through the kitchens ready to explode at the sight of the dog contaminating his canteen. Biohazards were just about the most serious threat we faced in Eden Five.

I shoved my way past the chuckling workers and took Baba Weseka by the arm. Everyone was staring at me, and I wished I didn't care quite so much. But it wasn't much use me being shallow and trying to act sharp. It's not like I was ever going to be popular.

"Baba, you're all tangled up in your suit. You need to go back to your homeroom and put your clothes on properly first. And lock Yango up—she's not allowed out, especially not to the canteen."

Baba Weseka peered at me with his pale eyes all wide and wondering, confusion clouding his face. "Who are you?" he asked weakly.

Urgh. He was having one of *those* days.

"I'm Adina. You know me—I work on the maintenance crew. Come on, let's go."

"But I'm hungry. I want my lunch. I have a card, see?" His trembling hands fumbled in his pockets, and he pulled out a piece of plastic that Yango had chewed down to a stump. There wasn't enough left to recycle, never mind swipe in the card machine.

"Come *on*, Baba, you need to leave now," I urged. The angry overseer was stomping across the canteen towards us, a grim-faced sanitation crew in tow. Yango was in for it if they got hold of her. It was bad enough she was in the canteen in the first place, but the yellow puddle soaking the floor was enough to get her sent back to the cages on the Slaughterhouse Level for good. Director Eshe would rather turn a blind eye to Baba's tears than tolerate a source of contamination on the Cookhouse Level.

"Please, Baba?"

But Baba Weseka was flustered and distressed. He flapped his hands in the air, the sleeves of his unzipped suit slipping down his bony arms and flailing about. The laughter in the canteen had died now. The air grew heavy with anticipation, the workers watching the overseer approach with eager eyes. There was going to be a scene.

Then suddenly we were rescued. A strong pair of hands grabbed Baba Weseka by the shoulders, propelling him back through the canteen doors.

"Come on, old man, let's get you back to your homeroom," Otienno said. He aimed a kick at Yango, sending her scuttling for the stairs.

I followed behind him like a puppy, my heart hammering. The double doors swung shut behind us, the cookhouse overseer stopping just at the edge of his kingdom and glaring through the plastiglass at us. He thought hard for a moment, the bulging veins in his neck throbbing as he tried to work out what to do next. When he finally turned away, my legs went weak with relief. I didn't need another behaviour report filed on me this close to the harvest. He must've decided he didn't need the hassle of all those forms to fill in either. The sound of his shouted orders to the sanitation crew followed us halfway down the stairs to the accommodation levels.

Otienno glanced over at me as we waited for Baba Weseka to fish his homeroom keycard from his pockets. "You're Adina? Maintenance crew, right?" he asked.

"Um, yes," was all I could think of to say. As first lines go, it wasn't exactly epic.

"I'm Otienno, planter." He held out a hand, and I shook it eagerly, my fingertips tingling when they touched his. "But then I guess you know that already from all the times you've stood staring at me in the Gardens." He gave a soft snort of laughter and grabbed the card Baba Weseka was fumbling with, slotting it in the lock and opening the homeroom door. I hovered in the entrance, my cheeks stinging with embarrassment, until he called, "Are you coming in or not?"

Damn it. Why couldn't I get myself together and act sharp? I must look like some dumb kid. I followed Otienno inside, trying to avoid his gaze as we helped Baba Weseka put a clean suit on the right way round and sort his boots. Instead,

I looked round the little room. It was depressingly familiar. The cramped kitchen area, the basic bunkbeds, the chipped plastic furniture. But somehow it was all so disordered, so unkempt and confused, it made my homeroom seem like a palace in comparison. His bed was undone, the thin blankets ragged and stinking. Mouldy food leaked out of tins by the sink he'd tried to open weeks ago but had given up on halfway through the attempt. Dog piss leaked out from under the door of the sanitation unit, the smell almost unbearable. The whole place was one giant biohazard.

"So, you got anything to do tomorrow night?" Otienno asked casually, ignoring Baba's yelp of pain as he pulled the sleeves of his shirt on too quickly over his scrawny arms.

I shrugged, my mind racing almost as fast as my pulse. He wasn't going to ask me out, was he? I mean, seriously?

"If you're free, then why don't you come and check out the game that me and some of the other planters have got going on down in the basement tomorrow night? It's a good laugh, and you might earn yourself some extra credits if you're willing to place bets on the winner. Up to you of course, but we don't invite just anybody."

I gawped at him in reply, my mouth hanging open dumbly. I'd heard whispers about the game the younger planters played away from the eyes of the overseers. They said it was dangerous. Kids got hurt. But Otienno was telling *me* about their secret game, asking *me* to go and watch. And they didn't invite just *anybody*.

"Sure, I might come along if I've got time," I said, trying to sound casual. It came out more like an excited squeak.

Otienno didn't seem to notice. He was just too sharp for words.

"OK then. Right, we're done here. Go to sleep," he ordered, pushing Baba Weseka back onto the bed and forcing him to lie down. Otienno shoved Yango off the blankets with the toe of his boot, kicking at her until she backed away under the bunkbeds. "Stinking mutt, someone ought to put her down."

I sort of agreed, but I felt bad when I saw Baba Weseka's eyes go all teary again. "But I want my lunch *now*," he whined, pushing the covers away. His skin had that waxy warning look that said if he didn't go to sleep right away he was going to have another fit.

"Look, you're not well, Baba," I said, sitting down on the edge of the bed and rearranging the covers for him. "Go to sleep, just for a little bit, OK? I'll bring you something from the canteen later when you're feeling better." *When the canteen's empty and there's no one left in there to laugh at me,* I added to myself.

"You promise?" Baba Weseka looked up at me the way Tash did when I swore on my life I'd bring her a hot chocolate when I'd got enough canteen credits.

"I promise. Go to sleep."

Baba Weseka relaxed, his waxy face softening as his eyes closed and his breathing slowed. I waited until I was sure he was fast asleep and wasn't going to have a fit before I let go of his bandaged hand. When I got up, I saw that Otienno was trying hard to hide an amused smile. I wasn't sure if he was laughing at me or Baba Weseka, but I felt my face go hot all the same.

"You coming or you want to stay and watch your boyfriend sleep?" he asked, throwing me a look that said he knew exactly which buttons to press to make me squirm.

Oh, right. So it was me he was laughing at then. For a brief second, I wished it was Dejen standing there with me. Then I wouldn't have any problem slapping the stupid smile off his face. But then Dejen wouldn't be laughing at me in the first place for helping Baba Weseka out. Damn it.

We left Baba Weseka to sleep, closing his homeroom door and heading back up the stairs. I didn't have the guts to face the cookhouse overseer or the grinning workers right away. I'd lost my appetite, but it might've been more to do with Otienno's eyes on me rather than the overseer's. Otienno didn't seem afraid of anyone. He wanted his lunch, and I was pretty sure he'd stare down a hundred overseers to get it.

As we parted ways at the canteen doors he looked back at me. "So, the game? Tomorrow night. Basement Level. Eleven o'clock. *Don't* tell anyone else." He stepped closer to me. "It's a secret, understand?" His brown eyes gazed down into mine, and I gulped, my mouth suddenly dry.

"Got it," I croaked. He nodded again, then he was gone, leaving me breathless and shaking. What in the name of the Gods was wrong with me? He was just some boy, for crying out loud. I got my head together as fast as I could, then went running up to the lab levels, skipping the stairs three at a time. I wasn't sure why I had to see Dejen right then, but my heart was bursting and I needed to talk. Dejen wasn't in the canteen, so there was only one other place he could be.

I knew as soon as I opened his lab room door that something was up.

Dejen wasn't peering into his microscope, typing data into a calculator spreadsheet or flicking through one of his books. He was staring at the blank wall, a deep frown on his face. For once, I couldn't read his expression.

"Everything OK?" I asked, sitting down on a stool and punching his arm.

He twitched in surprise, then his face relaxed. "Oh, hi, Adi. Everything's fine."

"Then why do you look so…"

"So… ?"

"Constipated."

"Haven't had my breakfast bran this morning," Dejen half-smiled. But his face didn't look right. His smile didn't reach his eyes. It made me nervous seeing Dejen like this, it wasn't normal. It made me feel unsettled, like there was something deeply wrong with the universe that wouldn't be put right until Dejen's smile was real.

I wanted to tell him everything—about Otienno, about the invitation to the game. But Dejen didn't like Otienno or the other planter boys. They'd given him a hard time in school, resenting the young kid who'd fast-tracked through the older classes and made them all look stupid. Besides, Otienno had said I couldn't tell anybody. I bit my tongue, holding back the secret that was trying to burst out, and asked, "What you doing?"

"Just… thinking," Dejen said vaguely. He picked up a sample kit and tried to look busy, but I wasn't buying it.

"You still thinking about the Amonston Corporation and those videopods locked up in Director Eshe's office?" I asked.

Dejen just shrugged. A horrible thought struck me.

"Dejen? You're not thinking about doing something stupid are you? Something *illegal*?"

He looked up at that, his smile a little more real this time. "Illegal's your area of expertise, not mine. Speaking of illegal, what was the secret job you went off to do yesterday afternoon?"

"Ah! Wait till you see this." I checked through the plastiglass window to make sure there was no one in the corridor, then I took the chocolate bar half out of my tool bag and showed him under the table. "Look."

Dejen shook his head in mock disapproval. "Should I ask how you made it?"

"Nope."

"Should I ask how much trouble you'll be in if you're caught with it?"

"Nope."

"Then I won't bother. It's pretty clever though, Adi. Tash'll love it."

He didn't even need to ask why I'd gone to all the bother of making a bar of chocolate. He knew me so well.

CHAPTER 9

TWO DAYS/37 HOURS TO THE END

I was right, and so was Dejen. Tash did love the chocolate. When I brought it back that evening she went crazy, running round our little homeroom like a bee in the flower gardens and jumping up and down on the bunkbeds in excitement. My mother just shook her head at me from the table and went back to planning her lessons. Her disapproval didn't quite stretch to confiscating Tash's illegal treat. My father, as usual, was at a friend's homeroom, but I doubt he'd have much more to say on the subject than an uninterested grunt.

It made me feel all warm inside when I thought of Tash's happy little face beaming up at me and calling me the best sister in the whole wide world. But later that night when I was walking back from a neighbour's homeroom where I'd been helping repair their recycling unit, I saw something that wiped out the warm glow and made me feel sick to my stomach. I'd just been looking forward to bed, wondering if Tash had finished the chocolate bar already, when I saw someone sitting on the stairs licking something brown that smelled of cocoa beans.

It was Chiku.

She had half of Tash's chocolate bar in her grubby hands, sucking on it like it was made of oxygen.

I was so mad I couldn't see straight. I worked for *weeks* for that little bar, hiding out on the factory level, shirking assignments and risking my job to steal enough power for the processor. And here was Chiku, the unwanted girl who'd destroyed my family, chewing on the fruits of my labour like a hungry dog. She must've been watching Tash with the chocolate through our homeroom door, peering and snooping like a thief. Then, when no one was looking, she'd crept in and stolen half the bar that was meant for my little sister. Or maybe it was worse. Maybe she'd taken it right off Tash, twisting her arm and hurting her to get at the candy. I went a bit nuts at the thought.

"Thief!" I yelled, clutching her round the neck and dragging her to her feet. "Give it back, you stinking little thief!"

Chiku took one look at me and my mad eyes and tried to stuff the whole half-bar into her mouth in one go.

"Drop it!" I ordered, trying to take the soggy bar from her. But she held it out of my reach, whining and crying that it was hers.

I grabbed her arm and thumped her wrist against the metal stair rail—once, twice, three times—until her hand went limp and she dropped the chocolate with a yelp of pain. She tried to catch it with her other hand, but it spun out into thin air, dropping down through the gap in the spiral staircase and disappearing from sight. Neither of us would get it back now. If it wasn't picked up and claimed immediately by one of the children on a lower level, then it'd be scooped up by the sanitation crew on their regular sweep before we could make it down the stairs.

All that work, gone in an instant.

I pushed Chiku hard against the wall, squeezing her scrawny chest with my fist. "I warned you what I'd do if I caught you near my family again," I hissed. "I said I'd throw you off the stairs. You ready, huh? Ready for a trip down to the basement?"

Chiku was struggling to breathe, whimpering in pain and fright. Her tears and snot dripped down onto my hand, and I wiped them off on her tatty shirt. "It was mine!" she gasped when the pressure on her chest eased for a moment. "Tash gave it to me."

"You're a liar!" I roared, "a thief and a liar!" I'd just grabbed hold of her neck again to drag her to the stair rail, when a man's hand was laid on my arm and a stern voice said, "Leave her alone, Adina. Let her go."

I looked up.

My father was standing over us. It was late and he smelled of tobacco ash and rice wine. I hated that smell.

"But she's a thief!" I protested. "She stole Tash's present!" I was ready to cry at the disappointment of Tash losing half the treat I'd worked so hard to give her.

"Let her go, Adina," my father warned. He was serious. I dropped my hand, stepping aside grudgingly to let Chiku stumble away. She turned back on the landing, fixing me with a stare full of malice and tears.

"I hate you," she sobbed.

"I hate you too," I threw back. I felt a brief flicker of triumph when the words hit her hard and I saw her wince.

"Go home, Chiku," our father ordered. He didn't turn round to look at her, keeping his eyes on me.

Home. What did that even mean for someone like Chiku anyway? She didn't have a family. She shared a homeroom on the bottom accommodation level with eight other unwanted children—one harassed, overworked nurse running after them all. They were all grubby and neglected, their eyes petulant and resentful. I loathed them all.

It wasn't until Chiku was gone that my father finally let go of my arm. "If you ever do that again, Adina, I'll lock you in our homeroom every evening for a month," my father said, his face strained and angry.

"How can you lock me in our homeroom if you're never there?" I shouted at him, storming off home. I knew he wouldn't follow me. It was too early for him to go to bed—he had friends to drink with and cigarettes to smoke. I was furious. Angry at my father for standing up for that ugly little brat instead of siding with me, his real daughter. Angry at myself for getting so worked up. But most of all, I was angry at Chiku. Why did she always have to go and spoil *everything*?

Luckily my mother and Tash were already asleep by the time I got back to our homeroom. I didn't want them to see my angry tears. I could hear my mother's soft snores coming from the bed in the dark alcove by the sanitation unit. I threw on my pyjamas and climbed into the bottom bunk, careful not to make any noise and wake Tash. She rolled over anyway, only half asleep.

She gave a loud yawn, and I whispered, "Tash?"

"Umph?" she muttered back down from the top bunk. I knew I shouldn't disturb her, but I wouldn't be able to sleep without knowing what had happened earlier.

"Tash, did Chiku take your chocolate from you tonight? Did she hurt you?"

"Hmph. Nope," came the sleepy response. "Gave her half."

I frowned in the darkness. "Why?" I demanded a little louder than I'd meant to.

"'Cause she's my sister," Tash yawned, "and she never gets nice things." She snuggled down against her pillow, drifting back off to sleep.

I lay awake for a long time, an unpleasant ache deep in my belly. Chiku didn't deserve nice things—her being born had spoiled everything. But somehow I couldn't shake the guilt that gnawed at my insides when I thought of her wrist hitting the stair rail and her wail of despair as the chocolate went spinning out of reach. I closed my eyes, willing the image of her tear-streaked face to fade from my memory.

When I finally did fall into an uneasy sleep, I saw the chocolate bar falling through the stairway gap to the basement far below. Only it wasn't a chocolate bar that was falling, it was Chiku. I was running down the stairs trying to catch her as she fell, but every time I reached out, she fell further away. I was screaming for help from the crowds of workers that stood on the stairs, but they were all laughing at me. Then there came a loud crack as Chiku's head hit the basement floor.

When I woke with a jerk, my hand was reaching out for her and my face was tight with dried tears.

CHAPTER 10

ONE DAY/14 HOURS TO THE END

The day before our pre-harvest assembly and official day off, everything got weird. And by everything, I mean Dejen. *Dejen* got weird.

He was kind of twitchy all day, fidgety and nervous when I went to see him in the lab before lunch and zoning out in the canteen when we went for dinner. He was so distracted he almost fell headfirst down the stairs when we made our way back to the accommodation levels late in the evening.

"What in the name of the Gods is the matter with you today?" I demanded, pulling him back to his feet.

"Sorry, I was just… thinking."

"You're not still obsessing over that stuff about the Amonston Corporation and the videpods in Director Eshe's office are you? 'Cause if you are, it's a complete waste of time."

"I know." Dejen did that thing where he nodded his head and disagreed with his eyes. I snorted in annoyance.

"Just forget it, Dejen. We're not going to find out anything else about the old times and how the world got this way. Even if there was something worth seeing on those videpods, Director Eshe isn't going to let anyone borrow them."

"I know," Dejen said again. I didn't like the way he said it. It sounded… dangerous. He saw me looking sideways at him and changed the subject quickly. "So, you still going to the basement to check this game out tonight?" He didn't sound too happy about that either.

I shrugged, trying not to look eager. "Thought I'd go down for a bit."

I hadn't meant to tell Dejen about Otienno's invitation, it just sort of slipped out. Didn't I say I couldn't keep secrets from him for long? Dejen had tried to talk me out of it, but I wasn't sure whether it was because he couldn't stand Otienno and his planter friends, or whether he knew something I didn't about the game. If he did, he wasn't telling me.

"You won't do anything stupid tonight, Adi, will you? Something you might regret later?"

Weird, I was just going to ask him the same thing. "No, of course not." When we finally reached my homeroom door, I was starting to feel pretty uncomfortable with the way he was studying me. "I'll see you tomorrow, Dejen. Go and get some sleep, you look like you could use it."

Dejen just nodded again with an odd frown and wandered away down the stairs. He looked sort of lonely and reluctant, like a man who knows he's walking off the edge of a steep drop to his death but can't stop himself. I wanted to run down and give him a hug. He'd probably think I was the one acting weird if I did. I mean, it's not like best friends hug each other all the time for no reason, is it? Instead, I swiped my keycard in the doorlock and stepped into my homeroom.

It was late and my mother was already in bed, fast asleep. She seemed to spend more and more time in bed these days, walking around in a permanent state of exhaustion when she was awake. I changed out of my work uniform and into a clean green shirt and trousers in the sanitation unit, careful not to wake her. As usual, my father was nowhere to be seen. But Tash was awake, leaning down from her bunk when I came back out.

"What's that funny smell?" she asked, sniffing the air and screwing up her nose.

"It's nothing, go back to sleep." I felt a bit stupid. I'd dabbed some scent on my wrists and neck, but it must've been stronger than I thought. Like most nice things in Eden Five that had to be specially made on the fly and sold through a chain of whispers, it hadn't been cheap.

"It's late, where are you going?"

"Out. Go back to sleep."

"But I'm not tired. Can I come? Please?" Tash was still wearing her day clothes. She swung her legs over the bunk and reached for the ladder. I pushed her feet back up and shook my head.

"Sorry, kid, another time." I felt bad. I remembered now I'd promised to spend the evening teaching her a new card game some of the techies had come up with in the breakroom. "We'll hang out tomorrow, OK?"

I hurried to the door so I didn't have to see her disappointed face, but then I stopped, hesitating in the doorway. "Tash? Does it really smell bad?" I couldn't help asking.

"Not bad. Just sort of a funny mix of stuff, you know, like the trash in the recycling bins?"

I rolled my eyes and rushed back into the sanitation unit, scrubbing at my wrists and neck to get the stuff off. The scent clung to my clothes, but I didn't have another clean outfit. It would have to do. I was going to be late.

"Go to sleep, Tash," I said, closing the homeroom door behind me and hurrying down the stairs.

The landing lights were dimmed, only the nightshift workers were up and about. I passed down the accommodation levels, the stairways growing quieter as I circled the Ventilation and Energy Level where the air was produced, recycled and purified, and electricity was stored in humming power units. By the time I reached the bottom level where the water was treated, the stairs were deserted. The air felt heavy down here, thick and stale, as though weighed down by all the levels above. It struggled out of the pipes with a thin hissing gurgle, and then I remembered why.

My assignment.

The one that was still scrawled at the top of my duty sheet waiting to be taken care of.

I'd forgotten again.

Damn.

But it was too late to do anything about it now. *I'll come back and fix the air filters tomorrow straight after breakfast*, I promised myself as I clattered down the stairs that led to the basement. My boots were too loud on the metal, the dull clanging echoing in the silence.

The stairs to the basement below Level Twenty-Eight ended in a metal door that was closed with a wheel, like the airlock leading to the outside. Only this door didn't lead to the wilds, it led to the maze of maintenance pipes tangling under Eden Five like noodles at the bottom of a bowl of soup. I'd been down here a number of times to fix the water pipes, but never without a map. It was easy to get lost in the labyrinth of dingy tunnels formed by the huge plastic tubes. I'd heard a techie got lost down here without a map years ago and couldn't remember the way out. By the time he was found, all that was left was a dried-up skeleton in a yellow suit. I was pretty sure it was just a story, but it made me nervous just thinking about it.

I hesitated for a long time in front of the door, wondering if I should knock. Then I realised how dumb that would look. I mean, it's not like the basement *belonged* to anyone, did it? I spun the wheel and pushed the door open, stepping into the poorly lit corridor beyond.

I heard it almost straight away. A loud roaring sound was coming from the darkness, the thunder of shouting voices and the rumble of many stamping feet.

I made my way towards the noise warily, my heart in my mouth. I realised now I had no idea what the game involved. People said it was dangerous, that was all I knew. I could turn back here in the maze of piping, before anyone saw me and knew I'd been a coward. But Otienno had invited me himself. I knew there were lots of other people here, but somehow I couldn't get the idea out of my head that this was some sort of date.

I turned the corner into the blaze of light and stood gaping at the sight before me. All along the huge pipes that circled an empty storage pit, teenagers stood stamping their feet and shouting. Fluorescent lanterns were shoved into the spaces between the plastic tubes, their light casting eerie shadows down into the pit below. I clambered up onto the nearest pipe and looked down. Two boys, bare-chested and panting, were brawling in the pit, their fists swinging at each other with deadly force.

Otienno was one of them.

"You're new here, huh?"

I nearly fell off the pipe when a stocky planter girl leaned over and shouted in my ear above the noise. I nodded, feeling nervous and out of place.

"Otienno said you might come. You're too late to place any bets on this fight, but you can put credit down on the next one if you want. It's a planter boy and a cookhouse assistant—you'll get good odds on the younger one." She held her book up to the light to show me her betting records. But I wasn't listening. I couldn't take my eyes off the figure in the pit.

Otienno's skin glistened with sweat, his muscles rippling in the lantern light. With the grace of a cat, he stepped out of the way of a swinging fist and landed another punch, staggering his opponent. A roar of approval went up from the crowd. The other boy struggled to stand, wiping the sweat from his eyes and spitting out a mouthful of blood. He was shorter than Otienno, but heavier, his own muscles taut across his beefy chest. Otienno stepped back with a wolfish grin, circling the boy impatiently as he waited for him to get back on his feet.

I wasn't sure what I'd expected the game to be, but whatever it was, this wasn't it. Violence was strictly against the rules of Eden Five. It was one of the few things that could get you locked up in the prison cell in Director Eshe's office. And that was something that didn't happen very often. Sure, there were arguments; workers pushing and pulling, pinching and slapping. The kids got in each other's faces all the time, shouting and shoving and letting off steam.

But not like this.

This was something different, something savage and dangerous. It sent a thrill down my spine, settling in my stomach with the sick, heavy sense that it was wrong, but I was loving it. I wasn't the only one. The crowds chanted Otienno's name as he went for the other boy again, his fists pummelling the planter's chest and smashing into his jaw. I found myself cheering with the rest of the kids, swept along in the wave of excitement that crashed round the basement and drowned the little voice in my head that said this was wrong, wrong, wrong.

The other boy went down again, this time for good. A line of blood trickled from his mouth, his eyes glazed. The crowd went wild, stamping and shouting themselves hoarse. I jumped up and down with them, clapping and whistling and letting myself go like I'd never done before. Gods, it felt so *free*.

I got a bit of a shock right then, though. I looked round at the other kids crowding onto my pipe, and I saw a face I recognised. Chiku was standing with an older orphan girl, watching me with those dark eyes of hers. What the hell was she doing here? This was no place for little kids. I peered round the crowds, seeing others who were Chiku's age or younger. What were the planters thinking, letting them watch this kind of violence?

The older orphan girl saw me looking and scowled, grabbing Chiku possessively by the shoulder and pulling her back into the crowd. I felt like I should go and say something, to send Chiku and the younger kids back to their homerooms where they belonged. But then Otienno was standing next to me, and I lost the ability to think straight.

"What do you think of the game?" he grinned, wiping his bare chest down with a towel. He smelled of sweat and musk and blood and secrets. I said something back that sounded like a string of nonsense words with no spaces in between. Then I cleared my throat and looked away, trying to catch my breath.

"It's pretty... extreme. Do you do this every week?"

"Most weeks. Not much else to do around here. You should try it—you've got strong looking arms, and you're smart. You'd do pretty well in the pit." He looked me up and down, his eyes lingering a little too long on my chest under my baggy shirt. I felt my face glowing with sudden heat. "I'd like to see you fighting down there, getting all hot and sweaty. Maybe—"

But I didn't get to hear the rest. An older girl who looked about nineteen had jumped down into the pit, the crowds going silent as soon as she started to speak.

"You ready for the next fight?" she yelled. The crowds roared their approval. She grinned up at them and checked the names on her list. "Next up is Idir from the planters and Jelani from the cookhouse. All bets are closed now."

Idir, the planter boy, was about fifteen, tall and skinny. The crowd yelled their support when he dropped into the pit. Most of them were from the planter workgroup themselves. The cookhouse kid was only about thirteen, but he was built like a 3D printer engine, all square shoulders and thick legs. The girl announcing their names made them shake hands in the centre of the pit, then she climbed out, shouting, "Fight!"

Fight.

The word echoed round the basement, chanted over and over by the eager kids watching the show. Otienno shouted louder than the rest, banging his fist against the plastic pipe and stamping his feet. I tried to join in, but somehow my heart wasn't in it anymore, not now that Otienno wasn't the one in the pit. The sight of all the younger kids yelling for blood turned my stomach. It just didn't seem right.

This fight wasn't as clean or practised as the last one. Otienno and the planter he'd been fighting looked fierce and confident, sure of their own strength. They blocked and dodged, stepping in to land each punch with graceful precision. It had almost looked like a sport, like the one the workers played up on the Recreation Level with balls and nets. But this wasn't a game. It wasn't even entertaining. The two kids looked nervous—I could even see the skinny legs of the older one trembling in the fluorescent lantern light.

Egged on by the crowd, they charged at each other, swinging wildly, clubbing each other over the head with clumsy fists.

"Come on, Idir, put him on the ground!" Otienno yelled. He kept looking round at me and grinning, as though he was trying to work out if I was enjoying myself. I smiled back weakly, wondering how long I'd have to stay and watch. If I left now, it would look weird, and Otienno might not ask me to see him after work again.

This wasn't what I'd wanted—sharing him with all these other kids, all the noise and confusion. I'd wanted it to be just the two of us, talking about our lives and our secrets the way me and Dejen did. I tried not to watch the two boys hurting each other in the pit below me. I kept my eyes up and scanned the crowds, searching for familiar faces. The fight didn't last that long anyway.

There came a groan of disappointment from the crowd. I looked down in time to see the planter boy crumple in a heap. His head hit the concrete floor with a sickening crunch, and I couldn't help thinking of the dream I had last night, of Chiku falling to the basement. Blood gushed from the boy's nose, one of his teeth glittering on the ground. That was it, I'd had enough. I turned to tell Otienno I was going, but he'd already swung down to the pit to help some of the other planters lift the boy up and carry him away through the maze of pipes. I hoped one of the kids from the medical team was back there.

The older girl was back in the pit again straight away, a girl of about twelve by her side. "Desta here's ready for her first fight—any of you girls up there brave enough to face her?"

Now they were getting little kids to fight for the crowd? Gods, this was sick. I started walking away along the pipe, wondering if Otienno would think I was a waste of his time for leaving. I wanted to like the game for his sake, but the sight of those kids down there clawing each other to bits made me mad.

I looked back one last time to see if Otienno had come back, and my heart skipped a beat. A ten-year-old girl was clambering awkwardly into the pit, her scrawny arms barely strong enough to hold her up on the pit ledge before she dropped down. She hit the concrete with a bruising thump, then got back on her feet and looked up at the crowd. They cheered her on, chanting her name when the older girl announced it.

I groaned. What in the name of the Gods was Chiku doing?

I hurried back, scanning the crowds for Otienno. He had to stop this fight; it was crazy setting two little kids up like this. The twelve-year-old girl was circling Chiku, taunting her as she waited for the order to fight. Chiku just stood there, gazing up at the crowd and turning round slowly like she was searching for someone. Her eyes finally met mine, and I realised it was me she was trying to find. Her face lit up, and she raised a fist in the air. The crowds cheered, but I felt sick when I saw it.

She wasn't looking for their approval. She was looking for mine.

CHAPTER 11

ONE DAY/12 HOURS TO THE END

Chiku had seen me cheering for Otienno and thought I'd cheer for her.

She stood there in the pit, gazing up at me with searching eyes. Her smile faltered when she saw the sick look on my face and realised I wasn't going to be clapping for her the way the other kids were. Her fist dropping limply back to her side, and she suddenly looked small and scared, like she wasn't sure what the hell she was doing down in that pit after all. But then the older girl shouted, "Fight!" and it was too late for her to back out.

It was slaughter from the start.

Desta threw herself at Chiku, pummelling her face with her fists. Chiku shrank back, covering her head with her hands. The crowd roared, and Desta came at her again, pushing her onto her back and kicking her in the ribs. I wanted to jump down and defend her, to shove the other girl away, but I was frozen, staring dumbly round for Otienno. Why wasn't he here to stop this? I felt helpless and small in the face of the baying crowd, too weak to defend the little girl whose blood they were shouting for.

Then, standing right behind me, I found the one person who gave me the strength I needed to act. Only it wasn't Otienno. It was Tash.

"What are you doing here?" I yelled. "You're meant to be in bed!"

"I couldn't sleep. I followed you down. Thought we could play." Tash's eyes went wide with horror as she stared down into the pit where Chiku was being kicked around the floor like a rubber ball. "Do something, Adina! Chiku's getting hurt!"

That was all I needed to hear.

I leapt down from the pipe, pushing past the older kids standing round the pit. The girl who announced the names grabbed me by the shoulders, trying to hold me back. "No interfering with a fight that's in progress."

"That's my little sister!" I growled, shrugging her off. The words were out before I even knew I'd said them. They felt weird on my tongue, foreign and false. The girl gave me a funny look and let me go.

I jumped down to the floor of the pit, pulling the girl off Chiku and shoving her back. She tried to slap me, but I grabbed her arm and twisted it hard, taking all the fight out of her. Chiku lay curled up on the ground whimpering, the arms covering her head already swollen with bruises. I tried to get her to stand up, but she batted my hands away, crying in fright.

"It's OK, Chiku, it's me—Adina. Get up. Come on, you have to go home."

Chiku sat up slowly, her face puffy and confused. The crowd had gone quiet. A low mutter rumbled round the basement in place of cheering. No one seemed to know what to do. Chiku was looking at me in a way that made me feel weird, like she couldn't quite believe she wasn't dreaming and that I was real. I didn't like it, it was too much like the way Tash had looked at me when I'd given her the chocolate. I grabbed Chiku under her arms and pulled her to her feet, wiping the spots of blood from her lip with my sleeve.

Just then, all hell broke loose.

"Bust!" someone yelled from behind the pipes. "We're busted!"

The crowd exploded in all directions like a swarm of butterflies scattering from the garden flowers when the planters got too close. The kids were gone in an instant, melting back into the basement labyrinth. They took their lanterns with them, the bright fluorescent light replaced by the sickly glow of the overhead strip lights. Within moments, the only people left were Chiku and me in the pit, and Tash crouching on the concrete edge above us.

We weren't alone for very long. Footsteps echoed in the corridors between the pipes, official-sounding boots thudding on the basement floor. A moment later, I found myself looking up into the stern face of Director Eshe. Three workgroup heads stood behind her, scowling and muttering to each other. One of them was Makena. Her gaze went from me to the younger girl with the bruised arms and bloodied lip, then back to me again. My mouth went dry. I knew how this must look.

"What are you and these children doing down here, Adina?" Director Eshe asked. *Demanded*, I should say. The Director wasn't the kind of woman to ask for anything she wanted.

"We just went for a walk," I shrugged, hearing how lame it sounded as soon as the words were out of my mouth.

"You went for a walk with two children down to the basement, which as you well know is out of bounds after working hours, and one of them just happened to suffer what looks like a collision with a fully loaded sanitation cart?" Director Eshe's lip twitched. It wasn't a good sign. She hated being lied to. I decided to tell a little bit of the truth to save myself.

"It wasn't me! It was another girl, but she's gone now."

It wasn't enough truth for the Director. She scowled at me. "I know very well what's been going on down here, Adina. I've been told all about the violent game you and the other youngsters have been playing. My only real surprise is that you'd involve your sisters. I'd thought you a little more responsible than that. I didn't believe you capable of letting me down any further, but tonight you've outdone yourself."

Her words stung almost as much as the look of disappointment in Makena's eyes. I clambered out of the pit, avoiding Makena's gaze as she helped pull me and Chiku up.

"You still haven't repaired that air filter on Level Twenty-Eight," the head techie growled. "You can hear it rattling from three floors away. Didn't I tell you it was an important job, Adina? All it would take is one small spark from a loose wire to start a huge blaze. I assigned that job to you because you're one of the best, and I thought I could trust you with it. Looks like I was wrong."

That hurt worse than anything.

Now that the roar of the crowd was gone and the basement was wrapped in a heavy silence, I could hear the humming filter myself. At least, that's what I thought it was until Director Eshe frowned. "The water system pressure's still too high, isn't it?"

"I've been looking into it with my crew, but we can't seem to fix the problem," Makena shook her head. "There's something getting into the pipes further up the line, something sending the pressure shooting sky high. It's really worrying."

"We'll shut down the system if we need to," Director Eshe decided. "I'd hate to see Eden Five going without water for several days, especially with the harvest coming up, but this is too important to ignore."

For a brief moment, I thought she'd got too distracted by the business of running Eden Five to worry about us. No such luck. The Director hadn't finished with us yet. "Where are all the others?" She looked round the empty basement. The pipes twisted off into the dark, nothing but silence in the labyrinth beyond.

"What others?" I blinked, trying to look surprised. I was angry at Otienno for going off and leaving me, but not angry enough to go ratting out the rest of the kids. The Gods only knew what that would do for my popularity.

"I know there are others involved in this so-called 'game' of yours, Adina, so stop wasting my time!" the Director snapped.

"It's not my game! And anyway, who told you about it?" I shot back before I could stop myself. From what Otienno had said, entry to the game was by invitation only, and none of the kids would want to piss him off by running to tell the Director about it. None of the kids who were invited, that is. My heart sank to my boots when I saw a familiar figure step out from behind the workgroup heads.

"I told her, Adina," Dejen said. "The game has to stop, it's too dangerous."

"Dejen? How could you? I thought you were my best friend!"

Dejen's eyes looked strange in the strip lighting. They were usually warm and bright, full of enquiry and enthusiasm. But now they were cold and calculating. He was up to something. I only wished I knew what it was.

"This isn't about you. It's about Otienno. He's the one who's been rounding the kids up and getting them to fight for his own entertainment. If he wasn't such a coward, he wouldn't have left you and your sisters alone here to take the blame."

He sort of had a point, but I'd be dammed if I was going to admit it. I was too mad at him. "So you ratted us all out?"

Dejen shook his head. "I just want to put an end to Otienno's violence."

I realised then that he wasn't trying to get me into trouble. He was doing this to get back at Otienno for all those years of bullying. Somehow it didn't make me feel any less mad at him.

Dejen was glancing round, peering into the shadows between the pipes. He was looking for something. Someone.

"It's a pity Otienno isn't man enough to come out and face us," he said loudly. "But then I guess a guy who watches little kids beat each other up for fun won't have much of a backbone."

It was a deliberate challenge. And it worked. There was a thud of something dropping from a high pipe, and Otienno stepped into the circle of light. He crossed his arms over his bare chest and glared at Dejen. "You brave enough to repeat that to my face, you stinking little lab rat?"

"I've had more than my fill of teenage attitude for one night," Director Eshe snapped. "The four of you are on punishment duty until further notice, starting six o'clock tomorrow morning."

"But the pre-harvest assembly!" I protested, "Couldn't we—"

"You should have thought of that before you broke the rules." The Director gave me a cold stare. "Perhaps spending the day weeding in the Gardens while everyone else is in the assembly halls enjoying the biggest event of the year will make you all think twice about rule breaking in future. But in your case, Adina, I doubt it."

She was wrong. I looked forward to the yearly pre-harvest assembly more than anything. The thought of missing it over some stupid game I didn't even enjoy watching made me clench my fists to stop myself from crying. Tash clutched my arm and wailed, burying her head in my shirt. This was so unfair. It didn't have anything to do with her. Chiku stared sullenly at the ground, the blood on her lip already hardening to an ugly scab. She wasn't crying for once. She was too used to missing out on nice things.

"Now, Otienno, while these girls go to bed, you will join me in my office where you'll write out a list of names for me. I want to know exactly how many children you've involved in your vicious little excuse for a sport."

"I think we both know that isn't going to happen, Director."

Otienno wasn't exactly smiling, but he had that sort of defiant look in his eyes that said he wasn't going to be pushed around by anyone, not even Director Eshe. Even though I was still mad at him, it gave me a thrill to see how sharp he could act under pressure.

Dejen walked up to Otienno and stared right in his face. They were nearly the same height, despite the planter being a year older. Otienno's shoulders were broader, his arms thicker, but there was a glint in Dejen's expressive eyes at that moment that made him look like the more dangerous one.

"You think this is funny, don't you? Little kids hurting each other so you can get off watching them. You're sick, you know that? But I guess I can't expect any more from some thick planter like you. I mean, if you had even half a brain, they wouldn't have had to find you a dumb robot job planting cabbages all day."

Otienno's temper snapped. He shoved Dejen hard, his face filled with hate. Dejen staggered, found his balance, and stepped forward again. Then he did something I'd never seen him do in my whole life. He swung his fist at Otienno, catching him on the jaw and sending him sprawling to the concrete floor.

We all stood there stunned for a moment. Dejen was a scientist, an award-winning scholar who'd fast-tracked more classes than anyone else had ever done. I guess we forgot sometimes he was also a teenage boy. Otienno hadn't forgotten. He lunged at Dejen, ready to knock his head off. The workgroup heads stepped in just in time, pulling the boys apart. It took two of them to hold Otienno back. I'd never seen him so angry. Dejen hadn't even broken a sweat. He didn't look mad. In fact, he was peering at Otienno exactly the same way he studied his soil samples under the microscope. It was weird.

"Enough!" Director Eshe shouted. "I will *not* tolerate violence in Eden Five, do you understand me? Dejen, I'm placing you in custody. We'll hold a disciplinary hearing tomorrow after the pre-harvest assembly. Until then, you'll spend the night cooling your temper in the holding cell in my office."

Dejen shrugged and looked at the floor, the same strange glint in his eyes. And then it all fell into place. He hadn't been trying to score points by ratting us all out to the Director about the game. He'd set this up so he could thump Otienno right in front of the Director and get himself locked up in the holding cell.

The holding cell in her office.

The office that had all the videpods from the old times he was desperate to get hold of.

I had to admit, it was pretty smart.

But stealing Director Eshe's private information stash right out from under her nose? It was also crazy dangerous. In less than a day, I would find out just how dangerous. For now, all I'll say is it nearly got him killed.

CHAPTER 12

20 MINUTES TO THE END

This was it. The day before the official harvest. The day we held the biggest celebration of the year. Everyone had the day off to prepare for the harvest week. Every single person in Eden Five would spend the morning in the assembly halls, singing, dancing, and exchanging cards and presents. Every single person that is, except me, Tash, Chiku and Otienno. And Dejen of course, but since us missing the celebrations was kind of his fault, I wasn't going to feel too sorry for him. I was too busy feeling sorry for myself.

"This sucks." I threw down my trowel in disgust and rubbed my aching back. I'd been bending over weeding cassava and yam plots on Level Six since the early morning, and I was tired and grumpy. Tash didn't look any happier than I did. The heavy gardening gloves were too big for her hands, and she kept stopping and taking them off, blowing on the blisters that were forming on her palms. Chiku sat as far from us as possible, pulling sullenly at the thick weeds on the other side of the plot. I'd made it clear she wasn't welcome to work with us.

Otienno was the only one who wasn't grumbling about the extra garden chores, but then again, he did this every day anyway. But that didn't mean he wasn't pissed off. He scowled and muttered to himself darkly as he worked, grunting in reply to my attempts at conversation.

Great.

My best friend was locked up in the Director's office in as much trouble as he could possibly be. I'd admitted publicly to half the teenage world last night that the ugly little orphan with the runny nose that everyone hated was actually my sister. And now the boy I'd been secretly obsessing over for months was mad at me. It just couldn't get any worse, could it?

I stood up, dumping the pile of weeds in the fertiliser bin and pulling off my gloves. I'd had enough.

Tash looked up in surprise. "Where are you going?"

"I'm supposed to have fixed the air filters down on Level Twenty-Eight by now. If I don't get the job done, I'll be in trouble with my workgroup as well as Director Eshe."

"But what about the weeding? We're meant to stay here till the dinner bell goes."

"I'll be back up as soon as I'm finished. Don't worry, I'm not shirking." I put that last bit in for Otienno's benefit, throwing him a defiant look. But he just shrugged like he didn't care either way. Gods, and I thought Dejen could be annoying.

"Can I come and help?" Tash pleaded. "I won't get in the way, I promise. We could have a quick look in the assembly halls on the way past—you know, check how the party's going... ?" She didn't want to be stuck there weeding any more than I did. But I couldn't risk her getting in any more trouble, not if she wanted to be fast-tracked in school after the harvest.

"Sorry, kid, this is a one-woman job. I'll be back up before you know it."

I turned away quickly and headed off through the vegetable plots before her sulky pout could make me change my mind. I had no intention of going down to fix the air filters. If I so much as breathed too close to the assembly halls on Level Nineteen this morning, Director Eshe would have me locked in the holding cell with Dejen. No, what I had in mind was far more fun. I had a date with a bright red apple that had been flirting with me for weeks.

The orchard was silent and still, the heavy branches undisturbed by the birds and insects that fluttered through the six garden levels. It was almost as if every living thing in the Dome was holding its breath, waiting for the coming harvest. The air under the heavy-laden branches felt cool against my skin, the thick green leaves shutting out the glare of the ultraviolet skylights. Now that I'd seen the real sky outside, I couldn't believe I'd ever thought the electric imitation enclosing the Gardens was beautiful.

I found the tree I'd been looking for and gazed up through the gnarled branches. There it was. My shiny prize. I felt I deserved it more than ever, what with being unfairly blamed for setting up Otienno's game and having to do extra chores and all. The apple was hanging too high for me to reach, so I grabbed the thick trunk, swinging myself up to sit in the fork where the branches divided. I reached out, my hand grasping for the crimson fruit.

"No!"

The sharp cry almost toppled me out of the tree. I looked down in surprise. Baba Weseka was stumbling through the orchard, flapping his hands at me to stop. By the look on his face you'd think I was about to burn the Gardens down or something. It was just a damn apple.

"No, no!" he cried, "you mustn't pick the fruit before the harvest!"

"Baba, it's just one apple," I sighed, "it's not going to do anyone any harm. There's thousands of pieces of other fruit, and they're all going to get picked this week anyway. What difference does a day make?"

But Baba Weseka just flapped his hands harder, his face all scrunched up in distress. Yango was right behind him, whimpering at the fear she heard in his voice and trying to twine herself round his legs. Gods, I swear that damn dog was one biohazard report away from being put down. I don't know what had got into Baba Weseka this week, but ever since that fit in the medical bay it was like his whole head had come unhinged and its crazy contents were spilling out all over the place.

"Please don't pick the apple, Adina?" Baba pleaded. "That's how it all starts."

I really wasn't in the mood for this. My hands were rubbed raw from gripping the trowel through the heavy gloves, my back ached, and my head was pounding. Between worrying about what my parents would say when they found out about our punishment duty, how it would affect Tash's chances of fast-tracking, and what would happen to Dejen at the disciplinary hearing, I hadn't got much sleep last night.

"Go down to the pre-harvest assembly with everyone else, Baba," I growled, "and leave me alone."

It wasn't a fair thing to say. Without me down there to shield him from the angry muttering of the other workers, there was no way he'd be welcome in the assembly halls. Besides, he looked like he was too confused to find his own backside never mind find his way down to the lower levels. But right now I just didn't care. He wasn't my problem. I was so sick of everything being my fault.

I reached out again, my fingers brushing the smooth skin of the apple. Something large and hairy scuttled across the back of my hand, and I yelped in fright. A spider as big as a plum shot up my arm, its spindly legs reaching for my face. For one awful moment I was back in the wilds outside the Dome, watching the dust swirling in the shape of a Nomaly with too many twitching arms and legs. I swatted the spider away with a shudder of disgust, watching it drop to the ground below. Yango snapped at it as it fell, gobbling it up and wagging her tail in delight. When she looked back up at me, she had bits of spider leg stuck to her muzzle. They were still twitching.

"Please don't touch the apple?" Baba Weseka was wringing his hands now, tears glistening in his eyes. "I saw it all happen, Adina. That's how it starts. It's bad! It's bad…"

If I didn't hurry up I'd have a full-scale hysterical fit to deal with. I grabbed the apple and tugged hard. It didn't want to come away, the stalk not yet ready to yield despite the fruit being ripe. But I was determined, twisting the apple back and forth and shaking the branch. A hail of other apples rained to the ground, sending Yango scuttling for cover. Baba Weseka wailed louder, covering his eyes with his hands at the sight.

My apple finally came free, and I held it up to the light in triumph. It was even more beautiful than I'd thought, its skin deep red and glistening under the skylights. It was so round and smooth I almost wanted to hold it in my hand forever. But there was one thing I wanted even more. I bit into the fruit, its flesh and juices cold against my teeth.

I knew as soon as I'd done it that something was badly wrong.

The skylights flickered, the whole Dome shaking with the vibrations that rose up from the underground levels. I dropped the apple, the bright fruit sinking into the shuddering soil.

And that was when our whole world fell apart.

CHAPTER 13

THE END OF EVERYTHING

It began with an apple, and ended in ashes, just like Baba Weseka said it would.

A noise like thunder rolled through the Dome, the floor of every Garden Level buckling like plastic sheeting. A piercing wail shrieked above the noise of the rumbling storm, Eden Five's emergency sirens blaring from crackling speakers on every wall. Even from way up here, thirteen levels above, I could hear the echoing screams of thousands of terrified people down in the underground assembly halls. That's what finally forced me to move.

My mother and father were down there.

I leapt from the tree and sprinted for the doors, the ground shuddering and swaying beneath my feet. Baba Weseka curled up in a little ball, rocking and whimpering and saying, "No, no, no!" over and over again. I didn't have time to comfort him. I had to find out what was happening.

The ultraviolet daylights along the spiral staircase were blinking on and off, the underground levels caught in some sort of electrical storm. I ran to the rails and peered down through the gap in the centre of the stairs. Many, many levels below, I could just make out the crowds of people stampeding up the stairs in the flashing lights. Their screams were almost drowned under the rumbling thunder that rolled up from the depths of Eden Five. They were heading to the safe rooms on Level Ten, the concrete bunkers under the labs that were designed to protect the workers from natural disasters like earthquakes. But even as I watched, my guts twisting in horror, I knew they weren't going to make it.

None of them were.

It started as a glow deep down in the gap through the centre of the spiral stairs. It grew brighter as it rose up through the levels, the dim yellow flicker blossoming to bright reds and oranges. It took me a moment to work out what I was seeing. My brain just didn't want to believe it. But then there came the loud whooshing sound of oxygen being sucked from the air, and the stinging heat hit my face. A sea of flames washed up the stairs faster than the shrieking workers, drowning them in a rising tide of liquid fire. One moment there were thousands of people stampeding on the stairs, the next there was only flames and heat and buckling metal.

But the fire wasn't satisfied yet. On it climbed—up and up towards the Dome. I staggered back—half screaming, half retching—stumbling through the doors into the Level Seven corridor.

And then Otienno was there, catching me in his arms and pulling me to my feet. He'd brought the others down from the Gardens with him when the alarms went off. Tash was holding Babaa Weseka by the hand, crying almost as hard as he was. Chiku took one look at my sickened face and knew at once that everyone was dead. She started shrieking, clamping her hands to her ears to shut out the thundering noise and wailing at the top of her lungs.

"Fire!" I croaked. "It's coming!"

"The safe rooms?" Otienno glanced at the doors to the lower levels. The roar of flame beyond was growing louder, heat rising up the stairs.

"No time. We have to get out!"

Otienno nodded. He knew what I meant by "out."

We raced down the corridor towards the airlock, dragging the kids and Baba Weseka with us. Yango trailed behind, howling in fear. She could smell death approaching. We all could. I swiped my keycard in the storage cabinet's doorlock, pulling biosuits out and thrusting them at the others. "You have to put these on—you can't go into the wilds unprotected."

I was just grabbing the helmets, when the memory of a familiar face flashed before my eyes.

Dejen.

What in the name of the Gods was I thinking?

Dejen was still locked in Director Eshe's office.

"I'll just be a second!" I shouted, racing back to the end of the corridor.

"Where are you going?" Otienno called.

"To get Dejen!" I yelled back.

I don't know how I could have missed him on the way past—it's not like he wasn't making enough noise. Through the small plastiglass window in the door I could see him thumping on the other side, trying to shoulder the door open. The gate to the holding cell inside stood open, as did the door to the private study at the back of the office. But this door—the very one we needed open to get Dejen out to safety—wouldn't budge.

"Didn't you steal the Director's keycard?" I yelled through the glass.

"It isn't working! I had to re-magnetise it to bypass the fingerprint recognition unit in the study doorlock."

"What the hell did you do that for?" I hammered on the other side of the door, swiping my own card uselessly in the lock. The light blinked red. Of course it did, but at least it meant the electrics up here weren't completely fried or we'd never get out of the airlock.

"I didn't think I'd have to open this door myself!" Dejen stopped hammering and looked at me seriously through the glass. He knew what was happening. He could feel the heat rising up through the buckling floor, the ultraviolet daylights shorting and popping on the walls in bursts of bright sparks. "You have to leave me behind, Adina," he said. "Get everyone else out—hurry! You've only got a minute before this whole place goes up."

"No!" I thumped the door again, beating at the plastiglass window that separated us. "Dejen, I won't leave you!"

"You have to save the others!" Dejen stepped away from the door and turned his back on me. "Goodbye, Adina." He was trying to make it easier for me to walk away.

Then Otienno grabbed me by the shoulders and gave me a hard shove. "Move!" he ordered.

"I'm not leaving him!" I sobbed. I could hear the roar of the fire beyond the doors that led to the underground levels. The heat was intense, sweat dripping from our scorched skin. The lights in the corridor began to flicker. If we didn't go now, the electrics in the airlock would fail before we got out. I had to leave Dejen if I wanted to save my sisters. Gods, it wasn't fair. How was I supposed to make a choice like that? I just couldn't.

But Otienno made it for me.

"I said move!" he yelled again, pushing me away from the door, away from Dejen. I stumbled back, tears blinding me. Otienno stepped up and swung something heavy at the doorlock. There was a flash and the crackling spark of electrics. Otienno swung the heavy maintenance wrench he'd pulled from the storage cabinet again, this time almost smashing a hole in the wall. The wires in the doorlock buzzed, the shattered light flashing green before the bulb exploded. The door sparked and swung open.

Dejen was free.

I grabbed him by the hand and fled for the airlock. Tash and Chiku were still struggling with the suits, trying to fit their legs into the rubbery material. Baba Weseka just held his cradled to his chest, rocking back and forth in distress. "Leave them!" I yelled, "there's no time!" I pulled the emergency survival packs from the cabinet, throwing one to each of them and grabbing a handful of biofilters from the shelf on the way past.

I swiped my maintenance card in the airlock door, praying the electrics at this end of the corridor were still working. They were. The heavy metal swung open, the air inside strangely cool and still.

"In!" I ordered, shoving Tash and Chiku through the entrance.

Without waiting for the automatic locking sequence, I pulled the door shut behind us, turning the wheel clamp. Before I swiped the card again to start the outer door sequence, Dejen quickly fitted us all with biofilters. The sharp needles stung when he held mine to the base of my neck and pressed the release button. I could feel the three metal prongs stabbing through my flesh and settling in my bloodstream, ready to start their cleansing work the minute we stepped outside.

I was just going to swipe my card again to start the outside door sequence, when Baba Weseka began pounding on the inner door. "My dog, my dog!" he wailed. "Yango! I need Yango!"

I looked back through the reinforced plastiglass window. Yango was still in the corridor, her legs tangled in a biosuit that was caught in the door of the storage cabinet. She struggled and whimpered, trying to free herself. All the while the yellow glow of fire surged up the stairs, ready to burst into the corridor.

"Leave it," Otienno growled, "it's just a dog. Adina, quick! Open the door."

I tried not to look at Baba Weseka's distraught face, my hand hesitating above the doorlock. It was all the time Dejen needed. Before I could stop him, he'd spun the wheel, opening the inner door and racing back along the corridor.

"Dejen!" I yelled, "come back!"

I could see the bright flicker of approaching flames behind the doors at the far end of the corridor. Dejen reached down, pulling the whining dog's legs from the biosuit. Then the corridor exploded in heat and light, the doors bursting open. With one arm around Yango and the other pumping the air, Dejen raced back towards us, the flames shooting down the corridor towards him.

He almost didn't make it.

The fire slammed into the airlock door just as I spun the wheel shut behind him, the thick metal absorbing the full force of the flames. But it wouldn't hold for long.

I swiped my card in the outer doorlock, holding my breath until the whooshing gases cleared and the green light blinked on. But then the light flickered and died, the electrics fried in the fire's relentless onslaught. My heart hammered in my chest at the thought of dying here, in this tiny box stuck halfway between the terror of flames and the dread of the wilds.

"Is it open?" I cried.

Otienno put his shoulder to the door and shoved. It opened with a loud screech of metal. I was almost gasping with relief when we all tumbled through into the barren wastelands outside. Otienno picked Tash up, grabbing Chiku's hand and bolting for the cover of the small hills in the distance. Dejen and I dragged Baba Weseka with us, half carrying him as we fled from our burning home.

We'd just reached the dust dunes that rose up round the dry lake bed, when the whole Dome went up in flames. The solar panels exploded outwards in a fountain of sparks, glass shards raining down on the lake bed like glittering tears. The fireball burst through the roof and shot to the sky, the metal support beams ripped apart in the blast.

The violence was over almost as soon as it had begun.

The Dome collapsed, every floor of the Gardens destroyed in an instant. The flames settled back down over the ruins, licking almost gently at the charred remains of what had once been Eden Five. There was no point going looking for survivors now. No one even bothered suggesting it. We watched, numb with grief, as the smoke billowed from the wreckage of our home, the ashes of what had once been plants and flowers swirling in the wind.

Tash and Chiku clung to each other, sobbing in each other's arms. Baba Weseka curled up with Yango in his lap, while Otienno stood with his arms crossed tightly over his heaving chest, staring in disbelief at the ruins of the Dome. Dejen sat crouched on his heels, his head buried in his arm. He sat up after a while, his cheeks wet. He walked slowly over to where I stood watching the flames with dull, uncomprehending eyes. I could feel him coming up behind me and squeezing my shoulder. I think he would've hugged me if I'd let him. But I shrugged him off, stumbling away towards the ruins and sinking down into the dust. I couldn't let him comfort me. If I did, then I'd start crying. And if I cried, they'd all know the truth.

The truth was that this was all my fault.

I'd killed everybody. Every single person in Eden Five. I was supposed to fix the wiring in the air filter on Level Twenty-Eight. The assignment had been on my duty sheet all week. I'd ignored it for days on end, shirking off to see Dejen in the labs and make chocolate in the factories and pick an apple in the Gardens. I'd even gone all the way down to the basement for Otienno's game, walking right past the air filter I couldn't be bothered to fix.

And then it had happened, just like Makena warned me it would. A spark from the faulty wiring must've caught fire in the oxygen tubes, sending up a fireball that brought the whole of Eden Five crashing down. Everyone was dead. *Everyone.* I killed them all.

No one must know, I told myself, my fear of being found out almost overwhelming my grief. *No one must ever know.*

And that meant I mustn't cry, not ever. I couldn't give the others any reason to suspect me. Tash could never know I'd killed our parents. Otienno must never know I was the one who destroyed our home. And Dejen? I felt sick at the thought of him knowing what I'd done. He'd abandon me, and I couldn't bear the thought of my best friend walking away in disgust any more than I could bear him trying to comfort me.

I'd have to be careful. Chiku and her suspicious little eyes would be watching me, seeing everything I was trying to hide. I'd have to be on my guard every moment so they wouldn't suspect. And that meant not giving in to grief. I couldn't afford the luxury of even one little tear, not anymore.

I took a deep, shuddering breath, the taste of smoke and dead ash filling my mouth. Then I stood up and walked back to the others, my true face hidden behind a grim mask of determination. I could never show my real face to them again. It was the face of a killer.

"Come on," I growled, "we have to get moving."

"To where?" Otienno said, his jaw set tight with grief. "Everything's gone."

"We have to find Sanctuary Seven. It's our only chance."

I pulled a compass out of my survival pack and found south-east. Without looking back at the others, I started walking. We had thirty days before our biofilters packed up and we all died out here in the wilds.

Fourteen thousand seven hundred and fifty-six people.

That's how many people I'd killed by shirking my work duty. If I counted Baba Weseka's mangy dog, then only seven of us had survived the fire. If I'd known right then that before the thirty days were up and our biofilters gave out another four of our group would be dead, I probably would have just lain down in the dust and given up.

But I didn't know, not then.

All I knew was we had thirty days to get to safety, and the countdown had already begun.

PART 2

THE COUNTDOWN

CHAPTER 14

DAY ONE

B y the end of our first day in the wilds, we'd almost given up hope.

Everything was dead, *everything*. I'd thought when we trekked over the dust hills surrounding the dry lake bed we'd see something living—a few weeds maybe, the remains of trees. But there was nothing. Only rolling dirt plains clouded in a permanent fog of restless dust. It stung our eyes, lining our throats and coating our tongues like a layer of burnt chocolate. It made me sick to think of that chocolate bar now, and the job I'd shirked to make it. I glanced over at Chiku whenever I thought of it, remembering the dream of her falling to the basement. I almost wished she had now. Her eyes were always on me, watching me as we marched across the dust plains. I'd have to be careful, or those little eyes would find my secret out, peering right through to my rotten soul the way Director Eshe's eyes once had.

Maybe I should poke them out first and be done with it. My hands trembled at the thought, itching for action.

We walked in silence for most of the day. Every time we opened our mouths the dust found its way down to our lungs, making us cough and spit painfully. We couldn't afford to lose fluid like that; the water flasks in our survival packs wouldn't hold out for more than a few days, and there was no knowing when we'd have a chance to refill them. We took bandages from the medical kits in our packs, binding them round our noses and mouths to keep out the worst of the dust. Baba Weseka tried to tie his around Yango instead, but the dumb dog thrashed and howled like he was trying to kill her. Dejen shouldn't have rescued her. She didn't have a biofilter, and the invisible poisons in the air would kill her slowly. I didn't want to watch more death.

We stopped a couple of times for food—once under a rocky outcrop, another time in a low depression between two high dust hills. None of us had any appetite, especially not for the dry, chewy protein bars in our packs, but we needed to rest and regroup. At least, the others did. Dejen tried to get me to talk, but I shook my head and walked away, holding Tash in my arms like a protective shield to ward him off. It was all about my little sister now—nothing was going to stop me getting her to safety. To get to Sanctuary Seven, I had to keep the group together. And that meant keeping my secret to myself, despite the pain I saw in Dejen's eyes when I brushed his concern off and ignored him.

"What do you think those are?" Otienno asked the second time we stopped, pointing at the dust swirling over the plains in the distance.

I shrugged. "Just dirt clouds." I nearly told him what Makena said about techies seeing things their first time out of the Dome. But then I remembered the job she'd assigned me to do down on Level Twenty-Eight. The job I shirked. Her death was my fault.

I choked back the reply and stared at the dust cloud instead.

It was like the one I'd seen a few days before, all spiky legs and strange bobbing head. Only this one looked like it had split in two, scuttling and darting between the dust dunes far behind us whenever the wind picked up.

"I don't like the look of them," Dejen frowned, shielding his eyes against the bright sun. "They look too alive to be just swirling dust. They almost look like…"

"Nomalies." Baba Weseka's voice trembled, his pale eyes peering at the dust clouds in the distance. "They're coming for us."

It was the most coherent sentence he'd put together since we'd escaped from Eden Five. I wished right then he'd just go back to babbling nonsense.

We all shivered despite the heat, Tash and Chiku clutching each other's hands. I shivered harder than anyone. Baba had been right about the apple and the fire. Whatever he'd seen in that fit he'd had last week in the medical bay, it had somehow happened just like he said it would. And if he was right about that, how could I keep pretending to myself that his stories of Nomalies in the wilds were just made up?

I had to try, though. If the others realised he wasn't just talking crazy nonsense, they might actually start listening to him. And what if he told them about his visions of the apple and the fire and they made the connection that it was all my fault? I couldn't let them get that close to my secret. I was going to have to keep a close watch on Baba Weseka to make sure he didn't say anything that might give me away. But he hadn't finished talking just yet.

"They'll eat you up, Nomalies will," Baba Weseka muttered. "Gobble, gobble, crunch—you'll be gone just like that. Nothing left but bones turned to dust in the wastelands. That's what we're standing on right now—the bones and dust and ashes of all the people who used to live here in the old times before the Nomalies. That's what we're walking on— layers of death so deep our feet can't touch the bottom. Soon we'll be ashes too, just like the people in Eden Five."

"Baba, that's enough!" I snapped. I had to admit, it wasn't just the kids he was scaring now. "Keep your crazy talk to yourself. There's no such thing as Nomalies. It's just the wind stirring up the dust. Come on, we've stopped here long enough."

I grabbed Tash's hand, pulling her away from Chiku and stomping off quickly so I couldn't see the frown Dejen threw my way. I'd never talked to Baba Weseka like that before, but I couldn't let myself feel guilty about that either. There wasn't time for guilt and regret, I had to stay numb and keep moving. The others followed me, and I kept up a steady pace across the plain strewn with dust dunes that rippled in the wind.

There's no such thing as monsters in the wilds, I chanted to myself as I walked. But deep down I knew it wasn't true. Something was following us. Something bad.

Dejen and Otienno knew it too. They kept looking back, shielding their eyes and peering into the distance when they thought the rest of us weren't looking. They didn't talk to each other, there was too much resentment simmering just below the surface for that. But now we were fighting for survival they kept it bottled, tense frowns passing between them instead of words whenever they looked back and confirmed what the other was seeing. I tried to ignore the silent conversation. Maybe if I pretended nothing was wrong, it would all just go away.

Tash had fallen asleep clinging to my back, her breath tickling my neck through her makeshift scarf. Chiku followed behind me, her face streaked with dirt and snot and dried tears. Gods, she was ugly. She tried to hold onto me once, slipping her thin, bony hands through the crook of my arm. I shrank from her touch, shaking her off with a few muttered curses. She didn't try again after that. I shrugged Tash higher up on my back, clinging tighter to her legs and marching forward grimly.

Despite everything that had happened, we were lucky that day. At nightfall, just as the sun was sinking below the distant mountains, we found shelter. The dust seemed to settle as the sun went down, the clouds parting at dusk to reveal what looked like an abandoned village. I'd seen villages from the old times in Dejen's books, but this was different. The pictures had made the small houses and streets between them look so alive, people sitting on doorsteps washing clothes in plastic buckets and talking to their neighbours while they plucked chickens and pounded corn. But there was no one here now. The narrow streets between the concrete houses were deserted, the corrugated roofing all caved in and rusted.

We walked until we came to a big building near the end of the dead village. It was still almost intact, its metal roof creaking and clanking in the wind. It had been white once, the paint on the outside walls faded and chipped. But we could still read the words painted in huge letters that said, "Amonston Corporation—Feeding the World." The door hanging on its hinges had a sign that read "Seed Bank" beneath the crescent moon and star picture. I was too tired to wonder what it meant. Without waiting for the rest to agree, I pushed the door open and trudged inside, setting Tash down and rummaging in my survival pack for the thermafoil sleeping bag.

The others followed me into the empty building without question. Dejen helped Baba Weseka and Chiku into their sleeping bags, slipping Yango part of a protein bar when he thought I wasn't looking. That really bugged me—it wasn't kind keeping the dog alive and prolonging the end we all knew was coming. I didn't have the energy to argue, though, not now. Before we could get any rest, Baba Weseka started thrashing around inside his sleeping bag, moaning and crying out while Yango howled in distress at his side.

"Great, he's having another fit—Dejen, don't just stand there, do something!" I yelled, shoving my own sleeping bag under Baba's arms to stop him from breaking his bones on the stone floor.

Dejen watched helplessly for a moment, then settled for rolling Baba Weseka onto his side so he wouldn't choke while his fit played out. "We're not hurting him, are we?" Dejen worried as Baba Weseka's yells got even louder. "I mean, what do you usually do when he has one of these attacks?"

"I usually call the emergency medical team and let them deal with it," I muttered, sick to my stomach when I thought again of Eden Five and all the people who were dead. "Just give him a minute and then it'll be over and he'll go to sleep."

Baba Weseka wasn't ready to pass out just yet, though. His body gave another shudder inside the sleeping bag cocoon, then his eyes rolled in their sockets and he started groaning, "The water, it's swallowing her whole! Pull her out! Quick, before it's too late!"

"There's no water here, Baba," Dejen tried to reassure him. "We're on dry land, no one's going to drown."

"She's going under!" Baba Weseka wailed, trying to grab at my face with his flailing hands. "You have to save her, Adina! Don't let her drown!"

A cold shiver ran down my spine. I'd always ignored Baba Weseka's ramblings before when he was having one of his fits, but the last time he'd warned of fire and death, it had all happened just like he said it would.

Dejen frowned at me. "What's he talking about?"

"It's nothing," I snapped. "His mind wanders and he says a whole bunch of random things when he fits—just ignore him." I didn't want Dejen suspecting for even a second that Baba Weseka might be seeing something that might come true. If he did, then he'd dig a little deeper, find out about the apple and my shirked duties and the fire, and put two and two together.

"Save her, Adina!" Baba Weseka gasped, grabbing my hand now and squeezing hard. "Don't let her drown."

Luckily for me he was all out of juice, and his eyes closed, his body relaxing as he passed out and lay limp in his sleeping bag. Yango gave a final whimper, then curled up beside him to watch over him while he slept. Dejen rearranged the bag round him and checked his airways to make sure he wasn't going to choke on anything during the night, while I went to reassure Tash who was sitting bolt upright, gazing at Baba Weseka with wide eyes.

"It's OK, he just gets overworked at times and has a bit of a meltdown," I said, tucking her in and wishing I could believe that's all it was. "Go to sleep now, you need to get some rest."

My back was to Chiku, but I could feel those dark eyes boring a hole in my head from behind. She must've heard what Baba Weseka said, and now she was suspicious. She might even have overheard what he'd been saying in the medical bay while she sat outside the door patting Yango. For all I claimed Tash was the brightest kid in the whole of Eden Five, Chiku certainly wasn't stupid. She'd work it out sooner or later, and then she'd go running straight to the others to tell them what I'd done. I would have to be very careful from now on.

"What did he mean, 'Don't let her drown?'" Tash asked me as I tried to get her to settle down in her sleeping bag. "Don't let *who* drown?"

"He was just talking nonsense, Tash, don't pay any attention to him," I said, stroking her hair till her breathing slowed and she finally fell asleep. I could feel his words spinning round and round my head, though, making me dizzy as I tried to work out what he might have seen. Was Tash in danger? Had he seen something happening to her? Was his vision some kind of warning? I wasn't sure, I just knew that I wasn't going to let Tash wander so much as two feet away from me until I got her to the safety of the Sanctuary. Whatever Baba Weseka had seen, I wasn't going to let it happen to her.

At least I didn't have to tell Otienno not to pay any attention to Baba Weseka's warnings. He'd walked away in disgust when the old man started fitting, turning his back on us and muttering darkly to himself. When I was done with Tash, I looked up to see if he'd gone to sleep yet. He hadn't. He was still standing silently at the small window that had lost one wooden shutter, staring out into the night with his arms folded across his chest. The way he stood there, his strong arms wrapped tight across his body, it almost looked like he was trying to hold himself together.

There were fluorescent lanterns in our survival packs, but I couldn't be bothered lighting one. The moon and stars were bright, shining through the half-shuttered window and the cracks in the roof. If it had been a couple of days ago, no doubt I'd be standing outside looking up and crying at the night sky's beauty the way I had when I first saw the real sky in the daytime. Now I just didn't care. I lay down in my sleeping bag beside Tash, holding her hand and listening to her gentle breathing. My whole body ached, but the hurt was deeper than that. It seeped right down to my soul, dull waves of guilt and grief that threatened to drown me every time I closed my eyes and saw the faces of my mother and father staring back

143

at me. I rolled over, watching Dejen instead through half-closed lids.

He had his little science backpack out, peering inside by the light of the fluorescent lantern he'd lit. He took out an infopad and two videpod cartridges, holding them up to the light and peering at them like they were precious jewels.

"What are those?" I couldn't help asking.

"These are the videpods Director Eshe was hiding in her office. Want to see?" He looked at me hopefully.

I shrugged and went over to sit beside him. It's not like I was going to get much sleep anyway. "Hey, Otienno, you want to see some stuff from the old times?" I asked.

Otienno shook his head without turning round, making a strange noise that sounded halfway between a snort of disgust and a sob. I didn't push it. Dejen clipped the first videpod cartridge into the infopad and flicked through the menu screen.

"Gods, there's *thousands* of entries." He whistled softly. "It'd take months to watch them all. Where are we meant to start?"

"Just start at the beginning," I said impatiently. I wasn't really that interested, but anything was better than being alone with my thoughts right now.

But if I'd known that what I was going to learn from those videpod cartridges would change my world forever, I'd have taken them straight off Dejen and smashed them into the dust.

CHAPTER 15

NIGHT ONE

Dejen selected the first entry. It was dated March the twentieth, 2023. One hundred years ago. He held the infopad up, and we watched the video playing on the small screen.

A young woman in a white coat was sitting down across a lab bench after pressing play on a personal recorder. Her skin was as dark as Dejen's, and at first I got the dates confused and thought she must be one of the early scientists from Eden Five, even though she was recording two decades before the Edens were built. Then she started talking, and I realised she was from somewhere else entirely.

"Good Morning." The young woman beamed at the camera. "And welcome to the personal videblog of Doctor Malathion, newly appointed geneticist at the Amonston Corporation's headquarters in New York. That's me, by the way. Hello!" She waved at the camera, her brown eyes shining happily.

"I'm so excited to be working on the Corporation's Africa project. It's taken years of research to develop the new strains of genetically modified seeds, but now they're ready for trial across the African continent. I'm sure the farmers there are just as eager as we are to start growing the first crops from these miracle seeds. They really will solve all the world's food security problems, so I don't know why the United Nations has taken so long to approve the seed trials in Africa."

The cheerful woman rolled her eyes and went on, "Luckily our Director, Doctor Gill Bates, managed to get enough board members into the US senate, or we'd never have pushed the vote through Congress, let alone coaxed the other countries into approving the trials. I dread to think how much money the Corporation's had to spend on buying up African land and encouraging the international community to agree to the new seed ownership laws." Doctor Malathion's smile faded a little for a moment, then she leaned forward again eagerly.

"Anyway, everything's finally in place, and the first superfarms will start planting at the end of the month. My job here will be to analyse the samples sent back to headquarters and monitor the growth patterns of the new seeds. I can't wait! Oh, hold on, I'll add some of the commercials." She flicked her fingers across a large infopad on the desk before her, selecting files to upload.

I shifted restlessly, not quite understanding. Her words seemed to make sense, but there were so many strange names mixed up with them, it came out half gibberish. "You got any idea what she's talking about?" I asked Dejen.

"Just listen," Dejen shushed me. He was frowning at the screen like he believed he could make sense of it all if he just stared hard enough.

The picture on the infopad screen changed, the gleaming lab room replaced by rolling fields of maize and seas of wheat that stretched off to the horizon under a blue sky. A man's voice with the same strange accent as Doctor Malathion began talking over the pictures. He sounded calm and reassuring, and I found myself trusting his words without really knowing why.

"Beautiful, aren't they?" the man's voice said. "Golden fields of wheat and maize, soybeans, cotton and rapeseed. What could be more natural than these plants that humans have been growing since the earliest times? But with the fast pace of life in our modern world, these healthy fields have become a rare sight."

The pictures now showed a dirty sprawl of smoke, concrete and glass all jumbled up in confusion. It took me a minute to realise I was looking at one of the cities from the old times.

"Food security in our overpopulated world has become a pressing issue," the man's voice continued, "and feeding the world's people is a challenge the United Nations has placed at the top of its agenda. Fortunately, they are not alone. We here at the Amonston Corporation believe that health and nutrition are the key to humankind's future, and so our goal is nothing short of feeding the world. To meet this challenge, we've been working with world leaders to pave the way for our new Africa project, which will in time lay the foundations of a farming system that will revolutionise food production, bringing health and nutrition to children in every corner of the globe."

The accompanying pictures were of official-looking men and women shaking hands in huge meeting halls hung with flags, smiling for flashing cameras as they signed documents. One man in a blue suit was in every picture, standing with the officials and whispering private jokes in their ears. His skin was pale, and his green eyes were sharp and watchful, searching out every opportunity to pose for the cameras.

I wasn't sure I liked him, until the picture changed again, and the man was standing in a field of maize, his shirt sleeves rolled up. He pulled back a curtain of leaves to show the most enormous yellow cob I'd ever seen. "Impressive, isn't it?" he said, and I realised he was the man who'd been talking over the other pictures.

"I'm Doctor Gilbert Bates, CEO of the Amonston Corporation, and this is the future of agriculture. The Amonston Corporation future. There are those who say that genetically modified foods aren't natural, that they're not as healthy as regular plants. Well, take a good look. Do these look healthy to you?"

The camera zoomed in on the huge maize cobs that glistened in the sunlight. "The truth is, humans have been adapting living things since the dawn of time. You only have to look around at the different breeds of dogs in your neighbours' yards to see how natural selective breeding is. Genetically modified food is no different. We take the best that nature has to offer, and make it better."

The picture changed once more, the camera this time flying high over a vast stretch of savannah. My heart jumped at the sight. I recognised the land, dotted with bushes and scrub. I'd seen it in Dejen's book. This was the Great Rift Valley in the old times. This was our home.

"The world's cities are struggling to feed themselves, and yet huge swathes of Africa remain empty and unused. This is going to change. The Amonston Corporation has signed an historic deal with the African National Congress, and before long, the empty plains you see will be filled with maize and wheat specially modified to produce high yields in an African climate. Not only will the world's food security problems be solved within a decade, but the jobs our farms create in Africa will revitalise local economies, providing the financial stability needed to pull struggling nations out of poverty."

The man looked at the camera once again, the giant maize cob resting in his hands. He held it up and smiled, his craggy cheeks dimpled like a schoolboy. "You can trust us. We're the Amonston Corporation, and we're feeding the world."

The menu on the infopad flashed up again, signalling the end of the first videpod entry. Dejen leaned back, frowning at the screen.

"Pretty smart, huh?" I said, still impressed by the giant maize cobs I'd seen. "How they managed to make enough food for everyone?"

"You think?" Dejen's voice came out somewhere between a spit and a snarl. I looked round at him in surprise. In the fluorescent lamplight his face was tight with fury, the hands that held the infopad shaking with anger. I'd never seen him look so mad before. But then again, our home had just been destroyed by a fireball that killed our families, friends, and everyone we knew, so I guess he had a good reason to be acting weird.

"The Amonston Corporation tried to feed everybody when the climate changed," I said defensively. "And they saved us from the biopoisons that destroyed the world. They made Eden Five and the other Gardens."

"You don't get it, Adi, do you?" Dejen was looking at me with wide eyes now, all his anger turned to sadness. I didn't like it. It made me want to cry, and I didn't dare cry, not anymore.

"Get what?" I demanded.

But Dejen just shook his head, stowing the infopad back in his pack. "It doesn't matter. Get some sleep, we've got a long trek tomorrow." He reached out to squeeze my hand, but I snatched it away before our fingers met. I had to make it clear he wasn't allowed to comfort me. I saw a brief flicker of pain in his eyes before I turned away, but I knew it hurt me more than it hurt him. I couldn't risk crying, I just couldn't.

I went over to where Otienno stood staring out of the window. I put my hand on his shoulder, rubbing it gently. His skin felt hot to my touch, his pulse beating faster when my fingers brushed his neck. It didn't make me sad to touch Otienno. If he found out my secret and walked away from me, it'd hurt, but it wouldn't break me. I could touch him without danger. In some strange way, the fire that rushed through my blood when I touched him made me feel safe; if it destroyed me completely it would take my secret with me, burning us both into ash.

"Go to sleep," I said in his ear. "It's late."

Otienno half turned, his lips brushing close by my cheek. I stayed looking out of the window, waiting for my heart to slow while he went back to the group and stretched out in his sleeping bag. I could feel Dejen's sad gaze on me, and I kept my back to him, staring into the dark instead.

Somewhere out there in the sleeping dust, strange, restless eyes were flickering in the moonlight. I shuddered. I was being watched on all sides. Sooner or later my secret would be spied out, and everyone would know what I'd done. The wind whistled through the cracks in the roof, gusting round the seed bank with a low accusing moan. *You're a killer*, it seemed to say. *You don't deserve to live.*

I looked around at the fading notices pinned to the walls, the regulations and terms and conditions of seed distribution. The Amonston Corporation had tried so hard to keep us all alive, and I'd gone and wiped out a whole Garden of Eden. The wind was right. I didn't deserve to live.

CHAPTER 16

DAY THREE

We were almost out of water by the time we found the stream. Well, I say "we," but it was really Chiku who found it. And not exactly "found." She fell in it, and nearly drowned. And I nearly let her.

By the third day, we'd finished the water in our flasks, and our tongues hung thick and heavy in our mouths, our feet dragging through the dust. Baba Weseka was in the worst state—he'd given half his water to Yango, and now he barely had the strength to put one foot in front of the other. Yango had given up whining. I think she'd finally figured out it was just making her more thirsty.

We'd just passed through a small valley between two crumbling hills, when the world changed beyond all recognition. Stretching out before us in every direction were thick patches of strange brown-green plants. Even from a distance, we could tell there was something odd about them.

They didn't look right. The healthy plants in the Gardens of Eden Five had grown in neat rows, each harvest batch a uniform colour and height. But these were all different. Some grew tall and spindly, others squatted near the ground, their stems too weak to support the weight of their misshapen grey fruit. I wasn't even sure what they were meant to be. At first I thought they might be maize, but when we got closer I could see sharp thorns growing from some of the stalks. Others had thin white fibres coating the withered leaves like a tangled layer of cobwebs. They were all covered in thick red pustules that burst when we passed too close, oozing poisonous sap down the rotting stems.

"What in the name of all the Gods are these?" Otienno whistled, picking one of the grey fruits and staring at it in disgust. It came apart in his hands, the putrid flesh inside stinking and full of fat, wriggling maggots. He dropped it on the dry earth. "I've never seen anything like this in my life."

"There must be water nearby," Dejen said, peering through the dense forest of shrivelled plants. "They can't grow here without some sort of water supply."

"Did you need all those extra years in school to work that out?" Otienno snorted. "You science kids think you're so clever, but without all your fancy lab equipment you're no smarter than the rest of us."

Dejen glared at him. He hated Otienno calling him a kid This was the way it had been for days now, the two of them circling each other, snapping and biting like bad-tempered dogs. I grabbed Tash's hand and shoved past them, heading into the strange fields of shrunken stems and withered fruit.

"If there's water here, we'd better get a move on and find it before we all die of thirst," I muttered. My tongue was sticking to the roof of my mouth, and my teeth felt almost as fuzzy as my pounding head. They could thump each other senseless for all I cared right now, just as long as we found something to drink.

Chiku followed behind sullenly, stepping where I stepped like a grubby little shadow. She'd barely said three words to anyone but Tash since we left Eden Five. I'd seen them whispering together at night when we lit the fluorescent lanterns and wrapped ourselves in our sleeping bags. I didn't like it. It made me wonder what she knew, what terrible secrets she was telling Tash about me. I was sure Chiku knew what I'd done. And so I watched her as carefully as she watched me, never letting her out of my sight for a moment.

We were so busy watching each other, we forgot to keep our eyes on the path ahead. She'd been following so close she kept treading on my heels. She did it once too often, and I gave her a hard shove, sending her tripping sideways round a patch of thorny plants. I heard the splash and Chiku's choked cry almost before I was aware she was gone.

Dejen dropped Baba Weseka's hand and came running through the withered weed field at the sound. He jumped over the plants where she disappeared, crushing them underfoot and calling her name. I ran after him, worried if I let him go he'd vanish too. We nearly toppled over the bank of the stream, but Dejen caught me before I fell.

The stream was brown and sluggish, barely deep enough to drown Yango, never mind Chiku. But it was the mud that was deadly. Chiku was floundering in the sludge that formed the stream bed, already sunk up to her waist in the thick slime. Dejen grabbed one of her arms and I grabbed the other, trying to pull her back to the bank. She was stuck fast, and she sunk further, the water closing in around her neck. If we didn't get her out right away, she wasn't going to make it.

"Pull harder!" Dejen urged, setting one boot on a flat stone and heaving with all his might. I planted my feet on the sandy bank and pulled as well. But I knew I wasn't pulling as hard as I could've done. Chiku knew it too. Our eyes met, her pupils blown wide with fear as she struggled to keep her head above the water.

How easy it would be, to let it all end like this. I was so sure she knew my secret. How could she not? She'd followed me round Eden Five every waking moment. With her gone, my secret would be safe a little longer. I loosened my grip, my hands sliding along her bony arm.

"Adina!" Chiku wailed. Her head dipped under the stream and water shot up her nose. She started spluttering and coughing, gazing up at me in terror. "Adina!" she pleaded again.

That was all it took to bring me back to my senses. Gods, what was I *doing*? I wrapped my hands around her arm properly, tugging with all my might. But it was too late. She'd slipped down too far.

"Chiku, keep your head up!" I yelled. She started thrashing her arms, panicking now she couldn't breathe.

I couldn't hold on. I could feel her slipping away from me, and in my mind I saw her falling down a deep stairway, the basement below rushing up to swallow her. Baba Weseka's words were echoing in my ears. "You have to save her, Adina! Don't let her drown!" I didn't know whether I was imagining them or whether he was yelling them from the maize field over and over again. All I knew was he had seen this happen, and he'd known I was going to let Chiku slip from my grasp.

"Chiku!" I cried. It was almost a sob now.

"Get out of the way!"

Otienno was there when I needed him. He pushed me aside and grabbed Chiku under both arms, leaning back and heaving. Muscles strained beneath his thin cotton shirt, and there came a soft sucking sound as Chiku was dragged free. Dejen grabbed her round the waist, lending his own strength to the effort, and together they pulled her from the mud and set her down on the safety of the bank. She sat there shaking and sobbing, brown water dripping down her face like great muddy teardrops. I should've sat down and put my arms around her, comforting her and wiping her tears away, I know I should have. But this was Chiku in distress, not Tash, and somehow I couldn't quite convince my feet to take that short step towards her.

It was Tash that took care of her, running down the bank to throw her arms around Chiku. She sat with her, patting her back gently until the half-drowned girl had finished hiccupping. Then she began washing the mud out of Chiku's hair and clothes, looking all the while like a miniature version of my mother. It was almost painful for me to watch. I pulled the water filter units out of our packs instead, setting them up by the stream and filling them up with the brown, muddy water. Dejen helped in silence, shooting me questioning looks now and then as though trying to work something out. I wondered if he knew what I'd almost done.

Gods, I hoped not.

When we finished we all sat down by the stream, pulling out protein bars and resting in the shade of the overhanging bank. It would take half an hour or so for the water to filter properly, and we could all use a break from the blazing sun. We didn't talk, we were all too tired and thirsty. Baba Weseka patted Chiku reassuringly on the head like she was a puppy, until Yango got jealous and nipped his fingers. His dog was looking happier now she'd had her fill of dirty stream water, her thin tail wagging whenever Baba Weseka scratched her ears. But her hair was starting to look thinner and more matted than usual, small clumps coming away under Baba's fingers when he stroked her back. He pretended not to notice. I don't think he wanted to know what it meant.

After a while Otienno got up and wandered a little way off into the field of plants, pulling at the stems and examining the fruit like he was trying to decide what they might be. Dejen sat hunched over his infopad, watching more of the videpod entries. He'd been obsessed with them since that first night in the seed bank, glued to the little screen every spare moment. I'd been too busy nursing my guilt and thirst to take much more interest in them. But now I needed a distraction, anything that would take my mind off Chiku's distressed little face looking back at me with sad, accusing eyes.

"What you watching?" I asked, stepping over the water filters and sitting down beside Dejen.

"More videpod entries," Dejen said, throwing me a sideways glance. He hesitated for a moment, then added, "That was kind of weird back there, wasn't it?"

"What?" I said just a bit too quickly. *Gods, does he know I nearly let Chiku drown? Did he see me holding back and watching?* I tried hard to meet his searching gaze, but guilt was burning my tongue, making me want to throw up and confess everything to him. I cleared my throat instead. "What was weird?"

"What happened to Chiku." He frowned, his eyes not leaving mine. I nearly choked with relief when he said, "It happened just the way Baba Weseka said it would. You think there's more to his fits than we thought?"

"Don't be daft," I snorted, keen to throw him off the scent of mystery he'd got hold of. Dejen was the best puzzle solver I'd ever known, and I wasn't about to help him get hold of all the pieces that would spell my guilt out loud and clear if he managed to put them together. "I've seen more of Baba's fits than anyone else in Eden Five—he's ranted about floods and hurricanes and rotting food and plagues and...Gods, I don't know what else, for years now. It was just a coincidence, trust me—next time he'll be raving about giant blood-sucking butterflies that'll eat us when we sleep. You don't want to go listening to him or you'll end up crazy yourself."

Dejen didn't look convinced, but I changed the subject to one I knew would distract him, and it worked like a charm. "So, you found out anything new from the stuff you've been watching?"

"Yes, you've got to see this, Adi. It'll blow your mind." Dejen went back to staring at his stolen videopod, and I let out a sigh of relief.

"These entries are from the second videopod cartridge," he said, pointing at the menu on the screen. "They're recorded by a woman called Nia and the other rebel farmers that tried to stop the Amonston Corporation taking over their land."

"Rebel farmers?" I frowned. "Why were they rebelling?"

"The Amonston Corporation bought all the seed banks, then they made laws to stop farmers from keeping seeds to plant from one year to the next. They were only allowed to rent the seeds, you know, like the books and videopods we used to rent from Director Eshe's office? The laws said that any seeds that contained even a trace of the genetically modified DNA belonged to the Corporation, but since the wind and insects carried pollen everywhere, all the seeds on every African farm eventually contained the new DNA, and the Corporation claimed all the plants belonged to them. The rebels fought for the right to keep their own seeds and grow them from one year to the next the way they'd always done."

He looked up expectantly, as though waiting for my reaction. I wasn't sure what he wanted me to say. The rebels didn't sound so clever to me.

"But why would they want to go on growing the old stuff anyway when the new seeds were so much better?" I wondered. "I mean, did you *see* the size of that maize cob the head of the Corporation was holding? The farmers were dumb if they didn't want to grow them."

"But the seeds *weren't* better." Dejen shook his head. "That's the whole point, Adi. They looked good in the lab, under certain carefully controlled conditions. But when they were planted in Africa, things started to go wrong. They had pesticides, bits of other plants, and even insect and animal genes spliced into their DNA. It wasn't natural like they claimed."

I shuffled my feet restlessly. I'd done a bit of science in school, I'd even been interested in some of the biology we learned. But I didn't want to hear a lecture on DNA and genes and all sorts of stuff when I was so tired. "So not all the trials were perfect." I shrugged. "So what? I'm sure they got it right in the end."

Dejen was looking at me like he wanted to shake me. I scowled back.

"Just watch this," he said. "Then you'll see."

He selected an entry from the infopad menu and held the screen up for me. A young woman's face filled the picture. The recording was shaky, and it was night, so I couldn't see her too clearly. From the look of the dimly lit concrete walls behind her, she was in some sort of large storage room.

"This is Nia Kutuny, member of the Rebel Farmers' Alliance. The date is November twenty-first, twenty twenty-nine." She spoke softly but urgently, looking over her shoulder at the closed door behind her.

"This is the day we've been dreading. We gave in three years ago and started planting the Corporation's seeds in our fields. We didn't have a choice, our plants were all contaminated by the genetically modified pollen, and we couldn't afford to fight the lawsuits. But the price of the Corporation's seeds has been going up every year, and we all owe money to the Corporation. Mosi killed himself yesterday over his seed debt—he's the third one this month." The young woman's eyes were round and sad, but there was a spark of fire in them that flashed in the pale light.

"The farmers met this evening and took a vote. It breaks my heart to say it, but we're selling our land to the Corporation. We're out of options. We were one of the last villages to hold out against them, but now we're being bought over too. It makes me sick to think of what they're doing to our land, to our traditions." Nia spat on the ground, her face twisted in anger. Then she took a deep breath and ploughed on.

"I'm making these video blogs as a record of what's happening here. I'll try to smuggle them out to the other continents for broadcast, but the Corporation has a stranglehold on the media. Now they own our entire food production and supply chains, they pretty much own our governments. But if this does get through, if anyone is watching, then please, you must help us! The Corporation says they're creating jobs, but they're forcing us to sell our farmland and then we have no choice but to work for slave wages on their superfarms."

The picture began to blur, the sound crackling as though the woman's recorder was running out of power. Before the battery died, she hurried on, "There's something wrong with the Amonston Corporation's seeds. No one noticed at first, but now it's clear. But any of the farmers who try to reach out to the media go missing, and we think the Corporation is—"

The picture on the screen faded, the infopad menu flicking back on to show the end of the entry. I sat staring at the dates blinking on the blue screen, working my way through all the strange words the woman called Nia had used. By the time I'd got to the end of the list in my head it still wasn't a whole lot clearer.

"Well?" Dejen prompted. "What do you think of the Corporation now?"

I shrugged and started filling the flasks up from the water filters. "So some farmers didn't like the way things changed when the Amonston Corporation came along and modernised the food production methods. Big deal. People hate change, Dejen, you know that. They always fight it and say it's bad and it's ruining everything. Look at the huge rows the workers had in Eden Five when the food technicians tried to update the cookhouse service in the canteens last month. It was just a few changes in serving lines and lunch times, but it nearly started a riot! People are dumb, they don't want to think."

I knew it was true, because I didn't want to think. I wanted to drink and drink until my throat stopped aching and my belly was full, and forget everything that had happened.

Dejen got up and brushed past me, a look of sheer frustration on his face. "What's the point of having a brain like yours if you don't use it, Adina?" he muttered. I made a rude sign behind his back. What was the point of having a brain like his if all it did was make you restless and annoyed at everything you didn't know?

I passed round the water flasks, making sure Baba Weseka didn't waste his on his dumb dog. He nodded and smiled, and said Yango was a "good dog," but I don't think he really understood. Once we'd drunk our fill and dismantled the filter units, we set off again through the field of giant weeds. That's what we started calling them—we didn't know what else they could be. In Eden Five, we'd stored the seeds of just about every species on the Biodiversity Level, planting them in rotation and harvesting them at the end of each season. But these plants weren't like anything we'd seen before. Nothing out here in the wilds was familiar, not even our own thoughts and actions. We were all acting weird, tangled up in the thick blanket of our own grief and snapping at anyone who got too close.

Otienno walked by my side the rest of the afternoon. Apart from Tash, he was the only one I let get so near me. Dejen was out in front, carrying Tash on his shoulders. He glanced back from time to time, making it look like he was checking up on Baba Weseka and Chiku behind him, but I knew he was really watching me and Otienno. I didn't care. My fingers tingled every time we stumbled on the uneven ground and our arms brushed against each other. I was dead inside, numb with guilt and grief, and this small spark was the only thing that made me certain I was still alive. This was all I could allow myself to feel, this sudden shiver of excitement that was so sharp it was almost painful.

But Dejen was wrong. I *did* use my brain. All afternoon I thought as I plodded through that endless stretch of rotting vegetation, trying to work out what it was that bothered me about the videpod entry I'd seen. It wasn't until the sun had set and dusk closed in that I finally figured it out. It wasn't what Nia had said that bugged me. I was pretty sure she was just mad at the Amonston Corporation because she and the other farmers had to change the way they did things. It was what I'd seen that unsettled me. The door with the poster on it, the walls filled with seed bank regulations—they could have been anywhere. But behind her there had been a window with one wooden shutter that swung back and forth in the breeze. I recognised that window. How could I not? I'd spent half a night gazing through it at the empty village beyond.

Nia's village.

Something bad had happened to her and the people she cared about, and I knew how that felt. I couldn't believe it had something to do with the Amonston Corporation, though, I just couldn't. They'd built the Edens and tried to keep us alive when the ecosystems collapsed, I was sure of it. They were the ones who'd saved us. I needed someone, *something* to believe in now our home was gone. And so I believed in the Amonston Corporation. They'd been trying to feed the world, hadn't they? How could that ever be wrong?

CHAPTER 17

DAY FOUR

By the afternoon of the fourth day, we were still in the weed fields. Gods, they seemed to go on forever. Only now we weren't alone.

I'm not sure when I first realised we were being followed. Maybe it was around midday when we stopped to shelter from the blazing sun, spreading our thermafoil sleeping bags over the tops of the high plants and stretching out to rest underneath. Or maybe it was some hours after, when we stopped again, this time to treat a deep cut on Otienno's arm. He'd tripped over Yango, stumbling forward and scraping his wrist on a sharp rock. He was furious at the dog, lashing out with his boot and catching her under the belly with such force she was lucky he didn't crack a rib. I managed to calm him down, pulling him a little way from the group and treating his cut with the antiseptic cleaning kit in my pack.

It wasn't really Yango's fault. She'd been nervous since daybreak, trailing after us with her tail between her legs and twining round our boots whenever we let her get close enough. At first I thought she was just in pain. Fat, warty blisters had developed across her back and sides where clumps of thin hair had fallen out, and she scratched at them constantly, rolling over and rubbing herself against the rocky ground whenever we stopped to rest. But that wasn't what was wrong with her, not really.

She was frightened. I finally figured it out when I saw her stop and look behind, sniffing the air and running back to the group with a faint whimper. I gazed back too, but all I could see were the endless clumps of giant weeds that swayed and rattled their rotten fruit in the breeze.

No, that's not all I could see.

There were flickers on the edges of my sight, quick darting movements that were there one moment then gone the next. The more I tried to focus on them, the less I seemed to see. Something was out there, following close behind us, keeping far enough back that we couldn't be sure it wasn't just our imaginations playing tricks on us.

It's just the wind stirring the dust, I chanted to myself as I walked. *There's no such thing as Nomalies or monsters in the wilds.*

But by now I was pretty sure there were.

I'd lost count of the number of times Yango had stopped, cocking her head to one side and straining her ears to listen to the wind rustling in the withered leaves. Then she'd dart back to us, tangling herself round our legs, desperate for comfort.

The last time she did it she tripped Otienno up, sending him sprawling in the dirt. After the blow he gave her, she wasn't likely to try that again.

"We ought to get rid of that stinking dog, it's no use to us," Otienno growled, wincing as I wiped his cut with an antiseptic swab. "It's going to die anyway, so it's pointless keeping it alive and wasting protein bars and carbohydrate pills on it."

I was pretty sure Otienno hadn't wasted any of the food rations from his pack on Yango, but I kept my mouth shut. I kind of agreed anyway—Yango was a nuisance we just didn't need.

"It's Dejen's fault, he should never have rescued the dumb dog in the first place," Otienno scowled. "He's the one feeding it—him and Baba Weseka. They're as bad as each other. I don't know why you like him." He looked up at me, a questioning frown in his eyes.

"Like who? Dejen or Baba Weseka?" I asked casually, playing for time. Otienno's face was close to my neck as I bent over to clean his wound and tie a bandage round his arm. I could feel the heat of his anger burning through the thin cotton of my shirt. It made me feel strangely safe somehow. I didn't have to think around Otienno. All I had to do was respond to his moods, reflecting back the flash of yearning whenever we happened to touch. It went just deep enough to make me shiver with excitement, but not deep enough to reach my soul and the secret I kept hidden there. I could give in to this without fear. Otienno was safe.

"I meant Dejen," Otienno said. "Are you and him…?"

"Of course not!" I snorted. "We're just friends." That's what I'd been telling myself for so long I almost believed it. Almost.

"Good."

There was a glint in Otienno's eyes, a spark of desire that burned brighter when he laid a strong hand on my neck and ran it possessively all the way down to my waist. I stared right back at him, a slow smile on my lips. When I looked into his eyes, I didn't see years' worth of shared memories staring back at me, weighing me down with their trust and expectation.

Not like Dejen. Dejen was dangerous.

Dejen could see into my very soul, and he'd snap my heart in two if he found the secret I hid there. No, better to feel without thinking, to let Otienno's rough hands squeeze my hips and remind me I was still alive.

"Are you two coming or what?" Dejen's voice called through the weeds, breaking the strange spell that Otienno's deep-set eyes cast on me.

"Be there in a minute," I called back, stepping away and shoving the antiseptic kit into my pack. Otienno and I exchanged glances, then we went back to join the others. Something had changed between us, and now every look and touch was charged with meaning. I felt a bit giddy as we walked together through the weed field, drunk with desire. But I didn't get to enjoy the feeling for long. Tash's scream put an end to that.

"Tash!" I yelled, running through the tall weeds to find my sister. She'd wandered a short way ahead with Chiku, holding hands and whispering together until they were out of sight behind the plant stalks. "Tash! What is it?"

"Nomalies!" she shrieked back.

Nomalies Nomalies Nomalies.

The word wailed over and over again in my head like a warning siren. But when I crashed through the curtain of dried leaves there was nothing there but the two girls, clinging to each other and crying. I picked Tash up, ignoring Chiku and rocking my real sister in my arms. "It's OK, don't be scared, I'm here now. What did you see?"

"It was a Nomaly," Chiku shuddered, clutching her bony arms to her chest and rocking herself the way I was rocking Tash. "We saw it through the weeds, clear as day."

"It was *horrible*, Adina," Tash sobbed. "All mixed up and wrong."

Otienno and Dejen exchanged glances as they strode through the plants, Baba Weseka in tow. None of us could pretend now. We all knew we were being followed. It was time to admit it, even if that meant making the threat real.

"What should we do?" I asked Dejen. He would know how to handle this. He always knew what to do.

"We have to get out of here as fast as we can," he said. "We should tramp the weed stalks down as we go so nothing can sneak up behind us and catch us unaware." Somehow his confident voice calmed us all down. It was alright, Dejen was in charge. Even Otienno didn't argue.

With Baba Weseka and the girls in the middle, we fanned out in a line, trampling down the plants on either side as we hurried through the weed field in the failing light. We weren't going as fast as I would've liked, but just being able to look back and see a clear stretch of open ground behind made me feel less shut in. The grey fruits burst apart beneath our boots as the stalks fell, their purplish flesh bleeding their juices into the dirt in thin, foul-smelling trickles.

We were so worried something would come sneaking up behind us, it never occurred to us to pay much attention to the path ahead. And that's where they attacked in the dark, suddenly, without any warning.

I'd just turned to ask Dejen if he thought we should make camp for the night, when something black and spidery twitched on the edge of my vision. A second later, three shapes burst from the plants ahead of us, sending us stumbling back with yells of fright.

Tash was right—they were horrible.

In the faint moonlight I didn't get much more than a vague impression of jumbled arms and legs in all the wrong places, twisted spines and huge, bobbing lumps that might have been heads, only they were so malformed I couldn't work out what I was seeing. All my brain registered were gaping holes that shrieked and snapped, and twitching bony things that looked something like claws. That was enough. I snatched Tash up and fled, racing through the weeds as fast as my legs could go.

I could hear crashing in the stalks behind, but I couldn't risk breaking stride to turn and see if it was one of my group or one of the Nomalies. Everything was a blur of motion in the moonlight. The shrivelled leaves whipped at my face as I ran past, and I couldn't tell if they were Nomaly hands clawing at my eyes. My lungs were screaming for air, my heart pounding so loud in my chest I couldn't hear the shrieks that were coming from the weed field behind me. Tash had gone limp in my arms, shaking so hard she could barely hold on to my neck. I was sure now there was a Nomaly following us. The air behind seemed to vibrate as it closed in, and I couldn't run any faster, I just couldn't.

And then I didn't have to.

The path in front opened up, and before I knew it I was out of the weed field and running across empty plains towards the incline of a little hill in the distance. Shadows raced across the face of the moon, the night wind picking up and stirring the dust clouds. I couldn't keep going. My lungs were burning and my legs were on fire. I stumbled to a halt and set Tash down, standing before her protectively and turning to face the thing behind me.

It was Otienno.

He had Chiku clamped under one arm, the other pumping the air as he ran. Chiku had lost her survival pack, her face all scrunched up with fear. Otienno stopped by my side and let Chiku slide down, hunching over with his hands on his knees to catch his breath. We didn't need to speak, even if we'd had the breath for it. We all stood there in the darkness, gazing back at the edge of the weed field and waiting. There was no sign of the Nomalies. But there was no sign of Dejen or Baba Weseka either.

My legs were wobbly, the adrenaline rush fading and leaving me drained and shaky. I strained my eyes to catch the slightest hint of movement between the stalks, cursing the wind that stirred the leaves and kept my heart leaping in hope until I thought I couldn't bear it any longer. When Dejen finally limped out of the field, one hand pulling Baba Weseka along with him,

I had to turn away to swallow the sob that threatened to bubble up from my throat. I couldn't cry, I couldn't. It was too risky. The others might guess my secret, they might suspect my guilt. I struggled to calm my breathing, finally getting it under control by the time Dejen made it across the plain to meet us.

There was a long cut running down one of Dejen's legs, and a deep gouge across his cheek. He looked like he'd been in a fight. Baba Weseka wasn't hurt. It was clear he'd had Dejen's protection. We all stood there together, half afraid if we turned our backs on the weed field and walked away we'd be followed again.

"Come on." It was Dejen who started limping off first, stirring the rest of us back to action. "We should get up to the top of that hill and make camp there. If the clouds clear we should be able to see across the plain. We'll take turns to keep watch from now on."

There was blood soaking his trouser leg, his knee threatening to give out every few steps. I wanted to take his arm and help him, but I dreaded my own reaction if I stood that close and let myself feel his pain. Instead, I lifted Tash up again, forcing my unwilling feet to keep walking. Otienno had to drag Baba Weseka behind him, trying to stop him from wailing for the dog that hadn't appeared and giving our location away to anything that was lurking just out of sight in the darkness.

Halfway up the hill we heard noises in the distance that sounded like strange shrieks and wails. There came a long whining howl, and then silence. We didn't stop and turn back—we all knew what it meant.

"Maybe that dog'll keep them from following us tonight," Otienno said quietly to me. "Whatever they were, they looked hungry."

Otienno's voice wasn't quiet enough. Baba Weseka heard and started sobbing, clamping his hands over his ears even though there was no more howling in the distance from his dog. "I have to go back and get her," he kept pleading. "She's a good dog, good dog, and I have to go back…" But Otienno had a firm grip on his arm. No matter how much he disliked Baba Weseka, he wasn't about to let him go back to be eaten by Nomalies. Not for some dumb dog at any rate.

We were all exhausted by the time we reached the top of the little hill. There was a shallow depression on the summit that hid us from view, but if we climbed over the rocks and sat at the edge of the slope, we could see out across the whole plain below.

"I'll take first watch," Otienno said, sitting down on the slope and letting the rest of us go on to the sheltered basin. "Adina, come and swap with me when you wake up." He looked Dejen up and down. Dejen was swaying a little in the night breeze, his lips pale. "You just get some rest," Otienno grunted. "You're not much use to us if you can't walk."

Dejen nodded, all the fight beaten out of him. We sat down in the sandy basin, spreading our sleeping bags out. I had a real struggle to get Baba Weseka into his—he was still trying to go back for Yango. "We'll find her tomorrow when it's light, Baba," I lied, "but you have to go to sleep now."

"I can't sleep without Yango," he whispered, passing a trembling hand across his eyes. He looked more confused

173

than ever, gazing round without recognising where he was. There was no use me telling him we were out in the wilds, I'd said it a thousand times and it still hadn't sunk in. All I got for my trouble was yet another story about Nomalies. That was the last thing I wanted to hear right now. "She sings me to sleep you know, Yango does. Sings me to sleep."

"No, she doesn't," I muttered, tucking his arms under the sleeping bag cover. "She's just a dog."

"But she's a good dog, good dog," Baba Weseka sighed. His head rolled back on the thermafoil, and he was asleep in moments, drool sliding down his chin.

I shook my head at the old man. Of all the people to get a second chance at living, why did it have to be him? Why couldn't it have been my mother or father? Not this useless old thing who'd probably be dead in a short time anyway. It just wasn't fair.

I silenced the nasty little voice in my head by promising to be kinder to Baba Weseka tomorrow to compensate for my wicked thoughts. I didn't want to think about what he'd said when he'd had his last fit and warned me about Chiku. It was just too crazy for me to process right now. I pushed it down into the strongbox in my mind where thoughts of my parents and all the dead people of Eden Five were buried, and locked the lid with as much determination as I could.

I set Baba's boots to one side and checked his water flask to make sure he still had some left for the next day. I already knew it was half full as I'd been keeping an eye on it for him all day, but it gave me an excuse to avoid Dejen for a while longer.

"Go and help Dejen clean up," I told Chiku, throwing her the antiseptic kit from my pack. "Make sure you get all the dust out."

"Don't bother, I'll do it myself," Dejen muttered. He took the medical kit from his own pack and began cleaning the wound on his leg, wincing when the iodine solution stung his raw flesh. He glanced over to where I stood, half watching him as I fiddled with Baba Weseka's pack. I knew what that resentful look meant. He couldn't understand why I would help Otienno when he was hurt, but not my best friend. The sob I had to choke off halfway up my throat was all I needed to remind me why I couldn't go to him. I wanted to wash the blood from his cheek and stroke his face gently, telling him how sorry I was that I'd blown Eden Five up and killed everyone. I was so, so sorry I'd ruined everything for him and Tash and Otienno. I wanted to tell him all my secrets, bare my soul and beg for his forgiveness. But I couldn't. He'd never forgive me, and I couldn't risk losing him like I'd lost my parents and nearly everyone else who'd ever mattered to me.

I settled Tash in her sleeping bag, biting back my anger that she'd have to share it with Chiku from now on. The dumb kid had gone and lost her pack when we ran from the Nomalies, and that meant sharing out the precious protein bars and carbohydrate pills that weren't meant for more than one. I could slap her stupid little face for being so careless. Chiku slipped in beside Tash before I could argue about it, turning her back on me and snuggling down under the cover. I left her to it—if I made a fuss, Dejen might suggest I share my bag with her instead. I think I'd rather bunk down with Baba Weseka and his waxy skin and drool.

I climbed back up the sides of the small basin, feeling Dejen's eyes on me the whole time. He knew where I was going. It was a relief when I skirted the rocks at the edge of the summit and was hidden from view behind the high boulders.

I found Otienno crouching on the balls of his feet, staring off at the weed field in the distance across the plain. He didn't look round when I sat beside him. He knew who it was and why I had come. We sat like that for a long time, watching the wind stirring up patches of dust on the plain and setting them dancing and shimmering eerily in the moonlight.

I could hear him breathing, and he could hear me.

Somehow that made us both breathe faster, our hearts beating louder in reply. Without a word, Otienno placed his hand on the small of my back, rubbing his thumb in slow, lazy circles that sent shivers up my spine. I leaned into the curve of his arm, half dizzy with the strong musk of sweat that soaked his shirt. My own hand found his chest, my fingers exploring the firm muscles under the layer of cotton. I could feel his pulse racing at my touch. Before I knew what had happened, his lips found mine, and for a long moment there was only his hands on my waist, his hot breath on mine and his stubble on my cheek as we fought to get closer. It was like a sudden hunger, and both of us were starving for comfort in this strange, bleak world.

Then there came a loud howl from the slope right in front of us.

We leapt apart, our eyes scouring the darkness, hands already clenched into fists. A pitiful whining came from a small shape that straggled and limped its way up the hill towards us. At first I couldn't make out what it was—my head was too full of the thought of Nomalies to see clearly. But then it got closer, and I recognised the matted fur and big sad eyes of Baba Weseka's stupid dog. Yango had come back to us, and she'd almost made it in one piece. She'd left half her tail behind her, though. The bloody stump she'd managed to keep wagged painfully when she finally reached the top of the hill and collapsed into my lap.

Yango's back was covered in deep scratches, her muzzle torn and gouged in a dozen places. Otienno edged away from her in disgust, muttering that we should just put her out of her misery. But for once I didn't mind the dog's bad breath and drooling tongue licking my face all happy and overexcited. I picked her up and carried her back to where Baba Weseka lay snoring softly in his sleeping bag, hushing the dog and patting her till she calmed down and stretched out beside him to sleep.

I knew deep down that Otienno was right. Dejen should never have rescued her, and keeping her alive to die a slow death wasn't kind. There'd been too much death already, far too much. But I couldn't help nursing a small spark of hope as I looked down at that dumb dog all covered in scratches and bites and sores and bruises. If Yango could survive the wilds and the Nomalies, maybe we could too.

CHAPTER 18

DAY SEVEN—MORNING

We didn't talk about the Nomalies after that day in the weed field. It was as though we were all scared the very mention of their name would bring them scuttling out of the dark after us. Besides, it wasn't as if we didn't have other things to worry about. Nomalies weren't the only danger we faced in the wilds.

Our biggest concern was finding water. Whole stretches of land were dry as the ashes of a long-dead fire, the sand and dust burnt to fine powder by the scorching sun. We looked down over the dead earth as we trekked south-east, crossing the ridge of the hills and searching in the gullies for any shaded pools that might have escaped the sun's full fury. It was days before we finally found one, tucked in a hollow beneath a rocky overhang. It was a dark red colour, stagnant and stinking, but we were too desperate to care. Besides, our water filters would drain most of the poisons clogging the small pool, and the biofilters in our necks would clear any toxic residue from our bloodstreams. We threw our packs down and began setting up the filters, glad of the chance to rest.

Dejen was more glad than any of us. His leg still hurt, and when he thought we weren't looking, his limp got worse. He shouldn't be walking on it just yet, but he didn't have a choice. We had to keep going. But first we needed to get clean.

We took turns washing with the filtered water, scrubbing away the dirt that clung to us after days of long trekking. It was such a relief to feel cool, clean liquid against my skin. It'd been so long since I last had a shower in the tiny sanitation unit in my homeroom I'd almost forgotten what being clean felt like. It was just a rub-down really, barely enough liquid to dislodge the layer of dust clinging to my skin. But it made me feel almost alive again, like a seed getting that first touch of water it needed to start sprouting.

Chiku needed it more than any of us. She was still caked in mud and grime from that dive she'd taken into the stream, and the dust was sticking to the streaks of snot from her nose like some kind of weird moustache made of dirt. It was just as well she submitted to me scrubbing her skin half raw with a sponge made out of a handful of bandages from the medical kit. If she hadn't, I'd have chucked her head first into the chemical pool and made her stay there till she either got clean or melted.

"Why's it such a funny colour?" Chiku grumbled, eyeing the crimson pool suspiciously while I washed out the clumps of dried mud sticking to her hair. She hadn't forgotten the dip she'd taken in the stream that nearly drowned her.

"It's from all the chemicals the Amonston Corporation let run into the rivers from their pesticide factories in the old times," Dejen said wearily. "They sprayed it on their GM crops in higher and higher doses. Over decades, the weeds and wildlife evolved in response and the mutations ran out of control. The whole water table's polluted with chemicals— even the rain's full of them. That's why we need to wear our biofilters."

"What's GM?" Chiku screwed up her face the way Tash did when she didn't understand. It annoyed me when she copied my little sister, reminding me we were all related whether I wanted to admit it or not.

"'Genetically Modified'," Dejen said. "The Corporation made loads of money in the old times by messing with natural seeds and plants, turning them into monsters. In the end, they destroyed everything."

"You don't know that!" I snapped, nearly knocking over one of the water filters as I leapt to my feet. "You always make them sound so evil. They weren't, they were just trying to help the world survive the collapse of the ecosystems."

"Open your eyes, Adina," Dejen sighed, rubbing at the scar healing on his cheek. "They *caused* the collapse of the ecosystems."

"No, they didn't!" I was so angry I was almost spitting. "They were trying to feed the world and save us all."

Dejen was too tired to argue. He just leaned back against the rock and muttered, "It's all in the videpod entries, if you'd just take the time to watch them instead of running off to play with Otienno every night like some dumb love-struck kid."

The accusation stung. I guess it's because it was true. Dejen had risked his life to get hold of those videpods, and instead of watching them and finding out about our world, I'd spent my evenings walking away from the group to have time alone with Otienno. I didn't want to know what was on those videpods, not really. I wanted to forget about Eden Five and the people I cared about and killed—forget about the old times and the beautiful world that was destroyed. Otienno helped me forget. Sitting next to him in the dark, kissing him and stroking his strong chest, made it easy to forget for a few brief moments each night that our world was in ruins.

But Dejen made me remember.

He was always pushing me with his words or his eyes to look back—look back at the world as it was and find the truth. I didn't care if what I believed wasn't true. It didn't matter now. All that mattered was that I believed in *something*. The Amonston Corporation had built my home and the other Gardens of Eden, giving us a chance to survive the biological disaster that destroyed the world. That was enough for me.

"You and your videpods can go to hell, Dejen," I growled. "I'm sick of them and I'm sick of *you*."

I stormed off before he could reply, striding all the way up to the top of the ridge to stare out over the landscape. My eyes were stinging, but it wasn't the dust or the wind. I'd have to be more careful. I couldn't let Dejen get to me like that or before I knew it I'd be sobbing in his arms and telling him everything. I looked out over the wilds below, taking long, deep breaths of the parched air. On one side of the hills where we were walking was a dead zone, a huge stretch of land that

181

was just dust and waste. But when I climbed a little higher to see over the ridge to the other side, I got the shock of my life.

The Rift Valley was green and lush and full of life.

Stretching to the horizon in every direction were countless giant polytunnels made of plastiglass, taller than the Dome of Eden Five and twice as wide. Even from way up on the ridge I could make out the fresh green of plants and vegetables growing in endless rows inside that were so long they seemed to disappear off into infinity. It was like looking at the garden levels of Eden Five through a magic mirror that multiplied the plants and maize fields and vegetable plots and fruit trees until my eyes just couldn't take the abundance of living things in.

We'd spent days searching for water, but now I knew where it had all gone. Standing between the rows of polytunnels were towering water tanks, humming in the shimmering desert air as they pumped the sluggish liquid up through plastiglass pipes and purified it in their chemical-filtration units. I watched the water in those spinning tanks whirring round and round as it was cleansed and the toxic chemicals were separated out, the pure water rushing down clear tubes into the polytunnels while the deep red chemical sludge was pumped down into stagnant pools that ringed the bottom of the ridge below me.

But it wasn't polytunnels or the plants or even the water tanks that made my heart leap in hope as I stared down into the valley. It was what I saw moving behind the plastiglass panes that made me open my mouth and yell for the others at the top of my voice. My mouth was so parched I had to try three times to shout loud enough for them to hear, but when they finally did, they packed up the water filters and came clambering up the rocks behind me double-quick time.

"What is it?" Dejen called. "Are you alright?"

"Get up here now—you *have* to see this for yourselves," I shouted back.

"What the…?" Otienno whistled, gazing down into the valley with wide eyes. Dejen cocked his head to one side and frowned like he was seeing something he couldn't quite believe was real. Tash and Chiku exchanged a high five and grinned like we'd already made it to safety.

"Is this it?" Tash asked me, grabbing my arm and squeezing it in excitement, "Is this the Sanctuary?"

"No, Tash, I haven't the faintest idea what this is," I muttered, pulling out a crumpled piece of paper from my survival pack that had a sketchy map of the area drawn on it. "Eden Five's here, and Sanctuary Seven's all the way over there on the sea coast." I traced my finger from the round Dome symbol across the page to the crescent moon and cross symbol on the other side. There was nothing else drawn on the map other than a few highland ridges like the one we were standing on, and the distant Dome symbols of Edens Three and Four at the far ends of the paper. The numbers detailing distances and coordinates scrawled across the map were all the help we were going to get crossing the wilds.

"What the hell is this doing here?" Otienno asked out loud like he was trying to work out what he was seeing. "Is this another Eden we haven't been told about?"

"Does that plastiglass and machinery look eighty years old to you?" Dejen said with a faint snort of contempt. "Look at it—it's all brand new. I've never seen vacuum pumps that powerful or hydroponic planting on that scale before. It's one of the Amonston Corporation's superfarms. Now that they've wrecked the land with their chemicals, they're growing everything in polytunnels to keep out the toxins."

"So they found a way to grow food again in the wilds. How is that a bad thing?" I snapped, defending the Corporation before I even knew what I was saying.

"They've taken our land off us, poisoned it till it's barren and useless and everything's dead, and now they're making more money by growing food on their giant protected superfarms." Dejen said slowly like he was talking to a child. "Exactly what's good about that, Adina?"

I scowled back at him, but I didn't have a reply handy.

"Where's all the food going?" Otienno frowned, staring down at the miles and miles of polytunnels. "I mean, all the Edens have their own Gardens, and the Sanctuaries probably do too. So who's all this food for?"

Dejen nodded. "Good question." I had a sneaky suspicion he already knew the answer, but I wasn't ready to hear it.

"Wait, is that…?" Chiku suddenly stood on her toes in excitement, peering at the plastiglass tunnels and pointing at the movement I'd seen earlier. "Look! There's people in there! Real people! They can help us, Adina, let's go down there and talk to them."

"Not so fast." Dejen grabbed her by the arm before she could go tearing down the slope and banging on the plastiglass walls of the polytunnels to get the attention of the people she saw moving about in between the rows of plants. "We don't know if they're friendly or not."

"What's that supposed to mean?" Otienno said, looking at Dejen like he was crazy, "We're a bunch of kids lost out here in the wilds, of course they'll help us, why wouldn't they?"

"The Amonston Corporation built the Gardens to keep us off our own land," Dejen said. "If you'd bothered to watch the videopod entries, you'd have worked that out by now. You think they want any of the prisoners they locked up in their Eden cellblocks turning up on their superfarms and asking for breakfast?"

"Don't be stupid, the Edens were built to keep us safe from all the biotoxins out here," Otienno shot back. "It's not some big conspiracy the Amonston Corporation thought up just to piss you off, Dejen. Come on, let's go."

Before he could start down the slope, Dejen pulled him back too. "This is crazy. We don't know if it's safe down there," he snapped. "We should stick to the plan—stay on the map path and head for Sanctuary Seven. We don't have time for detours."

"You're not in charge here," Otienno growled, taking a step closer and trying to cow Dejen with an angry stare.

Dejen just raised an eyebrow and stared back. "Neither are you," he said softly. Somehow he made it sound like a threat.

Otienno sensed he'd need backup. He did what I was dreading he'd do. He turned to me. "What do you think, Adina?" he asked. "Should we keep walking through the wilds and risk being eaten by Nomalies, or should we take a chance and ask the people down in the polytunnels for help?"

Dejen looked at me too, his eyes searching mine for some small sign of support. I knew what they meant. They were asking me to choose between them.

Damn boys. Damn them all to hell and back.

Why did they always have to make everything so difficult? Even when we were struggling for our very survival, it was all about them and their stinking little egos. I scowled at them both and walked a little way down the slope to get a closer look at the superfarm before I made up my mind. That was all it took for me to decide. Once I was out from under the overhang of rock that blocked our view to the east, I knew we weren't going to be able to just walk straight across the plains to Sanctuary Seven.

"We can't follow the path on the map. Come here and see what's blocking our way," I called back up.

To the east the whole earth was in motion. In the distance beyond the last of the superfarm's polytunnels, huge machines were walking across vast stretches of land that were pitted like honeycomb. Inside each crater, giant mining drills were gouging at the earth. Metal engines that looked like monstrous insects crawled between the drilling machines, pounding at the earth with piston-like legs.

A few short weeks ago, if I'd been asked at the Sunday assembly in Eden Five to describe Hell, I wouldn't have known where to start. Now I did. This was it. Hell was a nightmare of metal beasts glinting under a pitiless sun, tearing the earth into an infinite abyss of deep craters. And there wasn't just one devil. There were thousands. They were steel-clad giants that strode between the pits, turning their heads this way and that to survey the wreckage that was once a vast stretch of the Great Rift Valley.

I wanted to cry at the horror and ruin and waste of it all. Instead I gritted my teeth and said, "We have to go down to the superfarm and see if we can get help, it's our only option."

This time Dejen didn't argue.

It was only when we were halfway down the slope that I realised I hadn't seen Baba Weseka for ages.

"Wait, where's…? Damn!" I gazed back up the ridge, but I couldn't see him against the sun's glare. "Didn't any of you check that Baba was with you?" I said accusingly, glaring at Otienno and Dejen.

Dejen looked guilty, but with his injured leg he'd had a hard enough time getting himself up the ridge carrying his own pack, never mind helping Baba Weseka with his unsteady feet. Otienno just shrugged. "What, you mean babysit that freak as well as filling the flasks, packing up the water filters, and making sure the girls are safe and have their kit bags with them when you snap your fingers for us to come running?"

I made a face, but he did have a point. "OK, I'm going back to find him. Wait here for me, and don't go any closer to the polytunnels till I'm back."

I'm not sure why, but from a distance the people moving about behind the plastiglass made me nervous. There was nothing about them in our official history. They shouldn't be here. I wanted to make sure I was holding tightly to Tash's hand when we got up close to speak to them.

I hurried back up the ridge, out of breath and panting by the time I found Baba Weseka sitting on a rock down by the pool where we'd left him. Yango was pawing at his legs and whining, and at first I thought he'd had another fit and was zoning out. Then I saw he was staring up into the sky with a fierce look of concentration on his face.

"Baba?" I said, shaking his shoulder to get his attention. "Baba, come on, we have to keep moving, the others are waiting."

"They're waiting too," Baba Weseka said, pointing up into the sky. "Waiting for us to die so they can pick our bones clean."

I looked up. Circling in the sky high above us was a flock of ominous black shapes. The only birds I'd ever seen in Eden Five were the fat chickens and turkeys bred on the Biodiversity Level for the cookhouse ovens. The bee and butterfly colonies reared on the garden levels for pollinating the plants were too precious to be exposed to predators, so when the Edens were built all the unmutated birds were shipped off to the Sanctuaries along with the wild animals to preserve the gene pool.

The birds circling us weren't like anything I'd seen before in Dejen's old books, though. These were mutants, their DNA ripped to pieces by the biotoxins in the wilds. I was too numb by now to be surprised we'd been lied to in all our biology classes and there were actually things living out in the wilds after all. I'd already had all the surprise knocked out of me by the sight of the Nomalies the other day.

I shuddered as I watched their bloated bodies circling awkwardly above us. The eyes staring down at us hungrily were red ringed and bloodshot in the swirling dust, their hooked beaks ending in sharp points. They had no soft plumes like normal birds, just shrivelled grey skin and wings covered in long thin scales that rippled in the breeze like flight feathers. They looked like they were ready to follow us till we dropped dead so they could feast on our corpses. By the way they were eying us, I wasn't entirely convinced they had the patience to wait that long.

"I saw them in my dreams," Baba Weseka muttered, half to me and half to himself. "But they're bigger than I remember."

I'd been ready to grab him and get moving, but what he said made me pause and squat down beside him. For the first time I had a chance to talk to him about his visions away from the watching eyes of the others, and I wasn't about to waste it. "Baba, what you see when you have a fit—does it always come true?" I asked hesitantly, hoping he'd look at me the way Otienno did and say I was crazy. But he didn't. He just nodded, confirming all my worst fears.

"I tried to tell people about the Nomalies, but they didn't listen," he sighed. "No one ever listened. Not even you, Adina." He looked at me sadly now. "You didn't listen when I warned you about the fire and the death. It started with the apple. You shouldn't have picked it."

A strange feeling of guilt mixed with fear shivered up my spine, and I felt my blood run cold. "You mustn't talk about that, Baba," I begged him, "or everyone will know it was my fault. And you mustn't tell anyone else about your visions. If you have any more, just keep them to yourself, OK?"

"But I have to warn them if I see what's coming," Baba Weseka said, "don't I?"

"You can tell me, but no one else," I said, "especially not Dejen. If he finds out the fire was all my fault he'll never forgive me."

"But it wasn't your fault, Adina." Baba Weseka was looking at me without confusion for the very first time since we'd left Eden Five.

I gazed into those milky eyes, wondering what on earth he meant this time. "I know the fire wasn't caused by me picking an apple, Baba. It started because I—" I stopped suddenly before I could give my secret away. Gods, I was an idiot. I'd nearly opened my mouth and blabbed to the one person who'd go dribbling my secrets out as soon as he had his next fit.

"Just don't say anything to anyone, OK? Come on, Baba, we have to get going."

I helped him get his pack on and grabbed his hand, pulling him up the slope with me. Yango was even more relieved than I was to get going. Even though her paws were rubbed raw and weeping pus, she scampered up the hill away from the birds like she had an electric motor attached to her backside.

By the time we crossed the ridge and started down the far side, the others were already heading for the polytunnels. I cursed, seeing Otienno out in the lead, bullying the others along behind him. He'd clearly got tired of standing around waiting. Dejen kept looking back at me as if to say, "This wasn't my idea", but I was too far away to hear what he was calling back to us.

It was only when we got down to the bottom of the ridge and drew level with the run-off pools of toxic sludge pumped out by the water tanks that I realised he was warning us about the stench. Gods, the smell! The deep pools of chemicals bubbled and fizzed ominously, stinging our eyes and burning the back of our throats till we were coughing up the fumes. We covered our mouths, treading carefully on the narrow walkways between the huge pools. One slip and that would be the end. I was pretty sure that whatever was in the run-off from the filter tanks, it was stronger than any acid I'd ever seen.

We finally caught up with the others before they'd got right up to the row of polytunnels. At first I thought they were waiting for us, then I realised there was something blocking their way. The humming I'd heard all the way down the slope was louder here, and it suddenly dawned on me it wasn't coming from the mining drones in the distance. It was coming from the wire fence strung up around the polytunnels' perimeter.

"What the hell do you think this is?" Otienno said, gazing at the long rows of wire stretched between metal posts in front of the polytunnels. Just a short distance behind the fence the green plants inside the plexiglass seemed to call to us invitingly. We were too desperate to get to safety to pay close attention to those buzzing wires. We wanted in, and we wanted in now. But I was the techie—I was the one who should've figured out what that humming noise coming from the metal meant. I shouldn't have got so carried away with thoughts of getting out of the wilds and away from the Nomalies that I ignored the obvious warning signs.

"It doesn't sound safe," Dejen muttered. "We ought to keep back till we figure out how to get past without touching those wires."

"It's just the wind making them vibrate," Otienno said, reaching out to grab hold of two wires to clamber through. "I'll go first if you're too scared, lab boy."

Just before his hand touched the wire I worked out what the buzzing sound was. It wasn't that I remembered all my training on electricity and live wires and humming generators right when I needed it. It was what I saw when I glanced away down the length of fencing that made me scream. In the distance, lying in tangled heaps along the whole length of the metal fence, were bloated bodies with long spiderlike legs. Some of them were still twitching.

The fence wasn't to keep people out after all. It was to keep the Nomalies out.

"Otienno, no!" I yelled as his hand touched the wire.

But it was too late.

CHAPTER 19

DAY SEVEN— AFTERNOON

There was a loud bang, a flash of sparks, and Otienno went flying backwards, landing in a heap in the dust. For one awful moment, I thought he was dead.

"Otienno! Are you OK? Can you hear me?" I threw myself down in the dust beside him and checked for a pulse with trembling fingers. His hands were burnt and his boots were smoking ominously, but his eyes flickered open when I called his name. He rolled over with a loud groan.

"What the...? Gods, what hit me?"

"The fence is electrified. Damn it! I should have seen it. I'm so sorry."

Otienno struggled to his knees, but I didn't have time to help him up. Dejen was already calling me over urgently.

"Adina! Look—the people in the tunnels!"

I ran back over to the fence and peered into the polytunnel nearest us. Inside, a group of scientists in white coats and plant technicians wearing green overalls were gathering behind the thick plastiglass to stare at us. They were all talking at once, their eyes blown wide with surprise at the sight of us. Unlike Eden Five, where several generations of blending had made it hard to guess where some people's ancestors' had come from, here it was obvious. The scientists and technicians had every skin tone under the sun, ranging from pale white to deep brown. The digital equipment they were carrying looked like it was a whole century in advance of anything we'd had in Eden Five.

One of the scientists pointed to me, then over to the dying Nomalies twitching further down the fence, making a silent connection.

I stepped back in shock. They weren't just looking at us like we were the strangers on our own land. It was even worse. They thought we were Nomalies too.

Dejen was the first to make a move. "Hey!" he yelled as loud as he could. "Help us! Let us in!" He lifted Tash up in his arms so they could see we had a small kid with us who needed help. There was no way they could hear him through the reinforced plastiglass, but they could clearly see that Tash and Chiku were just kids and that Otienno had been burned by their stupid fence. One of the scientists stepped forward, peering out at each of us as though trying to make up her mind about something. In the sunlight, her eyes flashed green like the leaves of the plants inside the polytunnels. There was an odd look in them, something between suspicion and…something else.

I pointed to the biofilter on my neck, pointing out Dejen and Tash's too so they'd know we weren't contaminated. The woman's eyes narrowed, sweeping over us to take in Baba Weseka and his dumb dog. I'm not sure, but I think the sight of the waxy skin on his bald head and his shivering dog covered in festering sores might've been the deciding factor. Just as she made up her mind and reached for a button on one of the support beams, I recognised the look I'd seen in her eyes.

It was disgust.

She pressed the button. The heavy air, trembling with the hum from the water tanks and the distant vibration of the mining machines, was suddenly ripped apart by the screaming of a siren that wailed from speakers on every polytunnel. Dejen stumbled back, nearly dropping Tash as he tried to cover his ears against the noise. Chiku grabbed my arm and gazed around in fright.

"What are they doing, Adina?" she gasped. "Are they going to let us in?"

A moment later, even before I could shout a reply over the noise, she got her answer. Two hatches opened at the top of the polytunnel nearest us, and a couple of weird-looking silver discs shot out. For a moment they circled the air above us, lights flickering over their surface as though they were mini 3D printing machines processing a new template. Then they opened fire.

Dejen was ready for it before I was. I think he'd been in permanent defence mode ever since we'd left Eden Five. He shoved Chiku out of the way just as a crackle of energy hit the dust where her feet had been moments before and kicked up a cloud of sparks and burnt earth. It only took me a split second longer to react.

"Move!" I yelled, grabbing Otienno round the shoulders and breaking into a run. Dejen still had Tash in his arms, but Chiku and Baba Weseka were going to have to look after themselves. Chiku knew the drill by now, though. She grabbed the old man by the hand and took off at top speed.

Everyone was following me now, dodging the beams of light spitting down from the small discs whirling in the sky above us. I had no idea where I was going. I ran on autopilot, half carrying Otienno as I fled from the strangers with their eyes full of disgust and their polytunnels full of the food we needed to survive. I was so focussed on getting away from those defence drones, getting my sister and my friends somewhere safe, that I barely even noticed the bodies of Nomalies by the fence that we leapt and stumbled over as we ran.

A flash of energy sliced down so close to my face I could smell the bittersweet tang of my singed hair. Before I knew what I was doing, I plucked up a fist-sized rock and launched it into the sky above us. It was just dumb luck that it hit one of the drones square in the belly, knocking it off course. I think it would've landed, recalibrated, and come at us again if it got the chance. But the ground here wasn't safe. It was covered in chemical run-off pools from the water filters. The drone dropped sideways, straight into a bath of toxic waste. Instead of a splash there was a loud fizzing sound, followed by a bang and a shower of sparks as the electrics fried in the acid.

One down.

The other drone backed off, as though reassessing the situation. We weren't about to waste the opportunity. We doubled our speed, veering away from the fence, the chemical pools and the ridge and out onto the open plain.

"Where are we going?" Otienno gasped, leaning heavily on my shoulders. He was still groggy, and he was peering through dust-stung eyes like all he could make out was a blur of burnt earth and sunhaze. Dejen knew where I was heading, though. He knew it as instinctively as he knew my favourite colour and my secret hiding place where I stored food I'd stolen from the cookhouse. He even knew when I was cheating at cards. He knew almost everything that went on in my head. That was why I was so afraid of him.

"We have to get back over the ridge, Adina!" he called to me. "We're heading straight for the mining machines!"

"We'll never get back up the slope in time with that thing shooting at us! There's got to be a hole or a tunnel this way where we can hide until dark. Maybe by then that drone will have run out of juice and leave us alone."

It was a long shot and we all knew it. No one argued, though. They just kept running along right behind me towards the mining robots and the drilling machines. When it came to escaping from danger, it seemed like I was in charge.

I wasn't just guessing, though. I'd seen books that Makena read in the techies' breakroom about mining operations in the old days before the ecosystem collapse. I knew the metal drills dug deep shafts into the earth and scooped the precious metals up like electric vampires sucking the earth dry. If we could find a mine the drilling machines were already done with, we might be able to escape the second drone. It was our best shot.

We skirted the edge of the mining pits, trying to keep our heads down as the giant robots stomped this way and that, their eyes roaming the worksite as they carried equipment between the drills and processing plants. I wasn't sure if they were fully autonomous like the drones or whether there were more of those scientists inside controlling them, but I wasn't about to get close enough to find out.

"Adina, look! That drone's coming back, and there's more of them!" Chiku suddenly grabbed my arm, making me stumble.

I cursed at her and shrugged her hand off, but it was really the sight of a whole fleet of metal discs bursting from the polytunnel hatches that made me swear out loud. I guess that first drone had decided to call for reinforcements before it came at us again.

"Down here," I decided, picking the first pit entrance that didn't have a huge mining drill blocking the way. "Maybe they won't follow us into the dark."

"We don't know what's down there!" Dejen hesitated, torn between the known danger of the drones and fear of the unknown depths. "What if—"

"Look, there's an access stairway and a bunch of diagrams screwed to the wall, so people have been down here before. It's safe, OK?" I snapped, clattering down the metal steps with Otienno in tow and trying to pretend I wasn't just making it up as I went along. There *were* mine schematics on the wall by the tunnel entrance, but I'd only just noticed them. There wasn't much time to take more than a quick glance at them before the drones were circling overhead again ready to strike.

I managed to catch the words "South-Eastern Plains Access Tunnel" and what looked like a passageway straight under the mining site to the other side before we stumbled down into the tunnel and the darkness closed around us.

We took about a hundred hesitant steps down into the tunnel's depths, then stopped, turning back to look at the entrance that seemed much smaller and narrower in the distance. The drones were hovering there, the lights on their casing flashing. They weren't firing at us, but they weren't leaving us alone either. It was like they were watching us, just waiting for us to come back out again so they could finish us off.

"Do you think we're safe in here?" Otienno gasped, struggling for breath and rubbing his chest. I was pretty sure that blast of electricity had nearly blown his heart to pieces. If it had, it would've taken mine with it.

"I don't think they're going to come after us," I said, giving Tash's hand a reassuring squeeze. I knew how much she hated the dark, but she was brave enough not to complain.

"Maybe they know something we don't." Dejen frowned, setting Tash down and peering into the depths behind us. It was pitch black down there, but anything was better than heading back towards those drones and their energy beams right now. "Maybe this tunnel just stops at a dead end and we'll be trapped down there."

"That wall map showed an exit at the far end of the mining site," I said. "We can't get back out this way with the drones sitting there waiting, so we'll have to head through the tunnel."

"Sounds like a plan." Otienno let go of my shoulder and started forwards shakily on his own. He was trying to look brave, but I could see how much it was hurting him.

"The light out there burns, but the dark in here bites," Baba Weseka whispered ominously in my ear as we hoisted our packs up on our shoulders and headed down the tunnel. His eyes were wide and confused as he looked back at the drones hovering in the circle of light that was rapidly disappearing in the distance. "The light burns like fire, but don't forget—the dark bites like ice."

He said it softly so the others wouldn't hear. I was half afraid he was sharing one of his visions with me after I'd told him not to say anything to the rest of our group. But I didn't have time to ask him a million questions to cut through the layers of crazy and work out what he meant. I had plenty of other things to worry about. Dejen was limping badly on his injured leg, Otienno was barely vertical after that shock nearly blew his insides out, and Chiku had a laser burn right across her back that I'd need to dress pretty soon or it'd get infected. She hadn't said anything about it, not one word of complaint. But when the darkness closed around us completely and we got our fluorescent lanterns out of our packs, I could see the tear in her shirt and the deep red wound underneath as she walked ahead of me.

Maybe she was being brave like Tash, or maybe it was just the thick blackness and close air of the tunnels that was keeping her from opening her mouth. Even Yango was silent, trailing along behind us with the stump of her tail between her legs and her tongue hanging out. She wasn't even whining. Maybe she just didn't have the energy. But every time the tunnel opened up and passages branched off into the dark on either side, she shivered in fear and pressed closer to Baba Weseka's legs. It was times like this I was afraid it wasn't just Baba who could see things the rest of us couldn't.

We lost track of time down there in the dark. The tunnels seemed to go on forever, and as we passed yet another branching passageway, I was starting to get stressed that we weren't going in a straight line anymore. The walls of the tunnel were damp, toxic water trickling down from the roof to pool on the floor. When we finally came to a bulge in the tunnel where the roof was higher and there was room for us to spread out, Otienno called a halt to the trek.

"Let's rest here," he said, throwing down his pack like the decision had already been made. "We can find the way out tomorrow when we've all had some sleep."

None of us wanted to stay down in that dark tunnel any longer than we had to, but no one had the energy to disagree with him. We all squatted down on the tunnel floor, emptying out our sleeping bags, water filters and protein bars. The huge mining drills had made smooth work of gouging out the passage, and when we cleared some of the bigger rocks out of the way there were enough flat surfaces for us all to lay our thermofoil bags down and get some sleep. I set up the water filters to catch the run-off water where it dripped down from the walls and tunnel roof, then I got to work bandaging up Chiku's back and re-dressing the wound on Dejen's leg before I let them curl up for the night. After the scare Otienno had given me on that electric fence, I wasn't about to take chances with anyone else's safety.

We were all so exhausted I could hear the snores and deep breathing start almost as soon as the others put their heads down. No matter how hard I tried, though, I just couldn't get to sleep. I tossed and turned in my thermafoil bag, the faces of the scientists in the polytunnels staring back at me, the intensity of their disgust burning my closed lids. *Why didn't they help us?* I asked so many times in the dark that my blood began to boil. *Why did they set their drones on us? Couldn't they see we were just a bunch of kids who needed help?*

Details I'd missed in the panic of flight came back to me now, so sharply focussed they seemed to cut the edges of my mind as they passed before my eyes. I saw symbols and signs along the fence and polytunnels, a star-shaped "A" and a crescent moon marking the food inside as property of the Amonston Corporation. The mining robots and defence drones had the same symbols stamped across their metal casing. Everything in this world was the property of the Amonston Corporation, everything that had any value. Only the dust and the dead ashes were left to us. I had a wild idea that even the people born into the Edens belonged to the Corporation somehow. The impression of my arm being stamped with the Corporation's star and moon symbol was so strong my skin started itching and I had to scratch my wrist.

But the Corporation's symbol wasn't the only thing I'd seen when I was standing by that fence. No matter how hard I tried, I just couldn't shake the image of the dying Nomalies twitching in the dust from my mind. There were more of them out there than I'd ever imagined, and the thought chilled me to the bone. I'd had the horrible feeling we'd been followed ever since that night in the weed fields. Maybe there'd been a group of them on our tail the whole time as we climbed the ridge, hiding out in the hollows and watching us with their hungry eyes and snapping, gaping mouths. Maybe it wasn't the drones we'd find waiting for us on the other side of the tunnels. Maybe we'd come out of the dark and run straight into their snapping jaws. Maybe they'd even venture down into the tunnels to come looking for us. I sat bolt upright at the thought, peering into the shadows cast by the fluorescent lanterns and imagining spidery legs twitching just beyond the circle of light.

I wasn't going to get any sleep tonight, that was for sure.

As my imagination spun into hyperdrive, I got to wondering what the Nomalies were and how they'd come into being—were they some kind of mutated animal maybe? Or a breed of insect, their DNA twisted by the chemicals like Dejen said until they reached monstrous proportions? I didn't know. And the more I tried to work it out, the more it bugged me.

I looked over to where Dejen lay curled up on his side, his back to me. His pack was between us. His pack with the videpods.

I sat up and put my hand into the bag, drawing the infopad and videpod cartridges out carefully. I didn't know why I was trying not to wake him. I mean, it's not like he would mind me watching the videpod entries on my own. But somehow I didn't want him to know I still had a small spark of curiosity about the old times. It would make keeping up the mask of indifference I wore around him even harder. Besides, it wasn't the Amonston Corporation's experiments or Nia's Rebel Farmers' Alliance I wanted to know about tonight. It was something far more important. Something far, far scarier than science gone wrong or people fighting against change.

I slipped the first videpod cartridge into the infopad port and selected the "search" option from the menu screen. There was one thing I wanted to know about more than anything else. I typed in "Nomalies" and hit the enter button, waiting impatiently as the programme searched through Doctor Malathion's videblog entries. It seemed to take forever. Finally a message flashed up on the screen. "Zero entries matching search criteria found. Please refine search and try again."

Damn.

I tried the second videpod cartridge, searching through Nia's secret recordings for any mention of Nomalies.

Nothing.

I nearly threw the infopad against the wall in frustration. How could there not be information on something so important?

"If you'd bothered to ask I could've told you it was a waste of time," Dejen said quietly without turning round. "There's nothing on there about Nomalies." Then he rolled over, fixing me with a half-serious, half-amused stare. Damn it all. How did he always *know*?

I glowered back in the darkness, fighting the urge to punch him on the arm and laugh like I used to when he guessed my thoughts. I didn't want him guessing my thoughts anymore; it was too dangerous.

"Well, what's the point of watching them then?" I muttered, "if they're not going to tell us anything useful."

"If you want useful information out of a jumble of data then you have to ask the right questions. Here." He sat up and took the infopad off me, typing in his own search request. I leaned over to see what he was looking for. His search for "mutant plants" turned up hundreds of entries. He handed the infopad back to me. "You'd learn a whole lot more about the Amonston Corporation if you'd just admit the possibility that they weren't feeding the world like they said they were."

He shouldn't have said that. I switched the infopad off and tossed it back in his pack. "Suit yourself," he muttered, rolling over again and drawing the covers of his sleeping bag up.

I sat there in the darkness, listening to the soft breathing of the others and trying to think of something other than Nomalies and mutant insects. My restless mind spun round and round, making the shadows dance until I couldn't stand it any longer. Very carefully, I put my hand back into Dejen's pack and pulled out the infopad and videpod cartridges again. I put them in the pocket of my shirt, pulling my boots on and heading a little way down the tunnel without a backwards glance. It's just as well I didn't look back. If I had I would've seen Dejen smiling to himself in the dark.

CHAPTER 20

NIGHT SEVEN

That night was one of the longest of my life. Before it was over and dawn finally chased away the dark, I was bruised inside and out.

I'll start with inside. My brain took a beating from everything I saw on the videopods. I mean, it was *mind-blowing*. I sat there in the dark, watching entry after entry about experiments going wrong, African superfarms churning out plants mutated into toxic weeds by the Corporation's meddling, and chemical factories ramping up production every few months to keep up with pesticide demand.

Gods, why didn't they just *stop*?

In the entries recorded ten years after she first joined the Amonston Corporation, Doctor Malathion didn't look happy or excited about the Africa project anymore. She looked nervous and drawn, fiddling with her infopad as though trying to make the statistics there match the figures she wanted to see in her head.

"It's the weeds that are the main problem," she said in one videblog entry. "The transgenic DNA had been transferred by the wind and insects to the other vegetation, and it evolves so fast our pesticides can't keep up. The rebel crops are taking over everything."

Transgenic.

I knew that word from biology lessons. It meant genetic material transferred from one thing to another. The Amonston Corporation said it was natural. Only it wasn't. Genes got transferred through a species all the time in natural breeding. I had the genes for my father's eyes and my mother's wide, curved lips. Tash had most of my mother's features, and Chiku? Well, I tried not to see any of my family in her, even though the eyes that stared back at me from her snotty little face mirrored my own. That was another reason I hated her. Anyway, dogs passed dog genes down the generations, maize passed maize genes down the generations, and that was the way it had always been since the dawn of time.

Until the Amonston Corporation changed everything.

It wasn't that what they put inside their new plants' DNA was *bad* exactly, it was just that it was *wrong*. Foreign. From completely different species. They made plants produce their own pesticides to save money on spraying. So instead of eating plants covered in toxic chemicals that could be washed off, people were eating plants with pesticides coded into their very DNA. If the pesticides killed insects by bursting their stomachs apart, what were they doing to the people who ate them? The Corporation's infoclips—"commercials," Doctor Malathion called them—kept saying the plants were safe for people to eat. But looking at Doctor Malathion's worried face, I was starting to seriously doubt it.

"The problem is," the Doctor went on, "we've had to use so much herbicide to deal with the rebel crops, the insect and bird populations have been almost wiped out. The Corporation's financial team have kept it out of the news by buying up all the media outlets in the West and forcing what's left of the African governments to restrict visas to visitors approved by the Corporation, but we can't keep it secret for much longer, even with the Corporation's tight control of the Internet. The United Nations is demanding information, especially now that the African wildlife reserves have all been turned into superfarms and the animals sold off to international zoos. The local animal populations have mostly died out now that their natural habitats have been turned over to the Corporation for farmland."

I gritted my teeth at this. The Corporation said they were feeding the world. I guess they forgot to mention that didn't include feeding the animals too. I flicked through a few more infopad entries, selecting one near the bottom of the long list.

Doctor Malathion's face was so drawn in this one, I wondered if she was sick. She looked even more worried, her usually neat braids scraped into a clumsy knot at the back of her head.

"We just got the latest medical statistics from the African superfarms this morning," she said, "and the news isn't good.

There have been a lot of anomalous results reported on every farm and village in the herbicide spraying zones. Now that the insects are all dead, we have to spray the GM pollen over the fields as well, and it's causing major issues for farmers caught in the pollen clouds. I can't go into details on record, but the Corporation has sent out a team of medics to contain the emergency. Hopefully Doctor Bates has managed to get enough Corporation board members into United Nation positions to keep the anomalous data hushed up for now until we can sort the problems out."

Doctor Malathion looked grim, but then she brightened up a little when she read another report from her infopad. "The GM crops are selling well on the international market now that the Corporation's pushed through its anti-labelling laws in Europe and Asia. I don't know why some countries were so stubborn about the anti-labelling laws in the first place." Doctor Malathion shook her head, a wayward braid coming undone and straggling over her face.

"Some countries were so determined to make sure our GM food was clearly marked and labelled it took years to buy off enough government leaders to stop the supermarkets from doing it. Here's one of the commercials we ran as part of the anti-labelling campaign."

The picture was filled with Doctor Bates's smiling face. He looked older now, but there was something strangely young and frozen about his brows and eyes. Standing in a narrow lane between two wheat fields, he reached over and plucked an ear of wheat from either side, holding them up to the camera. "Look closely," he said, in that calm, reassuring voice of his. "See the difference? No? Well, don't be surprised. Even with a high-powered microscope you'd have a hard time telling the ordinary wheat in this field apart from our new African variety in that one."

I frowned at the screen. The commercials from the start of the Africa project were all about how the Corporation's GM crops *were* so very different from the natural varieties. Now he was saying they were exactly the same? I was confused.

Doctor Bates smiled again, his green eyes glittering in the sunlight. "The supermarkets are telling you that GM foods should be labelled so you know what you're eating, but that will drive food prices up by hundreds of dollars. Why pay more for high quality food, when without the red tape of labelling, you'll get our very best products for the same price as you're paying now for inferior brands?"

Doctor Bates held the wheat ears up to the camera once more. "You might not be able to see the difference, but I guarantee you'll be able to taste the extra goodness and nutrition in our African variety. That's the Amonston Corporation promise. Say 'no' to labelling laws, and 'yes' to good food at unbeatable prices."

He dropped one ear of wheat, holding the other up to the sun so it flashed golden yellow against the blue sky. The Amonston Corporation symbol appeared in white writing, the words "Feeding the World" written underneath.

I hit the "stop" button, my hands shaking with anger. I was starting to understand more of the strange names I heard on the videpod entries now, enough to know that what the Amonston Corporation was doing was wrong. They weren't giving people the choice to eat their GM food, they were forcing it down their throats.

"If you think that's bad," said a voice in my ear, "try this one."

Dejen leaned over my shoulder and changed the videpod cartridges over, selecting another entry. I shrank from the arm that brushed my own, from the warm breath that tickled my cheek, shifting on the floor so there was room for him to sit beside me without us touching. He tried to pretend he didn't notice, but even in the dark he couldn't hide the small flicker of sadness that flashed across his face.

In this entry, Nia scowled at the camera. Going by the date, it must've been about seven years after the last recording of hers I saw, and the harsh worry lines carved into her forehead made her seem much older.

"If anyone is watching," she said, "then these are the diaries of Nia Kutuny, head of the Rebel Farmers' Alliance. Be warned, the images you are about to see are disturbing. Health problems in Africa have soared in the years since the Amonston Corporation took over our farmland and forced us all to work for them for practically nothing. All we have to eat is genetically engineered maize, soybeans and wheat. We have nothing to drink but polluted water from rivers contaminated by pesticides and industrial waste from their mining operations. Even the air we breathe is filled with herbicides and GM pollen."

I glanced at Dejen. He wasn't looking at the screen. He was looking at me, trying to judge my reaction. I looked away again quickly, trying to wriggle further away from his silent questions.

"The following secret footage was shot in one of the Corporation's medical camps. They're off limits to everyone. The official story the Corporation-owned Western press and Internet is telling is that an outbreak of the Ebola virus across Africa has resulted in large numbers of people being quarantined in the camps. But the workers on the superfarms know it isn't true. Only we know the truth. The truth is, the GM food is bad for us. The pesticides and herbicides are causing cancerous tumours, terrible skin conditions and organ failure across the farming populations. The Corporation is hiding these so-called 'anomalous results' from the rest of the world. And that's not the worst of it."

Nia's eyes were filled with rage and sadness, and she clenched her fists as she went on, "The worst is what's happening to our children. We don't know if it's the chemicals or the transgenic material in the plants we eat, but our babies are being born with awful defects. I can't explain it all." She broke off with a choked sob. When she'd taken a few shaky breaths, she screwed her face up and forced herself to continue. "Just watch," she said, "and you'll see."

"Dejen, I don't know if I want to see—" I began.

"Watch it," Dejen insisted. "You have to know the whole truth."

I didn't want the whole truth. What I knew already was bad enough. And if all the truth came out then maybe my own secret wouldn't be safe. But Dejen was determined, and I found myself watching unwillingly as terrible pictures unfolded on the small screen.

A shaky camera image weaved its way slowly round a crowded medical camp. Sobbing, wretched people lay on filthy blankets on the floor, covered in warts and lesions and blisters the size of fists. Their hair had fallen out, their teeth loose in their bleeding gums. Some had parched skin that rubbed off in long strips whenever they scratched it. Others wept blood and pus from eyes swollen and bulging in their sockets. Yet more shook violently, unable to control their spasming limbs.

And then there were the children. Gods, the *children*.

Little babies no bigger than a few weeks old lay in their mother's arms, their heads so badly deformed you could barely make out where the hollow of their eyes stopped and their noses and mouths began. Many were twisted and hunched, with half-formed arms and legs that poked out of their ragged blankets in all the wrong places. Amonston Corporation medics in biohazard suits walked between the jumbled rows of the sick and dying, poking, prodding and typing figures into their infopads with heavily gloved hands. They didn't seem to be doing anything to help. In fact, it looked just like they were collecting data on yet another failed experiment. Only these weren't plants that were dying—these were people.

"Stop!" I yelled, "I don't want to see any more." I pushed the infopad away and rolled onto my knees, fighting the urge to retch. I leaned over, keeping my head down and taking deep breaths so I wouldn't have to look at Dejen.

"But it's the truth." He laid a hand on my shoulder, trying to help me up.

"I don't care about the truth, not now that everything's gone!" I shook his hand off, but I couldn't get rid of him this time. He grabbed my arms and pulled me closer, forcing me to look into his eyes.

"Then what do you care about, Adi?" His face was close to mine, his lips near enough that I could almost touch them. Gods, how I wanted to.

You. I wanted to say. *You and Tash, and that's all that matters.*

But I couldn't. I couldn't tell the truth. If I spoke now it would all come tumbling out before I could stop it, and he'd hate me for what I'd done. I couldn't bear the thought. Now Eden Five was gone, Dejen was my whole world, my strongest link to the past and the people we'd once been, and my best hope for the future. I couldn't give in to the urge to find comfort in his arms, to share the burden of truth. He couldn't know what I'd done. I needed him too much. I needed him to love me as much as I loved him.

"Dejen…" I faltered, my lips fatally close to his. One more inch was all it would take. One more inch, and then—

We didn't get to close that gap.

A loud scream echoed down the tunnel from the chamber where the others were sleeping. Only they weren't sleeping now. They were yelling at the top of their voices.

Dejen had moved before I was even aware he had gone. I scrambled after him in the dark, my heart hammering. Was it Nomalies? I was supposed to be looking after Tash. If the Nomalies had attacked my little sister while I was too busy with Dejen and his damn videopods to pay attention, then…

214

It wasn't Nomalies. But it was something every bit as strange.

Our little camp was in confusion, water filters knocked over and sleeping bags all tangled up. At first all I could make out in the fluorescent lamplight were huge shadows on the walls and tubes of shiny white skin oozing from the connecting tunnels like liquid plastic from a 3D printer jet. Then my eyes adjusted to the pale glow and I felt sick to my stomach as the creatures crawled into focus. Two giant maggot-like worms were slithering across our campsite, the veins along their bloated bodies standing out against their oily skin like high tension cables ready to burst.

"Adina! We have to get out of here!" Chiku yelled, holding Tash behind her back with one hand and beating the worm sliding across the floor towards them with a fluorescent lantern. In the flickering light I thought I saw another shape crawling on the tunnel roof, but I didn't have time to look up as the second worm creature opened its mouth wide to reveal a huge set of jaws with sharp teeth. It lunged at Baba Weseka, clamping down on his boot and dragging him away towards one of the side tunnels.

"Help! Adina, get it off me!" he yelled, trying to reach back for me as the hungry creature hauled him across the floor.

Gods! Everyone was yelling my name at once and calling for help, and I didn't know where to turn. Otienno came to my rescue as I was trying to decide whether to go after the worm attacking Tash and Chiku, or whether to save Baba Weseka who was about to disappear into the dark. Ignoring the deep burns etched into his palms, Otienno heaved a large rock over his head, bringing it crashing down on the worm going after the girls and splitting its tight skin wide open. A spurt of angry red blood exploded out of the ruptured flesh, fizzing and melting everything it landed on.

"Adina, over here!" Before I could scoop Tash up in my arms, Dejen was already calling for help. He'd grabbed Baba Weseka under the arms and was trying to haul him back before the second worm could drag him off into the dark. There were more white bodies wriggling and squirming in the depths behind the first worms, trying to fasten their jaws around Baba and get their fill of him. I kicked at their writhing bodies, trying to beat them back while Dejen pulled Baba clear.

"Don't touch them!" Otienno warned a little too late. My boot slid off the oily back of one of the worms, the oozing slime it gave off burning like acid through the cotton of my trousers where my ankle brushed past. I could feel my skin around the hole begin to sting, and I grabbed one of the water filter units, tipping its contents over my leg and swinging it at the worms who were slithering from the side tunnel. They wriggled back, regrouping for another attack.

I picked up a fluorescent lamp, hoping the light would warn them off. Shadows danced across the roof of the chamber as I raised it above my head. It was only then that I saw what Yango was barking at. I should have realised right away that the dog barking herself hoarse was a bad sign. She'd barely had the energy to do more than whine since we left Eden Five, and the dust of the wilds had stung her throat so badly her tongue was little more than a shrivelled strip inside her parched mouth. But now she looked like she'd been hooked up to a battery pack and shot full of juice, as she was practically standing on her hind legs, barking up at the shadows on the chamber roof above us.

We all looked up.

The shadows burst into motion, thousands of stubby legs flickering in the pale light as a colony of giant centipedes came scuttling down the wall towards us. Their bulging balloon eyes stood up on stalks, glowing like lanterns in the dark as they charged our way.

"Run!" I ordered, shoving Tash and Chiku towards the exit tunnel. "Keep moving and don't look back!"

"We have to get the sleeping bags and water filters—we can't afford to leave them behind!" Dejen yelled, scrambling to gather up our scattered things as the centipedes and worms came charging towards us. I snatched up a handful of stones and threw them at the creatures while Otienno and Dejen grabbed our stuff. The small rocks weren't much of a weapon, but there wasn't time for us to get our knives out of our survival packs. Trying not to drop my fluorescent lamp, I turned tail and went charging down the tunnel after the girls, tripping over Yango in the dark and cursing in fear. I could hear noises in the tunnel behind me, but I didn't have the nerve to turn my head to see if it was Otienno and Dejen or something else entirely.

By the time I caught up with Chiku and Tash, I could see the light at the end of the exit tunnel. Dawn had already broken, pale sunlight struggling through the dust clouds to ring the exit in a sickly yellow halo. I'd never been so glad to see the empty expanse of the wilds in all my life.

"Keep going, don't stop!" I urged the girls on until we finally burst out onto the south-eastern plain, our legs trembling and our lungs gasping for air. Moments later Otienno and Dejen came tumbling out of the tunnel, their arms full of tangled sleeping bags, survival packs and broken pieces of water filter. Yango stumbled out behind them, her eyes bulging in their sockets from fear. One more nasty shock and they'd go popping out and rolling down the slope to the plain below.

"No more tunnels," Otienno gasped, doubling over and coughing in the dry morning dust clouds. "From now on we stay out in the open where we can see what's coming."

"I second that," Dejen muttered, squinting back across the plain where the security robots were stomping round the mining site behind us. We could just make out the bright glint of sunlight flashing off the plastiglass polytunnels in the distance. Inside were endless miles of food and safety from the dangers of the wilds, and stern-faced scientists who would rather set security drones on us than let us in. We were on our own, and with only three weeks left on our biofilters, we were running out of time. I turned away, the sour taste in my mouth ready to choke me.

Instead of looking back I bent down to check over the remains of our survival kits, rummaging around in the piles of acid-burned thermafoil and broken bits of water filter to see what I could salvage. It was only when I looked up to ask

Dejen if he'd rescued the carbohydrate pills I'd been handing out last night that I realised we were one person short. My eyes darted round our group, counting silently.

Yeah, I was right. There was someone missing.

Baba Weseka had been left behind in the dark.

CHAPTER 21

DAY EIGHT

We argued about it for half the morning. In the end Dejen insisted on going back to look for Baba Weseka on his own. It was just as well he made a definite decision, any more discussion and he and Otienno would've been swinging punches.

"We've got less than three weeks left on our biofilters," Otienno had snapped, "We can't waste any more time on some crazy old man who can't keep up."

"So you think we should just leave him in there on his own to die?" Dejen shot back. "Gods, you're a coward, Otienno."

I stepped between them before Otienno could get his fists up. "This isn't about bravery, it's about the simple fact that our biofilters will give us just enough time to get to Sanctuary Seven and no more," I said, trying to calm them both down. "If we double back, we aren't going to make it. We have to keep going. And anyway, if those creatures in there got hold of him in the dark, there's nothing we can do for him." I hated the words I could hear tumbling out of my mouth, but I said them anyway. Someone had to.

"Haven't enough people died already, Adina?" Dejen looked at me sadly, his eyes filled with disappointment. "Baba Weseka needs our help. How can you talk about leaving him behind like it's no big deal?"

I looked away. I knew I was letting him down, but I couldn't help it. I looked at Tash instead. She was the reason I didn't want to go back. If it was just me, alone in the wilds with my guilt, I'd go back into those tunnels to look for Baba Weseka in a heartbeat. I couldn't stand the thought of him stumbling through the dark all alone and frightened with monsters closing in on him from all sides. Maybe he hadn't even survived the attack. Maybe as we spoke he was lying in some deep tunnel, his eyes all white and glassy like the creatures that were chewing on his bones. I shuddered at the thought. But I wasn't alone in the wilds, I had Tash to look after. She was my little sister, my responsibility, and I had to get her to safety. Even if it meant being cruel.

Dejen followed my gaze. And then he understood. I could've flung my arms round him for the way his eyes softened when he read my thoughts and sensed my conflict. "OK," he sighed, "I get it. You and Otienno go on with the girls. I'll go back and see if I can find Baba Weseka myself."

"You can't go on your own!" I cried. "There's worms and centipede creatures and who knows what back in there! And anyway, your leg isn't right yet."

"My leg's fine, I'll be OK. I won't go too far in, and I'll keep to the main tunnel. I'll take Yango with me—if Baba's alive in there, Yango will sniff him out."

I wasn't convinced. I was pretty sure Yango couldn't smell anything other than the stench of her own rotting flesh anymore. She was in a bad state, that was for sure. Her hair had almost all fallen out and her skin had turned a sickly yellow colour, all mottled and warty. The blisters had started to burst, thick pus weeping down her back and stinging her eyes when she turned to lick them. The stump of her tail tied up with bandages from my pack was drooping. It wouldn't be long before the bit that was left rotted and fell off too. She was poisoned and sore and dying a slow death, but all she cared about was Baba Weseka. I kicked myself for not making sure my hand had closed over one more biofilter before I ran for the airlock. Just one second more and I could've saved her. But there was no life support system for her out here in the wilds. She would die, and that would be my fault too.

Before I could find another reason to stop Dejen going back into that tunnel on his own, the whimpering dog suddenly lifted her head up, took one long sniff of the dusty air, then went completely mental. She charged at the dark hole in the rock, barking so loud I thought she was going to bust her vocal chords. A faint light was heading our way down the tunnel, a strange glow that seemed semi-fluorescent like the pale skin of the worms or the huge eyes of the centipede creatures.

We all tensed.

Otienno, Dejen and I grabbed our knives from our packs, staring into the dark and waiting to see what would come out.

I could see the light more clearly now. It swayed and bobbed eerily in the tunnel depths, hiding everything that moved behind. I couldn't make out how many shapes there were. If there were more than three, we were in trouble. Otienno and Dejen would each take one and I would take another, but that would leave the girls undefended. I turned to look at Tash trembling behind me. Chiku caught my eye, giving me a small, determined nod. If there were more than three, she'd take care of the other one and keep Tash safe.

It didn't come to that.

A moment later I dropped my knife and ran forward, catching the figure that stumbled out of the tunnel and nearly fell headfirst in the dust.

"Quick! Get me some water!" I yelled, cradling Baba Weseka's head in my lap and trying to keep Yango from licking his face. Baba had burns down his arms from the worms' acid, and his trouser legs were all torn up by the centipedes' teeth, but he was alive and breathing, and that's all that mattered. I'd spent so long thinking of him as helpless that it never occurred to me he could make it out of the tunnels all by himself. He'd even managed to grab a fluorescent lantern in the panic, though his pack was gone and I was pretty sure it was more blind luck than anything else that had guided him to safety.

"Is he going to be OK?" Otienno frowned at the burns running up Baba's Weseka's arms. He didn't sound like he really cared either way, but I had a feeling Otienno wouldn't be too upset if we had one less problem to worry about.

"Yes, he'll be fine," I snapped, throwing Otienno a fierce look that shut him right up.

It took us a while to get Baba Weseka back on his feet again, and it was only with Dejen half carrying him that we finally managed to set off across the plains south-east. By the way Baba was gasping and panting, it was only a matter of time before he had another fit. But I couldn't keep my eyes on him. There were other things that needed my full attention as we walked.

There were shadows flickering behind the curtains of dust, closer now than they'd seemed before. *Please don't let it be Nomalies,* I prayed silently the whole afternoon. *Anything but Nomalies.* Even the thought of those snapping jaws and strange twitching limbs made me break out in a cold sweat, I held Tash's hand tighter and walked on. The rest of our group followed me across the wasteland in silence. The only sound I could hear in the vast emptiness was our footsteps shuffling up the dry dust. By the time the long afternoon gave way to night, even the wind was still, holding its breath. Waiting.

As the sun went down and the shadows closed in, Chiku clutched my other hand, her fingers tensing as she waited for me to push her away. For once I didn't. I still remembered her struggling in the mud and my hands loosening their grip to let her sink. This time I held tight and didn't let go. We walked on like that, Tash on one side, Chiku on the other, till I could see Dejen's face grow pale as death in the darkness and I knew he just couldn't carry Baba Weseka any further. He wasn't about to give up, though. If I didn't call a halt to our trek, he'd just keep going till he fell dead in the dust from exhaustion.

"We'll rest here for the night," I said, throwing down my pack by a big pile of rocks and making the decision for him. "We all need some sleep after last night."

"Shouldn't we wait till we find shelter?" Otienno said, looking round at the dark wastelands suspiciously. It wasn't a great place to stop. We were out in the open, surrounded by empty plains on one side and the dry dead stalks of a flattened weed field on the other. There was nowhere to hide if the Nomalies came hunting us. But with the state we were all in, we didn't have a choice. I grabbed my medical kit from my pack and started treating the burns, cuts and bruises of the others as best I could, knowing all the bandages and salve in the world wouldn't heal the wounds we were carrying deep inside us.

Otienno, Dejen and I argued again later that night when we'd set up camp. This time it wasn't about Baba Weseka, it was about light. We'd lost all but one of our fluorescent lanterns when we ran from the tunnels, and the other one Baba had carried out was broken, giving off only a pale, feeble glow. Now we all sat hunched around the two weak light sources that remained, shrinking from the shadows that swayed beyond the weed field.

"There's dead stalks all around," Otienno grumbled. "Why don't we just light a fire and be done with it?"

"Please, Adina?" Chiku said. "It's cold."

"Then get into the sleeping bag with Tash," I snapped, tired of arguing and tired of feeling so helpless in the dark.

"We can't light a fire, it's too dangerous," Dejen said for the hundredth time, backing me up like he always did. I was too tired to feel grateful.

It was bad enough that the pale light struggling from the lanterns gave us away. We couldn't risk the bright flare of firelight bringing Nomalies creeping out from every corner of the woods. Otienno had already gathered a big pile of dry maize stalks. He dumped them on the ground, scowling at me and muttering to himself. I knew why he wanted the fire. He was frightened of the dark. We all were. But right now I had something way more important to worry about than Otienno being in a huff with me.

Baba Weseka was in a bad way. His arms were burned by the worm creatures' acid, and he had deep bites down one leg where those weird centipede things had tried to chew him up. It was clear from the way Baba was trembling and muttering to himself that he was going to have another fit any minute now.

We got him lying down just before it kicked off. Dejen turned him onto his side, while I tried to soothe him as he thrashed and yelled and moaned. I knew that if I prayed for anything it should've been that he would be OK, but all I could think was, *Please don't say anything this time! Please don't let Dejen or the others suspect you're seeing more than just crazy visions!*

The fit passed and Baba Weseka finally lay still. For a long moment, I thought I was safe. Then Baba started whispering. Dejen leaned forward, trying to make out the string of words that tumbled from the old man's mouth.

"What? Who's going to die?" Dejen frowned. "What's not safe? We shouldn't go to sleep? What do you mean, Baba? What did you see?"

"Leave him be," I snapped, pushing Dejen away before he could hear any more. "He's just talking nonsense. He needs sleep, and so do you, Dejen."

"But this could be important, Adina," Dejen said, leaning back over Baba Weseka again despite my best efforts. "Last time he had a fit he talked about someone drowning, and then Chiku fell in that pool, remember? And he said he saw the fire before Eden Five went up in flames, and something about an apple too. I think maybe he might be seeing things before they happen, warning us somehow."

"That's crazy!" I yelled, getting angry now. I was so scared all my secrets would come out if Dejen poked too hard at Baba Weseka's visions that I gave him a hard shove. "He just says the first thing that comes into his head. Stop trying to make it into more than it is."

"But he just said that someone was going to die, Adi," Dejen said, looking up at me like he couldn't understand why I was being so mean. "That's what he said. 'He's going to die. Look up. Don't go to sleep.' Those were his words. What if he means—"

"Stop it! You're scaring the girls!"

It wasn't a lie. Chiku and Tash were staring at Baba Weseka with wide eyes, looking almost as afraid as I was. "Who's going to die, Adina?" Tash gasped. "What are you talking about?"

I threw Dejen a final silencing look, then went over to tuck them back into their sleeping bag. "I told you, Tash, it's just Baba talking crazy again. There's no need to go listening to any of that nonsense."

227

Chiku gave me a searching look as she snuggled up next to Tash, but she was too smart to say anything. If I was lucky this would all be forgotten about tomorrow. I was so busy trying to make sure everyone thought Baba Weseka's words were nonsense, I didn't even stop to consider what he might have been seeing. If only I hadn't been so obsessed with covering up my own secret, things might've turned out differently.

"I'll take first watch." Otienno heaped some more maize stalks on the fire he'd got blazing and threw Dejen a triumphant look. He'd got his own way about the fire in the end, and he wasn't about to let Dejen forget it. We didn't have a choice about lighting one now. Baba Weseka had lost his pack in the tunnels, and Dejen had given him his own sleeping bag. It was too cold for Baba to spend the night without one, now he was so tired and hurt.

Otienno got up to pace the edge of the weed fields, staring out between the rows of flattened stalks, his knife held tense and ready in his fist. I think Baba Weseka's words had disturbed him almost as much as they had frightened Tash and Chiku. Dejen frowned at his back like he was trying to decide whether it was worth arguing about, then shook his head and wrapped himself up in Otienno's sleeping bag, too exhausted to care anymore.

I waited till I thought he was asleep, then I walked over to where Otienno stood gazing out into the night, resting my head on his shoulder and looking for comfort. "You holding up alright?" I asked softly.

The night was cold and cheerless, the temperature plummeting when the sun went down. I only wanted a hug, some kind of reassurance that I wasn't all alone in the dark. But as usual, Otienno wanted more, his rough hands catching my neck and pulling me close. I pushed him away angrily, fighting against the lips that came searching for mine.

"What's wrong with you?" Otienno growled. "One minute it's 'yes,' the next it's 'no.' Do you want to be with me or not?"

"I'm sorry, I just…" I backed away, shaking off the hands that wanted more than I could give. "I'm just not in the mood. Wake me up in a bit and I'll take next watch, OK?"

I walked away quickly from Otienno's angry eyes. He was pissed off, and I didn't blame him. It's not that I felt differently about him. His kisses and caresses made me feel like they always did.

Excited.

Hungry.

Aching.

Empty.

I was tired of feeling hollow and alone.

I wasn't the only one who was restless. It took a while for the girls to get to sleep; they were too excited about having a real fire to settle down straight away. Naked flames weren't allowed in Eden Five, except for lab experiments, and the sight of the flickering red light turning the dry maize stalks to glowing embers was almost hypnotic. Once Taǝh and Chiku had stopped whispering in excitement and were asleep, I sat as far from the fire as I could, unable to get the image of flames roaring up the stairs from the basement out of my head. The others hadn't seen our families and friends devoured by fire as they screamed and clawed their way up to the safe rooms. They didn't fear the fire the way I did.

"What's wrong, Adi?"

Dejen rolled over in Otienno's bag, his soft voice parting the fog of flaming memories. We'd have to take turns using the thermafoil bags now, one of us watching while the other two slept. Otienno was meant to be on watch right now. Only he didn't watch the weed fields, he watched me and Dejen. I shifted uncomfortably under his gaze. I wanted to stroke Dejen's face and beg him never to leave me again, to throw my arms around him and never let go. Instead I shrugged and said, "Nothing. Get some rest."

Our eyes met across the fire, and I willed him to read my mind the way he used to. *I miss you,* I told him silently. *I miss you with every heartbeat.*

He only heard what I'd said out loud, rolling over in his bag and falling asleep in moments. I was asleep too before I even knew it, exhausted and sick with worry. I needed a night of rest, free from the memories of death and destruction that haunted me.

That's not what I got.

The fire followed me into my dreams. It curled round the edges of the barriers I put up to shut it out, licking at the walls in my mind. I saw the faces I'd tried so hard to forget, swallowed in tongues of flame that spat from the basement. Their screams echoed through the dark labyrinth in my head, chasing me down long corridors of tangled maize stalks and melting plastic pipes. All the while, the hum of the failing air filter grew louder, an accusing warning siren that wailed so loud in my ear it finally woke me.

It wasn't the siren that was wailing in the morning light, it was Baba Weseka. "But we have to take Yango!" he was saying to Otienno. "She's a good dog. I'm not going anywhere without her."

"Look, she's all in, Baba, she won't be able to keep up, and we can't afford to lose any more time," Otienno said, nudging the dog with his foot to make his point. She was lying on her side in the dust, struggling so hard to breathe it looked like her chest was caving in. She didn't even whine when Otienno's boot touched her raw flesh.

I got up stiffly, rousing the girls and helping Dejen gather up what was left of our sleeping bags and survival kits. I knew the end was coming for Yango. I'd just hoped it would be quicker.

"We have to go now, Baba," I said, slinging my pack on my back and taking his arm. "We've got a lot of walking still to do."

"But what about Yango?" he asked. "I can't leave her behind."

"Otienno will take care of her. He'll make sure she's alright, won't you?" I said, exchanging glances with him. Otienno knew what I meant. He took his knife from his pocket, opening the blade and throwing me a questioning look.

Wait till we're gone, I mouthed, taking Baba Weseka by the hand and leading him off. The others quickly gathered up their packs and followed, the girls looking over their shoulders at Otienno. They knew something was up, they just didn't know what.

"Yango!" Baba Weseka called, trying to pull his hand from mine. "I need Yango!"

"She'll be along soon," I said, holding on tightly. "Come on. We need to keep walking."

Dejen looked over his shoulder too, clearly struggling with himself. I caught his eye before he went back, nodding at Baba Weseka and throwing him a pleading look. Dejen understood. He couldn't do anything more for the dog now. The kindest thing we could do was put her out of her misery. He took Baba Weseka's other hand, helping me lead him away through the weed field.

There came a sharp yelp from behind us. Then a long silence.

"Yango!" Baba Weseka cried, clawing his hands free and running back the way we had come. He didn't have to go far. Yango came bolting through the maize stalks, her eyes all wide and staring in fright. She wrapped her battered body round Baba Weseka's legs, whining and growling and telling anyone who came near her they'd better stay away or else.

Otienno followed, shrugging when I threw him a look. There was a small spot of blood on the blade of his knife, and he wiped it on his shirt before putting it away. Gods, that dumb dog was so stupid she didn't even have the sense to just lie down and die.

But watching her claw and scratch for life, struggling for every breath and clinging to Baba Weseka like he was her very own life support system, somehow lit a small spark of hope in my heart that refused to go out. I was tired and sore and aching with grief, but if Yango was still fighting despite how hurt she was, then I could fight too.

We were going to make it to the Sanctuary. All of us. Alive.

CHAPTER 22

DAY THIRTEEN

I was wrong. We weren't all going to make it to the Sanctuary alive. If I'd known who we'd lose on day thirteen of the countdown, I might've just lain down in the dirt and let the dust of the wilds bury me and my sorrow in the ashes of the old world. But I didn't know then what was coming. If only I'd listened to Baba Weseka and not pretended to everyone he was crazy, I might have been able to save the one we lost.

His death is on my conscience now too.

For the next few days, we made slow progress. We were all stiff and sore and itching, bickering over the dwindling water supply and the meagre protein bar rations. Otienno blamed me for giving Tash more than her fair share, and I blamed Dejen for wasting food and water on Yango. The final straw came when I caught Chiku going through my pack and slipping out a couple of carbohydrate pills when she thought I wasn't looking. I slapped her face so hard for that I knocked her over. She crumpled in a heap, howling and refusing to go any further.

"Gods, Adina, do you have to be so mean to her?" Dejen snapped, kneeling down and wiping away the thin trickle of blood that dribbled from her nose.

"She's a thief!" I growled at the wailing kid, daring her to contradict me. "We're running low on food supplements as it is, and she's stealing them for herself! Greedy little pig."

I took a menacing step towards Chiku, but Dejen stood up and pushed me back. "What were you taking them for?" Dejen asked her, a lot more gently than I thought she deserved.

"She-she didn't give m-me any!" Chiku sobbed, pointing at me. "Not y-yesterday, not t-today. I was h-hungry!" She gulped and hiccupped and looked up at me all hurt and accusing.

I was just going to call her a liar and worse, when I checked the plastic pill bottle. I'd carefully counted how many carbohydrate pills we could have each day. Adding the two that were clenched in Chiku's fist, we were at just the right number. I thought hard. I was the one in charge of the food and water rations, carrying the remaining food supplements in my pack. Had I given her any carbohydrate pills the last two mornings? I couldn't remember handing Chiku her share.

I remembered skimping on her protein bar allowance to make sure Tash had enough.

I remembered giving some of her water share to Otlenno when he looked thirsty.

But I didn't remember giving her breakfast the last two days.

Damn.

No wonder she was thieving.

"Why didn't you just ask?" I muttered. "You're not a baby. It's not my job to remember to feed you."

"Didn't think you'd give me any if I asked." Chiku had stopped sobbing, and now she looked at me sullenly, rubbing her aching cheek.

"Why?" I didn't want to know the answer, but it was out before I could catch it.

She shrugged. "Because I'm not your sister."

Dejen frowned at that. "Of course you're sisters!" he said. "You and Adina and Tash—you're all one family."

He wanted us to make up, to take care of each other the way we ought to. But we weren't just plastic parts spat out of a 3D printing machine. He couldn't just pick us off the assembly line and fit us together smoothly like we were made for each other. We were joined in all the wrong places, for all the wrong reasons. As a family, we were broken, and all the glue in the universe wasn't going to bond us into something whole.

"Can we get going?" Otienno complained. "We don't have time for this."

He was right; we didn't have time for this. I didn't have time to waste on Chiku. I had Tash to look after.

We trekked another full day across dusty scrublands dotted with spiky, blackened plants that hugged the ground, sheltering from the wind. Towards evening we found a sluggish stream, the water thick and oozing with chemicals. We filled our remaining water filters and carried them from the stream, not daring to risk finding out what lurked beneath the surface. We were lucky, though. Nearby we found another abandoned village crumbling to ruins in the dusklight.

At least, I thought we were lucky.

I know now spending the night in that village was the wrong decision. Gods, I wish I'd listened to the small voice that whispered a warning in my ear when I pushed open the door of the seed bank. I wish I'd tried to work out why the hair on the back of my neck stood on end when I stepped inside and gazed round the dark walls. But all the wishing in the world isn't going to bring back the one we lost that night. If only I'd listened to Baba Weseka's visions. If only I'd just looked up before letting everyone go to sleep.

If *only*.

Like the first village we'd found, the only building still standing here was the seed bank. The old storage house had concrete floors and walls just like the last one, high wooden support beams crisscrossing the space under the sloping roof. We only had one fluorescent lantern now, so we couldn't see much more than a blanket of shadows where the sheets of metal roofing met the walls, but it looked solid from the outside. It looked safe. It even had a pile of old cardboard boxes stacked against one wall. We pulled them out and tore them down, spreading them on the floor for bedding. The night was warm, the air heavy. We didn't need to take our thermafoil bags from our packs for once, thank the Gods. If we had, we would've lost them too.

I made sure I gave Chiku the right amount of protein bar and vitamin supplements this time. I didn't want her accusing me of starving her again. Besides, Dejen was watching me dish it out. It kind of pissed me off he didn't trust me not to short-change Chiku, but seeing as how half her face was a purple bruise where I'd hit her, I guess I didn't blame him. I felt bad about lashing out now, so bad I even gave her most of my food share too. My temper was so short I felt like a bomb ready to go off, all the dynamite of my grief and guilt stuffed down deep in my guts, waiting for one little spark to set it off—boom! I'd explode in a storm of destruction, taking anyone too near with me. I had to make sure I didn't let anyone get that close. Tash was safe—she was too young to understand what I'd done to Eden Five or blame me for it if she found out. It was Dejen I had to be careful around.

I gave the girls the last of the water from the flasks, then told them to get some rest. They didn't really need me bossing them about; they were too exhausted to do much more than curl up together on the thick cardboard and sleep. Otienno went round the windows and door, sliding the wooden latches shut. For once we didn't need to keep a lookout. We could all get a full night's sleep. I watched Dejen out of the corner of my eye as I filled the flasks up from the water filter units. He was still hunched over that damn infopad, watching images flash across the small screen like his life depended on it.

"Can I have a refill?" Baba Weseka asked, holding out his empty flask that hadn't had anything in it for days. The plastic of the top was all chewed where his dumb dog had tried to get at the last drops of water. "Yango needs something to drink too. She's a good dog."

Yango lay on the cardboard at his feet, her ragged ears pricking up at the sound of her name. She might've wagged her tail too if she'd had even a bit of it left and the energy to move it. She was so covered in sores and swelling, you wouldn't have thought now she was a dog to look at her. She'd never been a good-looking mongrel, with her stinking fur and nose all wet and runny like Chiku's, but now it made me wince just looking at her.

"Baba, we can't waste water on—" I began, then stopped. Gods, what difference did it make? From her slow blinking and tired panting, she'd be dead soon anyway. If it kept Baba Weseka happy to think she was going to make it to the Sanctuary with us, then why should I stop him giving her water out of his own flask? The crazy old man was burned and hurt and tired and sad, and the one thing keeping him going right now was Yango. I filled Baba Weseka's flask and watched him feed water to his dog one small dribble at a time like Yango was a baby. I knew now why Dejen had gone back for the dog in the corridor. He wasn't trying to save Yango. He was trying to save Baba Weseka.

Dejen knew I was looking at him even before I realised it myself. I used to think Dejen knew everything. Now I only feared he did. He looked up, returning my gaze with those steady brown eyes of his.

"You want to watch some of these entries?" he asked, holding the infopad up. "I found some more about the medical camps."

I shook my head. I couldn't face any more death and suffering right now. Just watching Baba Weseka put his arms around his dying dog and curl up to sleep was hard enough.

"She doesn't want to see your stupid videpods about the old times," Otienno growled. "Hasn't she said that often enough?

It just upsets her." He came up behind me, rubbing my back possessively with one hand and leaning over to take a water flask with the other. I didn't like the way Dejen's eyes went suddenly dark when he saw Otienno's hand curl around my hips and squeeze my waist. I couldn't tell if he was angry or sad.

"You want to sit outside for a bit?" Otienno whispered in my ear. I say whispered, but it was loud enough that Dejen could hear. I knew Otienno did it on purpose. I glanced at Dejen. He looked away quickly, fiddling with the videpod cartridges to make it look like he wasn't listening. I don't think he really wanted to watch the videpod entries either. I think he just wanted an excuse to talk to me. The very fact he needed an excuse made my chest ache with sadness.

"You coming?" Otienno asked again, taking my hand.

I had a choice. I could sit with Otienno and forget, letting him caress away all my pain and memories until I was empty, a hollow shell of the person I once was. Or I could sit with Dejen and remember, feeling so full of guilt and longing that the truth would explode from my churning guts, turning us both to dust.

I didn't want to make that choice at all.

"I'm tired," I muttered, snatching my hand back. "I need to sleep." I turned away from them both, curling up on the carpet of cardboard as far from them as I could get.

It wasn't far enough.

I could still feel the intensity of Dejen's gaze from across the room and Otienno's angry eyes on my back. Gods, why did everyone have to watch me all of the time? Couldn't I have peace for just once? Couldn't I let my guard down for a fraction of a second? I was so tired. The mask of indifference I'd put on when Eden Five burned had melted into my very face, the web of lies I'd spun cocooning me like one of the biohazard suits hanging outside the airlock. It clung to me, my second skin, choking my air and sucking the life from me until everything I'd once been withered away and died inside.

Everything was dust and ashes in the wilds. Even me.

I'd almost managed to slip into a light sleep when the voices jerked me awake once more. Dejen and Otienno were talking. My heart skipped a beat when I realised they were discussing Eden Five.

"If you scientists were as clever as you thought you were, none of this would've happened," Otienno was saying. It came out as a low growl of pain in the dark.

"You think Eden Five exploding was the science team's fault?" Dejen snorted. "Gods, Otienno, you're dumber than I thought."

"It doesn't take a genius to work out who's to blame!" Otienno shot back. "You lot got all the best equipment while the rest of us had to beg and borrow to keep our workgroups going. And look what you did with it! You blew up our whole world."

"So the fireball came from the lab levels, did it?" There was a hard edge in Dejen's voice I didn't like. "Is that what Adina told you? Funny, 'cause she told me it came up from the levels at the basement. I don't remember the science team ever doing any experiments down there, do you?"

There was silence for a moment, followed by some angry muttering from Otienno I couldn't quite make out. My heart was beating faster now. Damn it all. Why had I gone and told them what I'd seen on the stairway? I could've said the fire came from the science labs and they would've believed me. I could've shifted the blame far, far away from Level Twenty-Eight and the broken air filter, and no one would ever have known any different. Of all the dumb things to be honest about amid so many lies, why did I have to tell the truth about what I saw before we escaped?

"If you're so smart then *you* tell me what caused it!" Otienno snarled. He didn't like being talked down to any more than I did.

"Something went wrong down in the lower levels. Something was broken that should've been fixed. Baba Weseka had a vision about it before it happened—he warned Adina about the fire." Dejen's voice was low and measured, as though he was telling Otienno a secret.

He was. He was telling him my secret. He knew. Oh Gods, he *knew*!

My heart nearly leapt from my chest in fear. How long had he known? Was he going to confront me with the truth and cast me from the group to make my own way through the wilds in guilt and shame? Or for the sake of the others, was he going to stay silent until we reached the Sanctuary, keeping us together long enough to get to safety before letting everyone know I was a killer?

"What was broken? What needed to be fixed?" Otienno asked.

I held my breath. Would Dejen tell him and turn him against me too? The silence seemed to stretch on for an eternity before Dejen answered.

"It doesn't matter now. Everything's gone. Get some sleep."

Otienno grunted. I'm pretty sure he swore at Dejen, but the blood was pounding so loud in my ears I couldn't hear him clearly. He flung himself down on the far side of the cardboard nearest the door and was soon snoring. It didn't seem to matter how bad things got, Otienno could still sleep. He was like Tash that way. She even slept through some of my parents' worst arguments late at night in our little homeroom. I used to curl up in my bunk when they argued, pulling the covers up over my head and wishing I was anywhere else.

I'd give anything to be back there now, listening to them screaming at each other in the dark. I'd give anything to have my family back the way it was before—broken, battered and limping along from day to day in a steady routine of mutual distrust and misery. I even missed the smell of drink and tobacco my father sweated at night, and the way my mother sighed and snapped at me when I got another behaviour report.

But they were gone. I'd destroyed my family along with everybody else.

And Dejen knew it.

I didn't dare take a full breath again until long after he put the lantern out and lay down on the carpet of cardboard. I couldn't be sure he was asleep, but after I'd stayed completely still and counted to ten thousand, my chest was beginning to ache from all that shallow breathing, and I had to scratch the acid burn on my leg which was driving me crazy. That was when I opened my eyes and finally remembered to look up.

I screamed so loud I nearly ripped my throat out.

I was staring right into the hollow eye sockets of a Nomaly. It hung down from the roof beams, its misshapen legs all twitchy and its arms tearing at my head. I leapt up, grabbing for my pack. There was no time to go hunting for my knife, but I needed something to swing at the creature.

"Dejen, Tash—Nomalies! Knives!" I yelled, terrified and incoherent.

The roof exploded just as the others were scrambling up in confusion. Nomalies came spinning down from the rafters above us, scuttling and snapping, clawing and biting. I could feel blood running down my face from their teeth as I kicked and struggled my way to Tash. I grabbed her hand and ran for the door, but my hands were covered in blood and they slipped on the wooden bolt. I couldn't get it open. Why, oh why had we gone and locked ourselves in?

Baba Weseka had somehow made it to the door, Yango struggling and whining in his arms. Terror seemed to give the skinny old man strength. He beat at the door while I scrabbled at the bolt, yelling almost as loud as his dog.

"Dejen!" I cried, "I can't get it open! I can't get out!"

Where was he? The lantern was bust and the shutters were closed, the seed bank a dark pit of seething bodies, bloody teeth and tearing claws.

"I've got it!"

It was Chiku who saved us. She'd never once let go of Tash's hand, and I'd pulled her through the mob of biting Nomalies too without even knowing it. She slid the bolt clear, shoving Baba Weseka out into the moonlight and taking off at a run through the village with Tash dragged along behind her.

I nearly followed them. But I turned back to look for Dejen.

In the moonlight I saw something so horrible I nearly passed out. A mass of creatures had scuttled from every dark corner, converging in the middle of the floor in a feeding frenzy. Bloated heads bobbed on stalky necks, up and down, up and down as they tore at the screaming boy beneath them. His dying cries ended suddenly in a long choking moan. Blood glittered in the moonlight, pooling round their scrabbling hands and feet. I gasped for breath, my mind refusing to believe the guts I saw spilling on the concrete were real.

This wasn't happening.

I was still asleep.

This was a dream.

Please, please tell me this is all just a dream! I begged.

Time seemed to slow down. I could see something crawling in slow motion towards me through the tangle of twitching legs. I took a step back, my feet lumps of lead inside my boots. Then time broke free of all the rules and flew past at twice its normal speed. Something covered in blood charged for the door, grabbing my hand and fleeing with me out into the night.

It was only when we'd found Baba Weseka and the girls cowering behind the last house of the village on the edge of the scrublands that we stopped, and I finally gathered up the courage to look closely at the bloody face of the boy standing by my side.

I know it was wrong, Gods help me, I know what I felt then made me an awful human being. My heart was shattered in a thousand pieces, my grief for the one I'd lost so sharp I could barely breathe. But I couldn't fight the wave of relief that made me so dizzy I had to grab his arm to keep myself upright.

Dejen was safe.

It was Otienno they'd killed.

CHAPTER 23

DAY SEVENTEEN

I don't remember much of the days that followed. It was all a blur of walking east and searching for water and fighting for sleep in the small hours of the morning. I pulled my armour of indifference around me so tight I could barely breathe. It was just as well I didn't let my guard down and give in to grief. There was more loss to come.

Dejen and I hardly spoke. He tried to talk to me, of course, the Gods know he tried, but every time I looked at him I heard his voice in my head say, *"Something went wrong down in the lower levels. Something was broken that should've been fixed."* And I shrank from him.

I felt like I was under a death sentence, and I was waiting for the fatal blow that would fall without warning, any time, anywhere. The death stroke would be a word, a look, delivered with such disgust and loathing it would cut me in two. The executioner would be Dejen. He held my life in his hands. So

I shrank from his words of comfort, snapping and biting like an injured dog, trying to delay the inevitable.

On day seventeen of the countdown we had to stop. Not because we were tired and limping and thirsty and hungry. We were, but we were almost used to the routine of misery by now. No, we weren't stopped by exhaustion; we were stopped by the robots.

The ridge of the plains ended in a steep slope that tapered down to another valley scarred with mining pits. This time there was no way we'd risk our lives down in the tunnels underneath the site. We'd have to pick our way through.

"Is there no way around?" Dejen shielded his eyes against the sun and gazed out across the humming swarm of mining drones.

I looked at the compass again and shook my head. Southeast was right across the drilling fields. "It'd take too long to go around. We're running out of time as it is."

This was the way we talked now, discussing the business of survival in a cold, clinical way, like scientists working on soil samples in the lab. Only this wasn't the way we used to talk on the lab level, Dejen and I. We used to laugh and joke and tease each other, whispering our secrets and sharing our dreams. Now we were standing right next to each other, staring down at the giant robots below, but we may as well have been on opposite sides of the Earth. He knew I'd been lying about Baba Weseka's visions, and I knew he'd guessed my secret. It was only a matter of time before it all exploded out in the open. For now we just played dumb and pretended the only thing that mattered was getting to Sanctuary Seven before our biofilters gave out.

"The robots are probably programmed to wipe out intruders they don't recognise," Dejen said. "From what I saw on the videpods, they're designed to go long periods without being repaired. They'll have defence systems against Nomalies and other mutated wildlife to make sure the drones can keep running without getting damaged."

He said it so matter-of-factly, like we came across giant killing machines every day of our lives. I wasn't the only one who was numb. Dejen was struggling to keep his head together too, retreating back to his science training and treating everything like a puzzle that had to be solved. Even me.

"So what do we do?" I asked. I could've worked it out for myself, but it took so much effort to keep my guard up all the time I didn't have the energy for anything else.

"We should wait here until night," Dejen decided. "It'll be easier to slip past them in the dark."

I wasn't entirely convinced. I'd seen the way the pits were lit up at night with spotlights and search beams that cut through the wilds. But we were out of options, and I didn't have any bright ideas of my own.

We settled down behind a screen of loose rocks, waiting for nightfall. The girls curled up in a sleeping bag, grateful for the chance to rest. Baba Weseka lay down on another, talking softly to Yango until he fell asleep. She could barely move without pain now, her whole body twitching and shivering in his arms. There was one more thermafoil bag, but neither Dejen nor I could've slept even if we wanted to.

We'd been lucky with the survival packs. I'd grabbed mine to swing at the Nomalies without even stopping to think that we needed the food it contained if we were to make it to the Sanctuary. Chiku had grabbed Tash's bag in the confusion to use as a shield against their biting teeth. Dejen was the only one who'd gone back for his deliberately. He'd braved the claws and gaping mouths of the creatures to snatch up a water filter too. If he hadn't, we'd all be dead by now.

Dead like Otienno.

I gulped and tried to forget what I'd seen. Forget the blood and guts glistening on the concrete floor in the moonlight. It was hard enough remembering Otienno alive, with his easy smiles and dark eyes that sent shivers down my spine. I should've been kinder to him. I shouldn't have pushed him away. Maybe if we'd sat outside and kissed that night he'd still be with us now. I was a killer, and his death was my fault too. I could have saved him if I'd let the others listen to Baba Weseka and not just brushed his visions off to protect my own secret. I shuddered, loathing the person who hid beneath my uncaring mask.

"You OK?"

Dejen looked up from his infopad, studying my face in the late afternoon light. I shrugged, wishing he wouldn't do that. It's not like I had any secrets left he didn't already know. But this was the new game we played together now. Instead of trying to guess each other's thoughts, we'd pretend we didn't already know what the other was thinking. It wasn't as much fun as the old game.

"Fine," I said wearily. "Just tired." For once, it wasn't a lie.

Dejen rubbed the sweat from the stubble that shadowed his chin and upper lip, looking like he was trying to make his mind up about something. Then he got up—slowly, deliberately—and walked over to the rock where I sat. "We need to talk," he said.

"About what?" I said it too quickly. I sounded guilty.

"About what happened." Dejen sat down opposite me, blocking my line of sight. I didn't have any choice but to look into his eyes.

"What happened in Eden Five you mean?" My mouth was dry. Why couldn't we just keep pretending it was still a secret?

"About what happened the other night in the seed bank to Otienno. And about Baba Weseka's visions. But we can talk about Eden Five too, if you want."

I breathed a little easier. The game wasn't over yet.

"What's the point?" I said, more naturally now. "It's not like talking's going to bring Otienno back."

"I know, but it might help. I know what he meant to you." Dejen leaned forward and put his warm hands on either side of my face. It was such a soft gesture, so comforting, I almost burst into tears right there and then. Almost.

I leapt to my feet like I'd been stung, pushing him away. "Stop touching me!" I growled. "I don't like it."

Dejen looked at me like I'd slapped him. "I'm not trying to take his place!" he protested, his face all tensed up with hurt. "I just want you to talk to me, Adi. Stop cutting me off like we're strangers."

"I just want you to leave me alone," I snapped, sitting down on the spare sleeping bag and crossing my arms protectively across my chest. I didn't want Dejen to leave me alone, not really. I wanted him to wrap his arms around me and hold me tight and never let go. But he wouldn't do that. He knew my secret. Why was he acting like he hadn't already worked out I was the one who blew up Eden Five?

Dejen said something under his breath and stomped back to his infopad. He stayed there, sitting on the rock and watching videopod entries the whole evening till it was dark. I lay down on the thermafoil bag, pretending to sleep. We'd taken turns of this bag every night, Dejen and I, one sleeping while the other stayed up to keep a lookout. It had been mine, but now there were faint traces of his scent on the covers. He smelled different from Otienno. Otienno had smelled of sweat and musk, something strong and new and strange. Dejen smelled so familiar it made me ache with every breath.

He smelled of our childhood in Eden Five.

He smelled of the memory of toffee cake in the canteen, of old books in the schoolhouse, of the harvest and the homerooms and the hothouses full of flowers.

He smelled of the time we'd kissed as a dare when we were nine, hiding out under the stairs and giggling when the workers' boots thudded overhead.

He smelled of our dreams, so distant and lost I wanted to hug the bag to me as though I was holding onto Dejen himself.

But I didn't. Instead I rolled over and listened to the videopod entries Dejen was playing. These were some of the last Doctor Malathion recorded in 2039. I guess the Gardens had been built not long after that. Her voice was nervous and strained. She didn't sound well at all.

"It's getting harder to keep the anomalous results of the Africa project from being shared on the Internet," she was saying. "Now that Doctor Bates has been appointed as the US foreign secretary, we've been able to keep the United Nations out of Africa, but the spiking cancer rates and organ failure problems in countries relying on our products have caused enough panic for the United Nations to impose a temporary ban on the sale of GM foods, despite his best efforts. Luckily the worldwide fuel crisis has meant our superfarms have been put to use as biofuel farms and mining operations, so the Corporation is still making money from its African land investments."

Our land, I thought. *Not the Corporation's land. Ours.*

"In order to contain the spread of the Africa project's anomalous results, the Corporation has banned all immigration to and emigration from the continent. Luckily, with enough of our scientists in key positions, we've been able to convince world governments that Ebola has caused the mass deaths across the continent of Africa. The whole land mass will remain under quarantine until we can either get the mutations under control, or they die out. Fortunately, with the new drone technology, this won't affect our mining projects."

I didn't hear any more. For all my weary anger and grief, I started to doze, giving in to the warmth and comfort of the thermafoil around me.

It was already dark by the time Dejen shook me gently awake.

"It's time," he said. "We need to go now."

The girls were already awake, rubbing their aching legs and helping Baba Weseka get his boots back on his blistered feet. It took ages to coax Yango up again. She wanted to lie where she was, tucking her muzzle under her swollen belly and whimpering to be left alone. If it had been just a week before, I would've left her there on the rocks, walking away without a backwards glance. But now I couldn't bear the thought of losing any more of our group, not even that dumb dog.

"Come on, eat this," I pleaded, holding out my share of the protein bar that I'd crumbled into my palm. "You'll feel better."

Yango had no appetite, but she was always eager to please. She licked at the broken pieces, trying to earn a pat even though she winced whenever we touched her.

"She's a good dog," Baba Weseka grinned proudly. "Good dog."

She finally struggled up onto her paws, following us down the slope towards the pits on shaky legs.

Lights burned in the darkness. The mining pits were lit up by the spotlight towers built around each deep crater. We planned on skirting round the edges, avoiding the worst of the yellow glare. But even then we wouldn't be safe. Enormous robot sentries prowled between the pits. Their eyes were searchlights in the dark, cutting through the gloom like great electric knives. We hunkered down on our knees just beyond the reach of the first tower's spotlight.

"Whatever happens, stay together," Dejen told us. "We don't know what weapons these things have been equipped with." He took a long strip of bandages from his medical kit and tied one end around Yango's neck, holding on tight to the other. She whined and chewed at the leash with her empty gums, but she didn't have the strength to fight back.

"Sorry, Yango, you need to keep up with the rest of us. Tash, Chiku, you stay with Adina. I'll look after Baba Weseka. Is everyone ready?"

I took Tash by one hand, holding firmly to Chiku with the other. Tash's lips were pale and trembling, but she nodded bravely. I didn't look at Chiku. Her eyes were the mirror image of mine, and I knew I'd see my own fear reflected there.

"Let's go," I said, trying to keep my voice steady.

We hurried forward, keeping to the shadows between the spotlight beams. There were three pits standing between us and the wastelands beyond, robot sentries patrolling the narrow strips of raised earth surrounding each crater. We cleared the first land bridge without too much difficulty, trying not to look down at the drilling machines that spun and whined and chewed at the earth like the fat, greedy worms we'd seen in the tunnels. Each drill was surrounded by a swarm of drones that looked just like giant locusts settled on a maize field. Their piston legs beat and pounded the ground, their wings made of great pulley wheels that whirred in the spotlights' glare. It was almost overwhelming to see such destruction.

By the time we reached the safety of the shadows beyond the first pit, Baba Weseka had slowed down. Dejen was struggling to pull both him and his dog along. Neither wanted to go any further.

"Can't we just sleep here?" Baba Weseka begged, looking around in confusion. "Lots of light, see? No more Nomalies."

"Baba, it isn't safe, we have to keep moving," Dejen urged, trying to stop him from sitting down. He looked to me for help, but I had my hands full with Tash and Chiku. One second later I didn't. Chiku let go and hurried to grab Baba Weseka's other hand, helping to pull him up. She looked older in the searchlight's intermittent glare, like she had in the woods when she'd told me silently she'd protect Tash from the Nomalies.

We waited for the robot sentry to pass, timing our passage and running for the next bridge when its searchlight crossed the beams from a spotlight tower, leaving a dark strip of unlit earth between them. There were two more sentries at the final pit, standing between us and the wilds beyond. They stood still on either side of the crater, their heads moving from right to left to sweep the earth with their searchlights.

We crouched down on our bellies, keeping our heads low to the ground.

"How are we going to get past them?" I asked Dejen in a whisper. "They've got the whole way across covered."

"We have to distract them somehow. Lure them both to the same side so we can escape on the other."

"How are we going to do that?" I expected Dejen to have all the answers when we needed them. My face fell when I realised he had no idea. We thought for a long moment, running through the few options we had left. Then, at the same moment, our eyes came to rest on Yango. Dejen looked away quickly, guilty at being caught in the act. I knew exactly what he was thinking. There was no time now to play the game and pretend I didn't.

"She's going to die any day now," I whispered. "It would be quicker this way. And it might save the rest of us."

Dejen struggled with the idea. I didn't want to sacrifice the dog any more than he did. But I had to get Tash past those robot sentries, and I didn't know how else to do it. We needed a distraction, and Yango would have to provide it.

"OK," Dejen said at last, "if she can buy us even a few moments we might make it past those robots without being seen."

But Yango wasn't going anywhere, not on her own. Dejen untied the leash, trying to push her round the side of the pit towards one of the sentries. She whined and dug her paws into the ground, winding herself round Baba Weseka and whimpering for help. When Baba Weseka figured out what we were up to, he started crying too, hanging onto his dog and wailing.

It turns out it wasn't just movement the robots were programmed to respond to. They reacted to sound too. They turned their heads at the same time, their searchlights coming to rest on our little group cowering in the dirt on the other side of the pits.

Laser beams slammed into the ground inches from where we stood. We were just outside their firing range. But then the robots moved towards us, one from each side of the pit. They must've had some kind of radio link, as the sentries guarding the other pits all stopped in their tracks, turning and striding between the craters towards us. There was no way back. We were surrounded.

"Move!" Dejen shouted, pushing us forward.

We sprinted past the third pit just as a volley of laser fire destroyed the earth where we'd been standing. It felt insane to be running *towards* the sentry that blocked our escape to the wilds on this side of the mining crater. But we had nowhere else to go. My heart was hammering with fear, and I had to force my feet towards the great machine, my head saying, *"No, no, no!"* the whole way. The robot raised its arm again, the huge gun taking careful aim. I lifted Tash and cradled her in my arms as I ran, praying the laser fire would hit me instead of her. Dejen dragged Baba Weseka along, Chiku pulling at his other hand.

Suddenly, Dejen wasn't running by Baba's side anymore. There was a flash of blinding red light. The ground where he'd been standing moments before smoked and burned, turned instantly to ash. I almost choked at the sight, forcing myself to keep running for Tash's sake. Then I realised Dejen hadn't been incinerated. He'd moved just before the laser fire hit, dropping Baba Weseka's hand and running sideways, right into the searchlight beam. He was sacrificing himself to give the rest of us a chance to escape.

The sentry turned, focussing in on the new target that was running towards the pit instead of away from it. This new threat became the priority. The robot turned, its gun following Dejen. It was all the time we needed. We bolted past its huge metal legs, slipping and sliding down the slope of churned earth on the far side of the pit and charging out into the dark wastelands beyond without a backwards glance.

We didn't stop running until Baba Weseka collapsed, his face screwed up in pain. Chiku helped him sit up, supporting him against her own heaving shoulders. Tash looked shocked, like she couldn't believe what Dejen had done or that I hadn't stopped him. How could I have? He was off before I'd even realised he wasn't there.

My mind was reeling. Dejen had been my best friend since we were in kindergarten. I couldn't imagine him being gone any more than I could imagine living on after I stopped breathing or my heart stopped beating. He couldn't be dead.

He wasn't.

He came running out of the darkness just as Tash was starting to cry. He stopped by my side, all hunched over and panting—waiting like he expected me to hug him or something. There was blood running down his arms where he'd been caught by the edge of the laser fire, and it was a miracle he hadn't gone and got his head blown off. If it had been anyone else, I would've said what he'd done was incredibly brave. But since it was Dejen, I was so relieved I felt like punching him for being so stupid.

We'd made it. We were all safe. Even Baba Weseka had managed to make it without dying of exhaustion. He was leaning against Chiku, his chest heaving as he patted Yango on the head.

"She's a good dog," he grinned.

But his smile was fixed, his lips trembling. I looked down at the dog he clutched in his scrawny arms.

Yango was dead.

It was only then I realised that Baba Weseka had taken off his biofilter some time before and fixed it to his dog's neck in a futile effort to stop the toxins tearing through her DNA.

It was too little, too late. Her body had fallen apart, cancers and lesions eating her up from the inside out. Now she was beyond saving, beyond suffering.

I walked away from the others slowly, out across the dark wastelands to a lonely patch of weeds. And there I bent down in the brittle grass and retched and retched until the fire in my aching guts had burned a hole right through the dull ache of grief.

CHAPTER 24

DAY TWENTY

Baba Weseka didn't last long after that.

He wouldn't let us re-attach his biofilter, leaving it fixed to the dog we buried under a mound of dirt and dust. Not that it would've done much good. Once the biopoisons in the air made so much as a tiny crack in the chains of your DNA, they'd keep working away, prising and splitting the molecules apart and rearranging them all wrong. Before you knew it you'd end up like Yango, all riddled with tumours and rot. That's what had happened to Baba Weseka the first time he'd got out of Eden Five and went running away into the wilds. But back then, the medical teams had stopped the radiation from doing further damage to him and managed to halt the chain reaction of the mutation process. Now there was no medical team and no way to stop Baba's weak body from crumbling under the toxic onslaught.

He died late in the evening of the twentieth day, lost and confused and crying for his dog. We sat by his side till the end, holding his hand and telling him everything would be alright. The lie came easily, like we were all born knowing what to say to someone whose life was slipping from our grasp. I wish the other lies I told tripped off my tongue so smoothly.

None of us cried when he closed his eyes and took his last breath, not even Tash. Her face was pinched and drawn, drained of everything but hunger, fear and an all-consuming need for sleep. We all looked the same, our eyes hollow and haunted. It's not that we didn't care that Baba Weseka was gone. It's just that our nerves were rubbed so raw from all the loss we could barely process our feelings anymore.

Dejen pulled the cover of the thermafoil bag over the old man's head, hiding his sunken cheeks and waxy skin for the last time. We hadn't discussed what we'd do with him once he was dead, but Dejen and I didn't argue about the bag. By rights we should've kept it—we were one short as it was. But we'd got used to sharing my bag, and we found comfort in taking turns at wrapping ourselves in each other's smell at night while one of us stayed up to watch, closing the silent gulf that yawned between us during the day. Besides, Baba Weseka's bag was so soiled and dirty inside from his fits it would take more than a water filter's worth of scrubbing to clean it. We let him be.

Chiku helped Dejen gather up stones and small rocks, laying them over Baba's body to form a protective layer between him and the creatures of the wilds. I sat and watched, rocking Tash to sleep in my arms and trying not to wish too hard that we could have done the same for Otienno. I'd thought it wasn't fair Baba Weseka got a chance to live while so many had died. Now I saw that fortune out here was just an illusion. The wilds took the weak and strong alike and ground them all down to dust.

Tash was sound asleep by the time they were done, her head resting on my shoulder. Dejen wandered off with his infopad, muttering something about taking first watch. I let him go without question, relieved he didn't try to reach out to me anymore. What was the point? We were too lost in our own heads to save each other now. Chiku sat down next to the mound of stones, running her hands across the rocks like she was stroking Baba Weseka's face. It was an odd, gentle motion, and I found myself slowly hypnotised by the fingers moving back and forth, back and forth in the dusk.

It was only when they stopped that I realised Chiku was staring back at me. "What?" she demanded.

"Nothing," I said quickly.

It was strange. For one brief moment while I was watching those hands weaving back and forth in the half-light, I felt connected somehow, like those hands were stroking my own face and soothing away my hurt. Then Chiku stopped and the contact was gone, like a circuit breaking in a skytube, the light refusing to shine. I wanted that connection back again. Chiku was my sister, but I had no idea how to put the broken wires between us back together again so we could communicate.

"You OK?" I blurted out at last.

"Fine," she muttered, all closed off and defensive.

I snorted out a dark, humourless laugh. This was the same three-word conversation I had with Dejen every day, right down to the "back off" look that Chiku threw me. Her eyes were so like mine that I got a glimpse of the sight he saw every time he tried to make contact. The stare was guarded and hostile, all glaring mistrust and suspicion. No wonder he'd stopped trying to reach out.

We sat in silence for a long time, watching the stars wheeling slowly overhead. I thought she'd gone to sleep at last, so it was a surprise to hear her voice say, "Adina?" from the dark.

"What?" I looked up. Chiku was sitting on her sleeping bag, twisting her fingers into knots. Maybe she couldn't sleep without Tash for comfort. But Tash was curled up snugly in my arms, all warm against my skin, and I didn't want to move her. I needed the reassurance of her soft breath on my neck. If she was alive then there was still hope, no matter what.

"I was just wondering," Chiku said hesitantly. "What d'you think Sanctuary Seven's like? I mean, will it be like Eden Five, only bigger? Or will it be something totally different? Will it be like those polytunnels we saw?"

I was going to snap a reply about her knowing all about it if she hadn't skipped so much school. Then I stopped. Not because I realised in time what a hypocrite I'd sound, but because I only vaguely remembered a few school lessons about the Sanctuaries myself. They hadn't told us much, and now I was starting to wonder if anything we'd been taught was true at all.

"I think it's like a big Garden of Eden," I said slowly, "only with more biodiversity levels. We just had farm animals and some domestic breeds like dogs and cats in Eden Five, but I think there's a lot more in the Sanctuaries."

"What, like lions and zebras and penguins and things?" Chiku asked eagerly. Her face was all lit up now, and she looked like a ten-year-old girl again, instead of a hunched little troll jealously guarding the bridge to her thoughts. In fact, with her face all shining with curiosity in the moonlight, she looked almost pretty.

"Um, yeah, I think that's what it'll be like. Lions and zebras and penguins and things." Were there penguins in Africa in the old times? I couldn't remember, and it bugged me not knowing something so basic. Dejen would know. Where was he with his head full of useless facts when I needed him?

"And the people?" Chiku went on, "do you think they'll be like us? Or will they be from the other places—you know, the big bits of land across the seas?"

"I guess they'll be like us. I mean, it's one of the African Sanctuaries, right? So that probably means the people will be from here."

As answers went, it was vague and unsatisfying, but it was the best I had to offer. I was starting to feel uncomfortable, unsettled by the gaping hole in my head that should be filled with facts. I shrugged, hoping she'd get tired of asking questions that didn't have an answer.

She didn't.

"D'you think they'll have better 3D printers than what we had? I mean, d'you think they can make boats and planes and spaceships and things?"

Gods, she didn't just look like me, she thought like me too.

"I always wanted to be a techie, so if we were someplace that had printers with decent programs, I thought I could make—"

"You're too dumb to be a techie!"

It was out before I could catch it. She'd hit a nerve and I couldn't stop the venom that spilled out from the old wound festering deep in the hidden reaches of my heart.

"You think you can just copy me and that'll make you my sister, but it won't! You're just an orphan that nobody wants, so stop trying to be me!"

Chiku's bottom lip trembled. "Why are you always so mean?"

It wasn't a growl or an accusation. It was just a hurt little whimper.

She curled up in the sleeping bag, hiding her head under the cover. I knew she was crying, and I knew it was my fault, but I couldn't force myself to go over and apologise. Anyway, Tash was real my sister, not Chiku. Why couldn't she just accept it?

I told myself Chiku only had herself to blame for my temper, the way she poked and prodded and hit all the sensitive spots I tried to hide from the world. It was her own fault, or at least her mother's fault for seducing my father and making him forget his real family. It wasn't my fault at all. At least, that's what I told myself. But deep down, I knew the real reason I hated her so much. It was my oldest secret, hidden away in the locked chambers of my heart where even I couldn't find it. I wasn't about to go looking now.

I got up, laying Tash on my sleeping bag and walking off to find Dejen. It was probably about time for me to take a turn of watching, and I was too riled up to sleep.

I found him hunched over on the balls of his feet on a little incline that overlooked the wastelands around our camp. He was facing away from me, looking into the night. At least, I thought he was. Then I saw his shoulders shaking, and heard the soft sharp breaths that he tried to stifle deep down in his throat.

Dejen was crying.

I stood there stunned, not knowing what to do. All my instincts were to throw my arms round him and kiss his tears away. But I couldn't; there was so much distance between us. I hovered behind him, my twitching hands hanging all awkward and useless. Finally, I moved forward, resting my hand on his shoulder and willing him to feel the strength of my love through the pressure of my palm.

"I'm sorry," I said. What else was there to say? "You did your best with Baba Weseka and Yango. It wasn't your fault."

"I know," Dejen gulped.

Then why are you crying? I wanted to say. *Stop making it harder for me!* But I didn't, I just waited until he'd calmed his breathing. His hand found mine and he took it from his shoulder. I thought he was going to push me away like I always did to him, but then I found him putting his infopad into my hands instead.

"Watch it," he said without turning round. "Just watch it. Then you'll understand."

Understand what? Why he was crying? After everything that had happened, everything we'd lost, I didn't think he

267

needed another reason. I walked away and found a quiet place behind a rock, sitting down and holding the infopad up. I could still see Dejen's back out of the corner of my eye, but I was far enough away that he couldn't hear the sound from the small speakers. I selected the entry he'd highlighted for me, and pressed play.

It was the last entry recorded by Doctor Malathion, on May the first, 2041. It must've been right around the time the Gardens were built. She was in a long white corridor, with doors leading off to rooms on every side. Her face was so haggard and twisted with worry now, that she looked like a shell of the excited young scientist she'd once been. She held the camera up in shaking hands, speaking softly as though she was in a hospital ward.

"The anomalous results of the Africa project are everywhere—we can't contain them," she said. "We've done our best, but the mutations have spread through the next generation. All we can do now is quarantine those not affected and hope the mutations die out by themselves in a few generations."

She walked down the corridor, stopping by a door that had a plastiglass window set in it at eye level. "In the meantime, the Corporation has created special hospital facilities to research the anomalies. They should yield some fascinating insights into DNA mutation and transgenic contamination in humans. Though I must say, at this point I'm finding the subjects a little difficult to work with, especially the youngest ones."

She held the camera up to the window. Inside, under the harsh strip lights, a group of three tiny figures was curled up on the floor. At first I thought they were children, no older than Tash. They stirred at the sound of Doctor Malathion's voice, looking up at the door. I nearly dropped the infopad in horror. Their misshapen heads bobbed on gangly necks, too many arms and legs unfolding in all the wrong places. With spiderlike movements, they scuttled to the plastiglass, snapping and shrieking like baby birds begging for food. Only these weren't birds, they were children. Malformed, mutated, sick, suffering children.

Doctor Malathion turned the camera back on herself. She looked queasy, her lips pursed and twitching. "Of course, we can't possibly house all of the anomalies in our testing facilities, but the Corporation's mining drones have been programmed to search out and destroy any that come too close to the drilling camps. With help from the US government led by Doctor Bates, we should be able to keep the anomalous results of the Corporation's failed Africa project from reaching the eyes of the world."

The camera image panned back to the mutant children scrabbling at the door, closing in on the face of the smallest, all empty sockets and giant nose holes and too many crying mouths. The infopad slipped from my fingers, falling with a soft thud in the dust.

I looked up, my eyes meeting Dejen's in the moonlight. He'd turned to look at me, the tears shimmering on his cheeks. And now I understood. He wasn't crying for Baba Weseka and Yango and Otienno and all the people we'd lost, not tonight. He was crying for all the children of the old times the Corporation had poisoned with their mutant seeds and chemicals. All the children of Africa who'd grown up twisted and clawing and biting and scratching through the ashes of our land for food that was rotting on its stalks.

I knew now why Dejen was crying.

The anomalous data weren't just a bunch of numbers on a lab report recording the results of a failed biological experiment.

The Nomalies were people.

CHAPTER 25

DAY TWENTY-FOUR

We'd already lost three of our group to the wilds. But before our biofilters gave out, we still had another one to lose. Only this time, we didn't have Baba Weseka to warn us about it in advance. There was no way to see this death coming.

Dejen's infopad didn't make it to Sanctuary Seven either. The batteries were running down, the images becoming blurred and grainy. I'd thought the final entries would just fizzle out while we were watching, but the little viewing device came to a far more violent end than that.

We trekked south-east all morning, keeping well away from the rundown buildings that dotted the landscape. We'd reached the end of the wastelands where the Corporation had experimented with their mutant crops and poisoned the land, and now the remains of towns lay abandoned around us like the empty shells of maggot-ridden fruit. For all his curiosity about the old times, even Dejen didn't dare go exploring in the ruins. He remembered only too well the Nomalies hiding in the rafters of the seed bank. The Gods only knew what twisted, malformed people were camped out in the burnt-out husks of long-dead buildings, watching with too many eyes or no eyes at all from the shadows.

I didn't want to think about the Nomalies, but I couldn't push the image of those misshapen little children from my mind.

"How come everything out here's all sort of, well, spiderish?" I asked Dejen, when we stopped to rest and hide from the sun under an old dried-up water tower. "The Nomalies, I mean, and the wasps? The plants have got those weird kind of webby fibres, and even those centipedes we saw sort of scuttled."

"It's the transgenic material the Amonston Corporation put in their seeds," Dejen said, chewing a bit of protein bar without much appetite. "They used silk genes taken from spiders. They were trying to strengthen the crops, to make their stalks more weather-proof and insect-proof. But genetic transfer's never been an exact science, you know, not even in the old times with all their advanced technology."

"It wasn't?" I blinked. As a kid I thought they could do pretty much anything in the old times. I had a kind of vague idea that their scientists were strange magicians waving wands in their laboratories, casting spells to create new technology, weaving magic into their machines and boiling up medical advances in test tubes. By the time I started as a techie I knew better, of course, but the idea didn't quite disappear even when I understood a bit more about physics and chemistry.

"They made it sound like gene transfer was so precise, going on about 'gene selection' and 'targeted insertion,'" Dejen snorted. "Basically, the best they could do was gouge out a lump of genetic material from one species, fire it into the host cells of a new species with a gene gun, and hope that whatever bits of plant cell survived would carry the new genes."

"That doesn't sound very scientific," I frowned. "So everything ended up with bits of spider genes?"

"Just the plants at first. To be fair to the Amonston Corporation's geneticists, it probably worked pretty well in the lab. But then those seeds got planted across Africa, and all those crops with spider genes got eaten by insects and birds and people, and everything got mutated."

Dejen was starting to look more and more like his old self, leaning forward eagerly to explain things the way he did when I shirked work and went to visit him in the labs in Eden Five. It was so nice to see the enthusiastic glint back in his eyes that I kept the conversation going, even though I really didn't want to know any more about the horrible mutations the Amonston Corporation caused.

"So how come Yango didn't grow extra legs?" I asked. "I mean, if she'd survived a bit longer would she have turned into a spider or something?"

Dejen smiled at that, even though the thought of the dead dog was another painful reminder of everything we'd lost. "Of course not, that's not the way genetics works. Most of the biopoisons came from the chemicals that were sprayed on the plants and polluted the whole water table, wiping out most of the wildlife and even the plants they were meant to protect. They're what made Yango so sick. No, it's the babies that suffered most from the foreign genetic material."

"How come?" I didn't really want to know the answer.

Dejen's eyes went dark. He glanced over to where Tash and Chiku sat dozing together against one leg of the water tower, making sure they couldn't hear us. "Babies growing in the farmers' wombs were surrounded by the Corporation's chemicals—pesticides, herbicides, fertilisers, all clogging up their bloodstreams. Add that to the foreign genetic material their mothers ate, and you end up with a mix so toxic it's amazing any of the children survived at all."

"And this happened all over the world?" I asked. "I mean, I know the videopod entries are all about the Corporation's Africa project, but the whole world must've been affected by the transgenic material in the plants that they ate. That must be what destroyed the world's ecosystems, huh, Dejen?" I wasn't so much asking for information, as asking for reassurance that not everything we'd been taught to believe in Eden Five was a lie.

"Adi," Dejen said, looking at me like his heart was breaking, "I thought you'd worked it out by now. You saw their polytunnel superfarm and the scientists inside it. The Corporation may have built the Edens to protect the survivors, but they never left Africa, not even when they destroyed our ecosystem."

My heart was breaking too. I'd suspected the truth for a long time now, of course, but I'd thought that if I just kept pretending, I could keep believing the lies we'd been taught. "But they told us the whole world was gone!" I protested, clinging to the familiar old story. "The ecosystems collapsed everywhere, the environmental damage, it—"

"Here." Dejen handed me the infopad again, getting up and leaning against the metal leg of the tower to stare off across the bleak landscape. He was waiting for me to watch, waiting for me to catch up with him and the truth he'd known longer than any of us. I guess he was tired of carrying the burden alone.

He'd selected Nia's final entry. The date was June the ninth, 2042. The infopad's power light blinked in warning as her proud, defiant face appeared on the screen, her voice crackling over the dying speakers. "This is it," she growled, "the end of everything we've fought for. The Amonston Corporation has built giant quarantine bunkers across Africa, and is housing the survivors of their failed GM food project there until the continent recovers. They're calling them 'Gardens of Eden,'" Nia snorted. "But they're basically giant prisons to keep the African people off the land while the Corporation sucks it dry of oil, natural gas and any other resources it can find. They're building huge protected polytunnel superfarms over the rest of the continent, saying they're needed to grow enough food for the rising populations in the rest of the world. They're able to keep the prices so low and flood the global markets with so much cheap food that none of the other governments are complaining about the African takeover."

I had to remind myself to keep breathing as I watched. Hearing the truth I'd suspected spoken out loud made me almost dizzy.

"The international community has been fed the Corporation's lies for so long they're willing to go along with the 'continent-wide Ebola pandemic' and 'natural disaster' stories. Foreign governments are too busy fighting over contracts for the Corporation's cheap natural resources to investigate the ecological collapse of the entire continent further. Can you believe the United Nations actually praised the Corporation for its handling of the crisis and its provision of Gardens for the survivors?" Nia scowled and shook her head.

"But the Rebel Farm Alliance won't be herded into the Gardens like cattle. We're going to keep fighting. One day we'll get the truth out to the rest of the world, one day we'll—"

The screen flashed, then went dark. The battery had finally died. I sat staring at the blank screen, willing Nia's face to appear again even though I knew the infopad was no more use to us. In the brief time we'd been sitting there in the shade of the abandoned water tower, my world had changed forever. No, not my world—the world was the same as it had always been. But the way I saw the world changed, and it was all Dejen's fault. If he hadn't been so determined to steal those damn videpods, I could've kept on pretending everything was just as they'd told us when we were children.

"They had to tell us lies to keep us happy in the Gardens," Dejen said without looking at me. "The Directors knew we'd go mad with anger if we were told the truth. That's what happened in Eden Two—some of the workgroup heads got hold of their Director's videpods and what they saw started a riot that nearly destroyed the whole Garden."

It was an answer to the silent question I'd been asking with my eyes, but not the one I wanted to hear. "How long have you known?" I asked, trying to keep the resentment from my voice.

Dejen turned, looking at me now with that calm, steady gaze of his. "Since we walked through the weed fields. I watched a bunch of Nia's entries about the building of the Gardens."

"Why didn't you tell me?" If I sounded hurt, it's because I was.

"Because you weren't ready to listen. You had to hear the story from the start to believe it. And anyway, you were too busy with Otienno." There was a sharp edge of accusation in his voice that cut the air between us, driving us further apart.

He'd known all about the Amonston Corporation's lies for nearly the whole time we'd been out in the wilds. And he didn't tell me. How long had Dejen known about my own lie, my own secret? And when was he going to stop pretending and just confront me? I was tired of playing guessing games. I stood up and shouldered my pack, shaking the dozing girls awake.

"We should get going," I said. "We still have a long way to go."

We walked in silence, trekking south-east in the blazing afternoon sun. Tash and Chiku walked in front, holding hands and kicking up the dust with their scuffed boots. Chiku kept glancing back over her shoulder at me and Dejen, noting the way we kept our distance, wrapped up in our own thoughts. She knew something was up, but she was too afraid of my temper to ask any questions.

I was so mad for most of that day I could barely walk straight. I knew for certain now that my whole worldview had been warped by the lies we were told in our little bubble world of Eden Five. We'd been wrapped in cotton wool, swaddled like babies and lulled to sleep by soothing stories that said there was nothing anyone could have done to stop the ecosystems from collapsing. The whole world was gone, and it was an accident, we were told—nobody's fault. We'd been lied to all our lives, lied to just to keep us from fighting to get our land back and hurting the Amonston Corporation's profits. Africa was a wasteland filled with monsters and machines, and it was all done for money.

But by the time we'd climbed a little slope and neared the top, my mood had changed. We stopped at the edge of a steep drop, the clifftop falling away to meet a slow-moving river far, far below. Looking out across the sandy hills that dipped and rolled their way to the coast, we couldn't help sighing in wonder.

Out there, its great blue depths joining the paler sky at the horizon, was the sea.

I'd never seen so much water in all my life. Water had been strictly rationed in Eden Five, the showers in our homeroom sanitation units giving out grudging little trickles in carefully measured amounts. But here was a whole ocean full of beauty and magic, and somewhere out there, somewhere in the haze of blue halfway between sea and sky, was Sanctuary Seven.

We were close.

Eden Five was gone, but there was still hope. The rest of the world wasn't all empty wilds. The rest of the world had a living present and a future full of promise. Maybe one day after we'd reached the Sanctuary we'd get a chance to go beyond, into the world that was still alive. I could've danced with joy at the thought.

Tash and Chiku were even more thrilled than I was.

"It's so big!" Tash cried, staring with wide eyes at the waves rolling in the distance.

"Is that where Sanctuary Seven is, way out there?" Chiku asked.

"Yes," I said, "the maps show it's out at sea due east from here."

"Then we have to go over the sea?" Chiku scrunched her face up, looking like a strange little cross between me and Tash. "How? We don't have a boat."

I opened my pack and pulled out the map. "There's a landing site marked on the coast. There must be ships there. Or a radio, or something." It dawned on me now that I didn't really have a clue how we were going to get to the Sanctuary. I guess I hadn't expected us to make it across the wilds alive.

I didn't have any more answers, so I asked the one person I relied on to know everything. "You think maybe they'll send a ship for us when we get to the landing site, or an aeroplane maybe?" I turned to Dejen, my hands and feet all tingling with excitement at the prospect.

Then I yelled at the top of my lungs.

There was a Nomaly standing right behind him.

"What?" Dejen half turned when I cried out, the teeth that snapped at him missing his neck by inches. I just had time to grab my knife from my pack and shove Tash behind me when another one came scuttling out from behind a rock, its many-clawed fingers twitching. It lunged at me, biting and shrieking for blood.

I was terrified, slashing wildly with my knife at the creature and yelling for Chiku to get back. She stumbled away to the edge of the cliff, cowering back as the Nomaly threw itself at me again. I was nearly as scared as the two girls trembling behind me, but somehow just knowing that the thing trying to claw its way under my skin was human, however malformed, gave me courage. We were so close to making it to the Sanctuary, so close to safety. I'd be damned if I was going to let anything stop me from saving my little sister.

I screeched out all my anger and fear and frustration, charging the thing and stabbing at its twisted, gangly neck. My knife found its mark, striking deep in the Nomaly's warty flesh. The creature staggered back, the knife stuck in its neck. It howled and heaved, clawing at me this time in desperation and pulling me down to the ground with it. It was gurgling and dying, but it wouldn't let go, its many twitching arms catching me by the wrists and holding me tight while its blood ran into the dust.

I squirmed in its grip, twisting round to look at Dejen. I wailed in horror at what I saw. The first Nomaly was sitting on his chest, pinning him to the ground as its fingers and toes and hands and feet squeezed at Dejen's neck. Dejen bucked and kicked, trying to throw the creature off, but his head and shoulders had slipped over the edge of the cliff, and if he moved back even an inch he'd go tumbling down the endless drop below. The creature had too many hands and fingers for

Dejen to prise off his neck, so he scrabbled about in the dust instead, searching blindly, frantically for his pack.

I could see his thrashing arms losing strength, the Nomaly choking the life out of him, its jaws hovering over his throat. I yelled and fought and struggled against the dying monster dragging me down, but I couldn't get it off.

"Dejen!" I cried, "Dejen, no!"

The Nomaly on his chest drew back the lips of the mouths all muddled up on its bulging jaws, its teeth flashing in the sun. Then it struck, its head bobbing down to clamp onto Dejen's throat.

Dejen yelled in pain, his hand finally finding his pack. He pulled out the first thing his fingers closed around, slamming it into the side of the Nomaly's head.

It was the infopad.

The screen shattered, plastic shards cutting deep into the Nomaly's flesh. It tumbled from Dejen's chest, its hands clutching at its bloodied face. It teetered for a moment on the edge of the cliff, then it fell, spinning and shrieking through the air all the way to the ground far below. The dust clouds closed over it before I saw it hit the base of the cliff, but I'd stopped watching it fall long before then.

I finally tore the hands of the dead Nomaly from my wrists, running over and grabbing Dejen by the shoulders, hauling him back from the brink of the cliff.

"Are you alright?" I asked over and over, my hands running across his neck and his face and his chest and checking frantically for serious wounds. He submitted to my desperate caresses, staring into my anguished face with a strange look of wonder that turned into a slow smile.

"Adi, I'm fine," he said softly, "it's just a few cuts and bruises."

He ran his own hands down my wrists, stroking the claw marks that cut deep into my flesh and soothing away the pain. For a long moment we sat like that, holding onto each other tightly, our fingers bridging the gap between us. Then Tash flung her arms around us too, burying her head in my neck and crying in relief.

"It's OK." Dejen stroked her messy hair, the little pompoms I'd spent so long tying up all undone now and covered in dust. "We're all OK."

Then his eyes darkened, the way they did when he saw something that worried him. "Chiku, get back from the edge!" he shouted, "it isn't safe."

I turned to look. Chiku was leaning right over on the cliff ledge, peering down into the dust clouds that swirled round the river far below, searching for the fallen Nomaly.

"I'm not some dumb kid!" Chiku pouted, pulling back and scowling at us. Now that the danger had passed, all her attitude and spikiness were back with a vengeance. Gods, she was so like me it wasn't real. "I was just looking." She stood up and glanced back over the cliff edge.

And that was when the thin ledge of soil beneath her gave way.

One moment she was standing there, looking down at the haze of dust far below. Then there was just an empty void where she had once been, a trickle of loose soil, a frightened cry fading into nothing, and my own voice echoing on the wind as I screamed and screamed and screamed.

CHAPTER 26

DAY TWENTY-FIVE

The night after Chiku died I nearly went mad.

My memories of it are vague. I know I was shaking so hard when I stopped screaming that I couldn't stand upright. I know it was Dejen who helped get me going again, half carrying me down the steep slope of the eastern trail, away from the cliff where I'd lost one of my sisters. I know he carried Tash in his arms, her weeping face buried in his neck until she'd cried herself senseless. I know he sat rocking her all night, his gentle voice soothing the tears, his warm hands holding her tight.

And I know I didn't cry. Not one single tear.

I had no reason to pretend now. Dejen knew my guilty secret, I'd heard him tell Otienno as much. But I couldn't get the mask off my face. I tried and tried, banging my fists against the wall of indifference that separated me from Dejen's soothing words and comforting arms. I wanted to run to him, but my feet were all tangled up in the suit of lies I'd worn for so long I couldn't find the place where it ended and my own true self began. I wanted to cry—I desperately needed the release of tears—but they wouldn't come.

All I could do the whole long, dark night, was sit and brood, watching Dejen rock Tash to sleep and finally fall into a troubled doze himself. He'd tried to reach me, and I tried to reach back for him, but my guilt wouldn't let me catch hold of his hands so they could pull me back from the brink of madness. There was one more secret he didn't know, you see, one more secret I'd kept hidden away from him for years. It was a secret so selfish and terrible it made me recoil whenever I caught glimpses of it down the long, dark corridors in the hidden reaches of my heart.

The secret was the reason I'd hated Chiku so much.

The memories came flooding back now as I sat all alone with my guilt through the endless black night. I remembered my parents arguing when the young factory worker got pregnant, my mother hurling accusations at my father, and my father throwing them right back. But that wasn't why I'd hated Chiku—my parents had been arguing for years before she arrived on the scene. I'd longed for a loving family that was warm and safe and peaceful and not broken and warring like mine was. I wondered now whether the happy times I thought I'd spent with my parents smiling across the dinner table were even real, or whether I'd just made them up in my head as a kid.

I remembered the sad nights my mother and I spent alone in our homeroom when Chiku was born, my father going off on his own to visit her in the hospital ward. He'd tried to talk my mother into bringing the baby up as part of our family, but she didn't want anything to do with the kid who was a daily reminder of my father's cheating. I could see her clearly still, her tear-streaked face crumbling in pain and resentment whenever Chiku's name was mentioned. But that wasn't why I hated Chiku either.

I remembered I used to pass by the nursery on my way to school, watching the little girl who was my sister but not my sister through the plastiglass door. She was a fat toddler, healthy and happy and giggling in her chair when I sneaked in to slip her bits of cake I'd bought with my canteen credits. I didn't hate her then—in fact I was desperate for a sister. I couldn't understand why we couldn't just take her home and let the laughing, chattering little girl chase away the gloom that hung in heavy clouds over our homeroom.

I remembered clearly the day I started to hate her. It was etched deep into my mind, an ugly wound that refused to heal. I was nine years old. My mother was making dinner, and I'd gone looking for my father, hurrying down to the bottom accommodation level to knock on his friend Faraji's door and ask him to come back before the food all burned and my mother started sobbing again. I'd just raised my hand to knock when I saw my father coming out of the orphans' homeroom, holding Chiku in his arms. He was dancing the little girl up and down, and she was shrieking with laughter as he tossed her in the air and caught her again. I'll never forget the look of sheer joy and pride on his face as he looked down at Chiku then, his eyes all lit up and sparkling. I'll never forget the way my stomach turned when I realised the girl giggling in his arms was the mirror image of me, only smaller and cuter and giving him more joy in those few moments than it seemed I'd given him my whole life.

And that was why I'd hated Chiku.

It wasn't because my father loved Chiku's mother more than mine; it was because my father loved Chiku more than me.

It wasn't my mother who he'd replaced. It was me.

At least, that's what I'd always believed, my jealousy gnawing away at me until I couldn't think straight around her. Now, out here in the dust and wind of the wilds, I was starting to see more clearly. I looked back now and saw all the times I'd hurt the little girl to gain attention from my father, all the times I'd made her cry to get at him. My heart ached with sorrow and guilt, each image sending a fresh stab of pain through my heart. The dam of memories broke and they all came flooding out, flashing before my eyes in a never-ending stream of accusation.

All the times I'd slapped her so hard my hand stung.

All the times I'd laughed at her, jeering and belittling her attempts to copy me.

All the times I took away her chance to have nice things, and left her with broken toys, broken friendships, broken promises.

All the times I made her sob with despair and loneliness.

Chiku was my little sister, and I'd let her fall. I'd tried to catch her, but it was too late—years and years full of harsh words and unkind acts too late. If I could only have her back again, I'd cling to her and never let her go. I'd treat her just like

Tash—I *would*—I'd comb her hair and read her stories and sing her to sleep and make her chocolate.

Make her chocolate.

Gods.

I fell forward on my knees and retched, the sickening memory of her wrist thumping against the stair rail and the chocolate bar tumbling away all tangling up with my dreams of her falling and the awful reality of her death.

"Adi?"

Dejen caught me before I fell too.

I shrugged him off and hugged my arms to my heaving chest in the half-light of dawn. I didn't deserve to be saved. I deserved to be the one falling down to the basement and lost in the labyrinth of pipes until all that was left was the dried-up skeleton of a techie who'd shirked her work and killed everyone. I was so tired and alone and aching for redemption I could barely breathe.

"Drink this."

Dejen was determined to save me whether I deserved it or not. He pressed a water flask to my lips, insisting I drink. After a few long, cooling gulps I stood up and pulled my compass from my pack with shaking hands, trying to get my bearings. We were still a long trek from the coast and we were running out of time. We'd have to hurry now.

"We can't go without finding Chiku!" Tash wailed when I shook her gently awake and gave her some carbohydrate pills. We'd lost so many of our group we didn't need to ration food supplements anymore. "We need to cover her with stones like Baba Weseka so the Nomalies don't get her."

Tash knew her sister was dead, lying at the bottom of the cliff somewhere all broken and battered, but she couldn't bear the thought of Nomalies chewing on her bones. I knew that's how she felt, because that's how I felt about it too. But I just shook my head and made her eat the pills.

"We can't go all the way around the bottom of the cliff looking for her," I said as soothingly as I could with my throat all raw and my tongue numb with hidden pain. "We've only got a few days left on our biofilters. Don't worry—Chiku can't get hurt any more now."

My hand burned as it clutched the plastic bottle, my palm aching at the memory of Chiku's sobbing face, all swollen and bruised where I'd slapped it. I was such a bad sister I'd even neglected to feed her properly, then accused her of stealing when she was hungry. Chiku hadn't just been scared of the Nomalies. She'd been scared of me.

I pushed the thought away and took Tash's hand, leading her along at a quick pace east. There wasn't time now for me to dwell on the past or what a crappy excuse for a human being I was. I had one sister left to save, and somehow I'd been lucky enough to keep Dejen. I had to make sure they got to the Sanctuary, I just *had* to. Maybe if I saved them—just *maybe*—it would make up for all the other people I'd got killed along the way.

We hadn't gone too far along the coastal trail that wound through knotted scrubland, when Dejen stopped, clambering up onto a rock and shielding his eyes against the sun.

"There's something over there," he said, gazing out past the tangled bushes.

"Nomalies?" I asked tensely, gripping Tash's hand tighter.

"No…" he said slowly, "it isn't moving. It's just sort of sitting there flashing in the sun."

He'd jumped off the rock and started striding away before I could stop him. I knew what this was, this agitated need for action. It was his way of hiding his grief. He had to hide it now because he knew I wouldn't share it, and that hurt him more than anything. I followed him at a safe distance, clutching my knife in one hand and holding on to Tash with the other.

When we cleared the last of the bushes I saw it too. Something large and box-like lay on its side in the dust, the sun glinting off its metal casing. It was only when we walked right up to it we realised it was a vehicle from the old times, one of the heavy-duty transport jeeps they used to take on long distance trips. It had crashed into the twisted remains of a water tower, and now it was all twisted from the inside out and burned up like the engine had exploded.

"You think it's been here long?" The strange sight woke Tash up from the dull stupor of grief for a moment, and she kicked at the tyres, her boots thumping against the thick rubber.

"No," Dejen and I said at the same time. We both saw the smoke curling from the engine, the embers of choked grass around the jeep still smouldering.

And then, of course, there were the bodies.

Two charred corpses sat in the overturned jeep, one in the driver's seat and one in the back. I could just make out the rubbery brown material of their biosuits beneath the layer of ash, and their helmets melted around their heads.

"Who d'you think they were?" Dejen frowned. "You think they were from one of the Gardens? Or from the Sanctuary, perhaps?"

"Dejen..." My voice faltered. I'd seen something only a techie would recognise. There was a patch of blue on the burned biosuit the driver wore. It was so small, so nearly consumed by the fire that had eaten up the jeep and killed its passengers that anyone else would've missed it. But not me. I was a techie, and I'd seen it before. It was the tail of a blue bird.

"Dejen, it's Makena!" I gasped. For one wild moment, I wanted to rip the helmet from her head and check to see if she was still breathing. But I stopped myself just in time. It was stupid. Her body was so badly burned you could see her blackened skeleton through the charred layer of her biosuit. I shuddered to think what her face looked like under that melted helmet.

"The head technician from Eden Five?" Dejen squinted at me like I'd grown an extra head. "You sure?"

"That's her suit." My finger trembled when I pointed at the bit of picture that was still visible on the blackened biosuit. "She painted it herself."

"What was she doing out here?" Dejen looked like he couldn't quite believe the jeep was real. I knew exactly how he felt. "And where the hell did she get a jeep from?"

"I don't know. I didn't know there were any vehicles in Eden Five. They told us—"

They told us a bunch of lies. They told us there wasn't any way to get across to the other Gardens or the Sanctuaries without walking. They told us there was no point going anywhere as all we had was biosuits and biofilters that only lasted thirty days. They told us all the vehicles from the old times were gone and we could only make things out of lumps of stinking plastic. They lied and lied and lied. I don't know why I was even surprised anymore.

"Adina, Dejen!" Tash yelled at the top of her voice. "Come over here."

My hand flew to the knife I'd stuck in my pocket, and I cursed myself for letting go of Tash's hand for even a second. She'd wandered off behind a screen of bushes while we looked at the overturned jeep, and the Gods only knew what was lurking back there.

I raced to find her, Dejen close on my heels. I guess I was expecting to see Nomalies, but what we found was even weirder.

It was Director Eshe. And she was still breathing.

CHAPTER 27

DAY TWENTY-SIX

Director Eshe was dying.

It wasn't from the biopoisons in the air that seeped through her smashed helmet, though they'd started their deadly work on her DNA the minute they found an opening in the reinforced plastic. No, it was the crash that broke her body, flinging her through the windshield when the jeep hit the water tower and shattering her spine.

She slipped in and out of consciousness through the long afternoon, blinking at us weakly when we raised our water flasks to her lips like she couldn't quite believe we were real. I knew the feeling. I was itching to ask her all the questions that were circling round and round my aching head, but Dejen shushed me, knowing the time wasn't right.

It wasn't until night had settled over the coast and the moon was high in the sky that I finally got my chance. Tash was curled up in her thermafoil bag, falling into a deep, exhausted sleep after crying herself hoarse over her lost sister. I sat next to Director Eshe the whole day, waiting for an opportunity to speak to her before she passed away. Dejen worked round us quietly, efficiently, finding a stream to fill our water filter and searching the jeep to see if there was anything we could salvage. There had once been a radio, but it was too melted and fused to be any use now. I was just starting to doze, my head nodding down onto my knees, when Director Eshe grabbed my hand.

"Adina?" she croaked. "Is that you?"

"Yes!" My head snapped up, and I squeezed her hand back, willing her not to die before she'd told me everything I needed to know. "Director Eshe, what are you doing out here?"

"I was just… just going to ask you the same thing," she wheezed. She tried to smile, but it came out as a pained wince.

"We got out through the airlock—we were up in the Dome weeding when the fire started," I said. I didn't need to remind her why we weren't at the pre-harvest assembly—I was sure she remembered.

"Good, I'm glad." Director Eshe patted my hand in a motherly way. It felt odd; she'd always been so cold before.

Dejen saw us talking. He set down the water filter he'd just refilled and came hurrying over. For a moment, I wished him a million miles away —I wanted to confess all my sins to Director Eshe and beg her forgiveness on my own. Then I remembered that Dejen already knew my secret. It didn't matter if he heard now.

"Dejen? You made it out too?" The Director peered up at him, her smile a little less forced this time.

"Yes, Director. How did you and Makena get out? The fire came up the stairs—there was no way out except through the airlock."

"Not for the workers, no," the Director sighed. "But Makena, Foreman Tafari and I were already outside that morning. We'd gone to check the water system access points three miles from the Dome. The pressure had been all wrong for days—it was dangerously high. We went during the pre-harvest festivities so we wouldn't be missed and start rumours spreading about a breakdown, but…"

She trailed off, fighting for air. We'd taken her smashed helmet off and covered her as best we could with a thermafoil bag, but there wasn't much more we could do for her, except wait and listen to her last words.

"And there was a jeep? You had transport?" Dejen prompted. I knew what he was really asking. He wanted to know just how much the Director had kept from us all.

"Just one jeep, yes," she said weakly. "It was parked out on the other side of the dust dunes. We only used it for maintenance work, to check the miles of water pipes that stretched above ground beyond the Dome. It was an almost impossible job, you know, trying to suck enough water from the earth and purify it for all those people. It was so difficult to keep the system working, the pipes were so old…"

She closed her eyes with a sigh of pain. She seemed to be almost asking for forgiveness. It was weird; *I* was the one who carried the guilt for what happened to Eden Five, not the Director.

"And when you were outside, and you saw what happened to Eden Five, that's when you drove away?" Dejen asked. He was frowning, trying to piece the story together like it was a set of anomalous data in the lab. "How come you only made it this far? We've been on foot the whole time and you were only a day ahead of us."

"We went to Eden Four first," Director Eshe said, "to warn them about the chemicals in the water system. We tried to call them, but the radio in the jeep was too old and we didn't have the parts to fix it." Her voice was starting to sound crackly, like she was sucking air through a straw filled with liquid. "They wouldn't let us in—they said we'd been out in the wilds too long with just our suits and we'd bring biopoisons into their Garden in our blood. Idiots. These things were designed to last for weeks, not days."

"So you were heading for the Sanctuary, you and Makena and Foreman Tafari?" I asked.

"Yes, where else is there?" She looked confused.

"Everywhere!" I snapped. "There's a whole world out here you didn't tell us about—a whole world filled with people who haven't had their land turned into wilds and their children turned into Nomalies."

I hadn't meant to blurt it out, but I was so sick of all the lies.

"How do you know? How did you find out...?" Director Eshe's eyes widened for a moment, then she squeezed my hand tighter. "I didn't want to hide those things from you all, but what choice did I have? I had to keep Eden Five running smoothly from day to day. What good would it do to tell you there were other continents filled with life, countries and cities and places you'd never get the chance to see? The whole of Africa's under quarantine—none of us can get out. They won't even let us anywhere near the Corporation's superfarms."

"Did Makena know about it?" I frowned. I didn't like to think of the friendly techie lying to me through her smiles as we worked side by side.

Director Eshe shook her head, even that tiny movement giving her pain. "Only the Directors of each Eden know. Only so we'd be able to get everyone ready if the quarantine was ever lifted, you understand. We took our instructions from the Sanctuaries—we were waiting for them to tell us it was safe to leave the Gardens."

"By the looks of it, we'll be waiting a few more generations yet," Dejen said, frowning at the dust-filled wastelands. "From what we've seen, the wilds might never recover."

"It's not too late for you three," Director Eshe said urgently, her hand fumbling in the pocket of her biosuit. Her fingers were numb, and Dejen had to help her extract the round disc of metal she was looking for. She pressed it into his palm. "It's a homing beacon," she gasped, forcing the words out now. "It'll let the people of Sanctuary Seven know you're on your way to the landing site, and once you get there, they'll send a helicopter for you. Eden Four radioed ahead for us to let them know we were coming, but now you three will take our places."

She smiled up at us through the pain, her eyes looking glazed in the moonlight. "They'll only let you into the Sanctuary if your blood's pure, though, so don't go taking off your biofilters, not for…for any reason…"

She had to stop for a moment, gasping for breath. I fought the urge to shake her. My nerves were rubbed so raw I had no patience, not even for her suffering. There was too little time; I had to confess now, or I'd never get the chance again.

"Director Eshe?" I held her hand so tight my own fingers ached. "I'm sorry. I'm so, so sorry I caused all of this. If I could just go back and fix it all, I'd do it in a second." My heart was in my throat as I gazed down at the dying woman. What if she didn't forgive me?

"What do you mean, girl?" The Director wheezed, her eyes half closed. "What's your fault?"

"The fire that destroyed Eden Five. It was me, I mean, it was my fault—I was the one who caused it."

Dejen was looking at me like I was completely insane. "What are you talking about, Adi?" he asked. "How could you have caused it?"

"Stop pretending you don't know!" I yelled. "I'm sick of all this pretence, all these lies! I heard you tell Otienno! I heard you say 'Something went wrong down in the lower levels. Something was broken that should've been fixed.' You've known all this time that I shirked off duty that week and didn't fix the air filter down in Level Twenty-Eight. I'm the one who blew up Eden Five. *Me*. I killed everyone."

I was panting by the time I'd finished. I'd been numb for so long, so dulled by guilt and grief I was desperate for a reaction, something loud and angry and hurtful that would make me feel alive again. Instead, all I got was confusion.

"Adi, what do you mean?" Dejen grabbed my arm. "I was talking about the water system in the basement. From what I saw on the videopods, it was obvious the Amonston Corporation had polluted the water table so badly with chemicals we'd have a hard time keeping them out of our water system pipes with our out-of-date equipment. Didn't you hear the humming down in the basement the night before we left? The water pressure was almost through the roof."

"But the air filter that needed to be fixed…" I said weakly.

"Adina," Director Eshe sighed, "how could one little air filter breaking blow up a whole Garden of Eden?"

"The pipes were filled with pure oxygen!" I protested, "Makena said it would cause an explosion if it wasn't fixed!"

"And you believed that?" the Director asked sadly.

I sucked in a great lungful of air and thought hard, all the way back to that last week in Eden Five when I'd been shirking off duty. And then I remembered. I remembered everything.

I hadn't fixed the filter because I knew if the wires blew and sparked in the oxygen tubes, the whole air system in the pipe would automatically shut down. There were safety cut-off valves built in triplicate down there, with no possibility that even a mini explosion could cause more than a hiccup in the air tubes. I'd known it all this time, but somehow I'd felt so responsible for what happened I'd forgotten all my training as a techie. The knowledge came crashing like a wave through my consciousness, drowning me in the sudden truth. It wasn't me. I hadn't destroyed Eden Five and killed everyone after all.

"It was the chemicals that seeped into the pipes, Adina." Director Eshe was struggling to get her words out. "The water pressure spiked and the chemical mix exploded. There was nothing any of us could've done."

I was gasping like a floundering fish, gulping for oxygen that just wouldn't come.

"You mean to say you believed all this time that it was your fault? That you killed everyone?" Dejen gasped. "Oh, *Adi...*"

I stood up, stumbling back on trembling legs. Then I collapsed, my whole body giving up. My mask disintegrated, my suit of cold indifference spontaneously combusting in the blinding light of truth. Before I knew it, I was sobbing so hard I couldn't breathe. All the pain and guilt and grief I'd shoved so far down into the depths came bubbling up, choking me from the inside out. I fell forward, my arms stretched out in the dust, my shoulders shaking as I was wracked with sobs that shot through my body like electric sparks.

I don't know how long I lay there crying. It felt like weeks.

I sobbed for Eden Five, my home filled with faces I'd never see again. I sobbed for my mother and father, turned to ash on the stairs before I'd got the chance to help them fix their marriage and make us into the happy family I dreamed of. I sobbed for the workers who died screaming, for the children clutching their parents' hands as they watched death approach.

I sobbed for Otienno, for his dark eyes that sent shivers down my spine, for his strong arms and confident smile that turned my knees to jelly and made the girls in Eden Five fight for his attention. I sobbed for the way he'd died, so brutal and ugly and cruel, with his lifeblood draining away into the dust.

And I sobbed for myself because I'd never see him again, and have him hold me to his chest and tell me I was beautiful.

I even sobbed for Baba Weseka and Yango, and the way they'd died so pitifully lost and clinging to each other in the wilds. I couldn't have saved them, but I cried because they were the weakest of us all and they'd never really stood a chance.

Most of all, I cried for Chiku. I cried for the little sister I hadn't realised I loved until she was lost. I cried for all the times I hurt her, all the missed opportunities to pick her up and hug her and tell her I was her big sister no matter what. I sobbed so hard for the little girl I'd treated cruelly for years that I was almost senseless by the time the tears stopped flowing.

I wailed with pain so loud and long I'm amazed Tash slept through it all. But she was exhausted, her face pressed against the thermafoil, looking almost peaceful despite the storm of emotions raging around her.

At some point while I was lying on the ground battling the demons of grief, Director Eshe died. I was half aware of Dejen sitting with her to the end, then gathering stones to cover her body the way he'd covered Baba Weseka. He didn't ignore me as he worked; I could feel his hand brush my shoulder or stroke my hair each time he passed to pick up stones, but he didn't stop to comfort me. He knew I wasn't ready yet.

Dejen knew everything.

He knew when my body stopped shaking and I sat up to wipe the snot and tears from my face that I was finally ready. He didn't say anything. He just sat down with me and pulled me close, his arms so tight around me I felt I never needed to be afraid of anything ever again. If only I'd told Dejen my secrets long before now, if only I'd been honest with the one person who'd been there for me my whole life, I'd never have needed to feel so alone. If only I hadn't given in to fear and pushed him away.

"I'm sorry," I hiccupped. "I'm sorry I was so mean to you. I thought if I told you the truth you'd hate me for destroying everything. I thought—"

"Shh," Dejen stroked my face, his fingers brushing my cheeks, my lips. "How could I ever hate you, Adi? You're my best friend. I love you more than anything."

He loved me.

There was nothing else left to say.

His lips touched mine softly, gently, kissing away the bruises of guilt and the wounds of grief. His hands cupped my head, his searching tongue sending thrilling sparks through my body when it found mine. Dejen was dangerous. But Dejen was also safe, because Dejen was home. *My* home. All the safety of Eden Five was wrapped in his arms, all the sights and sounds and smells I thought I'd lost forever were stored in the heat of his mouth and the taste of his warm breath. He was my whole world, and I loved him more than life itself.

I told him everything—everything I'd kept hidden away from him on the long journey. Instead of blaming me he just kissed me back even fiercer, our tongues and fingers fighting to pull each other nearer and close the gap of misunderstanding between us once and for all.

Later, emotionally drained, we curled up together in my sleeping bag. I lay cradled in his arms, my head nestled against his neck as I listened to his breathing slow. We were out in the wilds filled with Nomalies and mutant plants and biopoisons all trying to kill us. And yet there in that flimsy thermfoil bag, lying out in the wastelands exposed to all the elements, I'd never felt safer in all my life.

As long as I had Dejen, there was nothing in this ruined world I had left to fear.

CHAPTER 28

DAY TWENTY-SEVEN

I never believed in miracles before. Why would I? It's not like I ever thought the old Gods were real. But a few days before the end of the countdown, I changed my mind.

The day didn't start out too well. I got up early, leaving Dejen and Tash to doze a little longer in their warm bags before another day's hard trek. My guilt and grief were dulled to a low ache now, and a restless need for action and activity took their place. I took up Director Eshe's little metal homing beacon, examining it closely in the dawn light.

It was broken.

The disc must have hit the ground with force when the Director was thrown from the jeep in the crash, tearing the metal open on one side and ripping a bunch of tiny electrics loose. I went back to the burnt-out jeep to see if there was anything worth salvaging, but I wasn't hopeful. Dejen had already been over the whole vehicle once already. There was nothing. Everything was fried.

I was so lost in thought as I stood staring at the broken device that was our one link to the safety of Sanctuary Seven, I didn't hear Dejen come up behind me. He put his arms around me, drawing me close and nuzzling my neck. Somehow, with his body warming me in the cold dawn, the broken homing beacon didn't seem so much like a death sentence. Dejen was with me—there was still hope.

"What you looking at?" he asked, his breath tickling my ear.

"This." I turned and showed him the broken beacon. "The electrics are fused, and I don't have anything to replace them with."

Dejen took it from my palm and held it up to the light, frowning at it for a long moment. "There might be some more buildings between here and the landing site," he said. "Maybe we might find something in one of them we could use to repair it?"

I doubted it. We'd skirted a series of abandoned towns many miles back, their hollow shells stripped of any useful materials. As we got closer to the coast, we'd started seeing whole areas of flattened, bulldozed land that had once been the suburbs of a bustling city. The Amonston Corporation was clearly preparing more of the land for mining and polytunnel farming. We'd find nothing to help us along the way.

But I didn't say that to Dejen. I said, "Yeah, we probably will." Then I smiled and kissed the tip of his nose, revelling in the new feeling of closeness. No, it wasn't new, it was the same way I used to feel about him in Eden Five. It was the reason I went running to his lab to talk to him when I should've been working, why I told him all my secrets, and why I needed his approval and praise for every little plan I came up with on the fly. It's just that now, for the first time, I recognised the feeling for what it was: love.

Gods, I'd been so dumb my whole life.

Tash was still sad and silent as we walked along the flattened coastal land, looking back over her shoulder at the pile of stones covering Director Eshe until long after it had disappeared in the distance. She was sick of death, sick of waking up every morning wondering who she would lose next. I tried to cheer her up, telling her about all the animals she might get to see in the Sanctuary, but I couldn't shift the frown that clung to her face. At first I thought she was brooding over Chiku's death and what had happened to Director Eshe. It took a while for me to figure out it was something else entirely that was bothering her.

"Tash, Director Eshe passed away peacefully," I sighed when I saw Tash glancing over her shoulder for about the billionth time that morning. "It's no good you looking back every two minutes, she isn't going anywhere now."

Tash looked up at me, her lips pursed. One hand held mine, the other rubbed her stomach in tight, anxious circles. I was just going to ask if she had a belly ache, when I remembered what she used to do with her doll in Eden Five. Something was upsetting her, something she was afraid to talk about. I stopped and looked back carefully now, searching the distance for the thing that was making my little sister so edgy. It didn't take me long to spot it.

Something was following us along the coastal trail. Something dark and blurred that stuck to the shadows the sickly bushes and trees cast on the dead earth.

"Do you see it?" I asked Dejen. I didn't need to tell him why I'd stopped—the concern on my face was enough. He stared back into the distance for a long moment, then he nodded.

"I see it. Looks like a Nomaly."

I shuddered, my worst fears confirmed. "Should we wait and see if we can kill it together? Or should we try to outrun it?"

"I don't think we should stop any longer than we have to, we're running out of time to reach the landing site as it is," Dejen said. "And we can't be sure there's only one of them. It isn't going much faster than us—if we keep walking till nightfall we should be able to find somewhere safe where we can watch it."

There wasn't much else we could do. We took our knives from our packs, trekking on as fast as we could without stopping to rest from the midday sun. By late afternoon we were sweating and exhausted, and the thing was still gaining on us with determined, shuffling strides. Dejen and I had taken turns carrying Tash on our shoulders the whole day, and we were both exhausted. We had no choice; we had to stop and catch our breath.

"Adina, what's that?" Tash said suddenly, pointing to a gentle hill that rolled up from the coastal trail. At the top stood a squat little building with a tall tower, its sun-baked bricks crumbling with age. It was the only building I'd seen standing since the villages with the seed banks we'd passed weeks ago. I stopped and stared, wondering why on earth it hadn't been flattened with all the other buildings around it. Then I recognised the symbols carved clumsily into the worm-eaten woodwork around the door.

It was a chapel.

Dejen and I exchanged glances. He peered up at the church, back at the thing following us along the trail in the distance, then nodded.

We climbed up the little hill and stepped inside the tiny chapel. Its door was hanging on its hinges, the air inside cool and still. The windows were boarded up, the only light coming from a missing sheet of corrugated steel on the roof. One bright ray of sunlight streamed down through the dust swirling around the room that was long since cleared of the furniture and fittings I knew a church was supposed to have. At one time there had been paintings on the walls, but now the faces of angels were crumbling like they were crying at the ruin and waste of it all, the remains of their hands held up in pleading to the heavens to save us. I couldn't help thinking it was all just a bit too late.

"Stay with Tash," Dejen said. "I'll guard the door."

"We'll both guard the door," I shot back. "Just because we can only see one doesn't mean there aren't more." Besides, I couldn't just sit around waiting for that thing to ambush us in the dark. Dejen took one look at my determined face and just shrugged. He knew me too well to argue.

I settled Tash down in her sleeping bag for the night, then came to sit with Dejen by the half-open door. The sun was setting behind the chapel, the vast sea in the distance already turned blood red in the twilight. My eyes searched the trail in the fading light, but I couldn't see the thing that had been following us.

"You think it's still out there?" I whispered.

"Yes," Dejen said darkly, "and since it hasn't stopped all day, it'll be hungry."

I gulped and gripped my knife tighter.

We sat like that until the moon rose over the ocean, straining our eyes in the pale glow for signs of movement. Then at last we saw it. The creature was still on our trail, winding its way slowly up the hill towards our chapel.

"It's here!" I gasped, clutching Dejen's arm. "It's coming right at us!"

"Get ready," he ordered. "If it attacks, then go for the neck like you did last time."

I watched the thing with wide eyes as it limped towards us, searching its smudged outline for arms and legs and trying to count how many it had. It was too dark to see. All I could make out was a blur of stumbling motion that came on and on up the hill without stopping. There was something in that shape that I recognised, something in the hunched, shambling gait that reminded me of hurt and pain and a terrifying fear of rejection. A shiver ran down my spine, a tremor of such intense hope it nearly shook me in two.

"Here it comes," Dejen warned, "keep your knife up and—"

But I'd already dropped my knife.

Before Dejen could stop me, I'd burst from the chapel and run to the small shape all covered in dirt and stinking of chemicals. Even under a thick layer of mud, I'd recognise those eyes anywhere. Those eyes were my own. I picked my exhausted little shadow up and hugged her to my chest so tight I could barely breathe.

Chiku was alive. She'd come back to me.

Dejen followed close behind, ready to defend me from my own insanity. When he saw it was my sister I cradled in my arms, he nearly dropped his own knife in amazement. "Chiku? How...?"

But it didn't matter how, not to me. All that mattered was I'd been given a second chance to love the little girl I'd been so cruel to for all those years. I carried her into the chapel, tears streaming down my face and streaking the mud that coated her own.

"I thought I'd lost you!" I sobbed. "Oh, Chiku, I'm, so, so sorry!"

Tash woke up with all the noise, rubbing her eyes and blinking in confusion before giving a shriek of joy and running over to throw her arms around Chiku. We sat like that for what seemed hours, me rocking my sisters in my arms and telling them over and over how sorry I was, and them clinging to me tightly, crying out all their hurt.

It wasn't until Tash fell asleep that I realised Dejen had gone.

"Dejen?" My voice trembled in the dark. Where was he? I had sudden awful visions of him walking off into the night, sacrificing himself so that me and my sisters could take the three places in the Sanctuary's helicopter.

But he was back in moments, kneeling down by my side with the freshly filled water filter. "I went to look for a stream," he grinned. "Thought Chiku could use a bath."

"Don't think I ever want to see water again," Chiku mumbled, her head buried in my neck. But when I took her shirt off and started washing the layer of dried mud from her skin, she submitted willingly enough, watching my gentle fingers with wide eyes like she couldn't quite believe I was the same person who'd given her so many bruises in the past.

She told us in a quiet voice how she'd landed in the deep river when she fell from the cliff, fighting and struggling against the mud that carried her along for miles before she could claw her way out. She'd tried to find south-east and catch up with us, but she'd almost lost hope trekking day after day with only the water bottle she'd had in her pocket and a few protein bars to keep her going. I don't know how she managed to get so lucky, but her biofilter had stayed in place when she fell, keeping the toxins that soaked into her skin from poisoning her bloodstream. By the time she'd finished her story, she was cold and trembling and sobbing with the burden of being so alone.

I cried with her, wrapping her up in my arms and promising never to let go again. I told her all the things I'd never said to her—that she was my sister, that she was the one in my family who was most like me, that I was proud of her and that I'd look after her. I stroked her matted hair, promising I'd braid it for her when we got to the Sanctuary, promising I'd make up for all the bad things I'd done.

Chiku looked at me through all this like she was going to burst with happiness. It nearly broke my heart.

That night we drew the sleeping bags together, Chiku snuggling down with Tash while I rested my head on Dejen's chest in the other. In the dark I could hear Tash and Dejen's breathing getting softer and slower, but I knew Chiku was still awake even though her eyes were closed.

"Chiku?" I reached out across the thermafoil cover, taking her hand and squeezing it gently.

"Hmm?" She was almost asleep now, exhausted by the long trek.

"I love you." I wasn't just trying to make us both feel better. It was actually true.

"I love you too, Adina." Chiku squeezed my hand back, holding onto it as she fell into a deep sleep. All the hurt and resentment was gone.

I was forgiven.

I waited until I was sure she was as sound asleep as Tash and Dejen, then I crept from my sleeping bag, careful not to wake them, and tiptoed outside. There I sat down in the moonlight, my knife in one hand and the broken homing beacon in the other. I'd got the miracle I'd been silently praying for. I had Chiku back again; I'd been given a second chance to put right all the wrongs I'd done. My only shot at redemption was getting those three people sleeping in the chapel to Sanctuary Seven, but there was a broken homing beacon standing between me and their safety. I was a techie, and I knew how to fix it. But fixing it would mean keeping another secret from Dejen and Tash and Chiku, a secret that would break their hearts into a thousand pieces when they found out.

I took a deep breath and prised off the beacon's round metal cover. I was willing to risk breaking their hearts if it meant saving their lives. I could live with one more secret, but how long I'd live after it was discovered was anybody's guess.

CHAPTER 29

DAY THIRTY—THE COUNTDOWN ENDS

The last thing we'd been expecting to see was a city. Over the last few days of the countdown we walked through miles and miles of empty buildings, past crumbling skyscrapers and once-grand courthouses, along wide boulevards where cars had whizzed, across glittering bridges and under metal arches. I wished we had time to stop and explore, to find out first-hand how the people of the old times lived in those high-rise apartments and shopped in the marble-paved malls. But the beep of the homing beacon drew us on, reminding us we only had a few days left on our biofilters. We wouldn't die straight away once they packed up, of course, but Director Eshe's warning ran constantly through my head.

They'll only let you into the Sanctuary if your blood's pure, though, so don't go taking off your biofilters, not for any reason.

But I kept her warning to myself, wrapping it up tight and hiding it away with my secret. The others would find out soon enough, but I didn't want to spoil the closeness we shared on the final days of the countdown.

They were strange, those last few days we trekked to the landing site. Eden Five was gone, our home was in ashes, and our whole world was a lie. And yet for three whole days I felt almost happy. No, not happy exactly—it's not like the memories of everything that had happened didn't still make me want to cry for all we'd lost. It's more that I was finally at peace.

I held Chiku's hand the whole way, telling her all the stories about our parents and life in Eden Five she would've known if we'd only treated her as one of the family. I told her when she was born I wanted to take her home and look after her like she was my very own baby. I told her about the time I got thrown out of her nursery when I brought her jelly from the canteen when she was three, and instead of eating it she used it as face paint. I told her about the time my father sat up every night for a month making her a model aeroplane from offcuts that he'd collected from the factory assembly line. She didn't get the model in the end—I was jealous of the time he'd spent on it and complained so much my father gave it to Tash instead—but Chiku was happy to hear about the gift and the effort that had gone into making it all the same.

"I used to wonder whether we'd be able to make aeroplanes one day with the 3D printers," I smiled at Chiku as we neared the landing site on the last day. "Real planes we could fly away in to a new world with natural gardens out in the open instead of under glass."

"Yeah, me too." Chiku nodded. "I wish I could be a pilot. Do you think if they have a helicopter in Sanctuary Seven I could be a pilot one day?"

Her dark brown eyes were so eager, so willing to trust me now that she knew I'd never hurt her again.

"I think you're smart enough to be anything you want," I told her, ruffling her messy hair and stroking her cheek. "You could be a pilot, or a scientist, or a builder, or maybe even a techie like me."

"You think?" Chiku's face glowed with pleasure, and she grinned up at Tash, who was perched high on Dejen's shoulders. "Hey, Tash, if I'm a pilot when I'm older, you wanna come fly over the sea with me to all the other places in the story books?"

"Yes!" Tash nodded eagerly. "Long as I get a shot at flying too."

Dejen smiled at me. "You've turned out to be not such a bad influence on your sisters after all. I can't believe you missed so much school and still ended up clever enough to fix a homing beacon we didn't have the parts for." He looked down at the little metal disc beeping in my hand and shook his head in wonder.

My guts twisted at that. Gods, I hated lying to Dejen. I'd told him I'd managed to put it back together by joining the bits of wire and electronic parts that hadn't been burnt. He hadn't seen the scrambled mess the crash had made of the homing beacon's insides. He had no idea what fixing that little disc had cost me.

"Hey!" Tash shouted suddenly. "Look! Is that the landing site?"

We cleared the last of the buildings and stood looking out over the empty harbour and the wide concrete loading docks that bordered the sea. There on the ground in front of us, drawn in bright red paint on the stone, was a giant cross surrounded by a crescent moon. We stood blinking at each other in the sunlight, barely daring to believe we'd all made it.

"It is, isn't it?" Tash asked again, less certain this time.

I pulled out the map and looked. There it was on the paper—a red cross and crescent moon. We'd made it. "This is it," I gasped. "This is the landing site."

Tash slid down from Dejen's shoulders and Chiku let go of my hand. They ran for the giant cross, dancing across the paint lines and whooping for joy.

"What do we do now?" Dejen asked, looking confused now there was no more need for action.

"Now we wait," I said, sounding strangely sure despite my misgivings. "They'll be tracking the homing beacon's coordinates. Now we've reached the landing site they'll send their helicopter for us."

"We made it just in time," Dejen sighed in relief, fingering the small metal device at the base of his neck. "One more day and our biofilters would've given out. Poor Baba Weseka— even if he'd made it this far, they wouldn't have taken him to the Sanctuary with his mutated blood. Gods, he was only out in the wilds that day for a few hours without a biofilter, and look what the toxins did to him."

I shuddered. I didn't want to think about what the biopoisons in the air out here did to people who didn't have biofilter protection. Dejen felt me shiver and put his arm around me, thinking I was cold.

"Do you think it was the mutations that caused his fits?" he asked, still thinking about Baba Weseka. "You think maybe his visions were something to do with the poisons changing his DNA somehow?"

"I don't know," I shrugged. "I don't think we'll ever know. Maybe he was just born different—some of the other old people said he always was a bit weird, even before he ran off. Anyway," I tried to change the subject, "I'm pretty sure you'll get all the answers to every question you can think of when you get to the Sanctuary."

Dejen grinned at that and gazed out to sea longingly. He didn't see the tears I quickly blinked away before he looked back at me.

We sat on the steps leading down to the harbour, enjoying the fresh breath of the sea breeze that cooled our faces in the hot sun. The waves swept against the docks with a low bubbling sound that was filled with the simmer of expectation and the soft hiss of the unknown. It all felt so peaceful, so natural and right after so much had gone wrong, that I wanted to stop time and sit there forever with Dejen and my sisters in the fading sun.

But then I heard the low hum from the distance, and I knew it was all coming to an end.

We heard the helicopter long before we saw it, straining our eyes against the shimmer of sunlight on the wide stretch of sea. Soon a small speck appeared on the horizon, growing bigger with each passing moment. At first Tash and Chiku jumped up and down on the edge of the dock, waving their arms and shouting in excitement. But when the helicopter approached, looming larger overhead, they drew back in fear, coming to stand with me and Dejen and watching the huge machine with wide eyes.

I kissed Dejen then, before the helicopter landed. I needed to tell him how I felt one last time. "I love you," I whispered urgently in his ear. "I'll always love you no matter what."

"Adi, what do you mean?" He looked at me all confused and uncomprehending, like I'd said something strange. He knew me well enough to hear when I was hiding something. But the helicopter had landed, swirling up dust with its great blades, and we turned to watch the door slide open, half afraid of what would emerge.

Four people in brown biosuits clambered out, ducking under the whirling blades and marching over to where we stood on the steps. They looked us up and down, and I got a glimpse of a woman's face and three men's behind their thick helmets.

"Are you the ones Eden Four called us about?" the woman asked, pressing the radio at the side of her helmet, her voice coming out all robotic through the speakers.

"No, that was our director and a couple of our workgroup heads," Dejen said. "They died. We're the last survivors from Eden Five."

"You've all still got your biofilters in place?"

Dejen nodded. "We haven't taken them off for a second."

One of the men stepped up to look, taking out a little medical scanning device and running it over Dejen's filter. "He's clean," he nodded, stooping down to check Tash's filter.

"There were only supposed to be three," one of the other men said. "We can't take more than three. We don't have the fuel."

"The girls are only kids!" Dejen protested. "Both of them together wouldn't add up to an adult's weight."

The man exchanged glances with the woman who was in charge. She looked at the girls, back at the helicopter, then nodded.

Dejen let out a long sigh of relief. Gods, I hated being the one to break his heart all over again. But now I had no choice. The man with the medical device had checked my sisters and cleared them for riding in the helicopter. Now he was heading over to me. I tensed as he ran the scanner up and down my body. A red light lit up on the read-out panel. He scanned me again, checked the result, then shook his head.

"Your blood's mutated," he frowned. "We can't take you to the Sanctuary. Sorry."

My breath caught in my throat. I'd known this was coming, but now the reality hit me like a blow to the gut and I felt my knees go weak. "My biofilter's only been off for a few days," I said, trying to keep my voice from trembling. "You have medicine at the Sanctuary—can't you treat me there to stop the mutation in my blood from spreading?"

"No one gets into the Sanctuary without pure blood," the woman said briskly, stepping forward to check the read-out on the medical scanner. "We can take your friends, but you have to stay. Those are the rules."

The silence that followed seemed to stretch on for all eternity.

"Adi, what the hell?" Dejen gasped. It came out all choked, like he was being strangled by the secret I'd kept from him.

"I'm so sorry, Dejen," I said in a rush, "but I needed to get the homing beacon working and I didn't have the parts. The only place I knew I could get electronics that would work was my biofilter."

"But the green light's still on!" Dejen protested, as though the little green diode could contradict everything I was saying that he didn't want to hear.

I pulled the filter from my neck. It slid out easily, the needles dead and useless. I held it up, showing him where I'd stuck a little piece of wire to keep the light jammed on.

"I didn't want to worry you. Not when there was no other way to get the beacon working. Oh, Dejen, don't look at me like that!" I wanted to cry at the way his face crumbled, but I had to stay strong for the sake of my sisters.

"It's only been a couple of days," Dejen said desperately to the people in the biosuits who had already taken Tash and Chiku by the hand and were leading them to the helicopter. "Any damage the biopoisons have done can be stopped with the right medicine."

"The damage was done the minute she switched the filter off," one of the men said. "Sorry, but there's nothing we can do. We can't let anyone into the Sanctuary if their blood isn't pure—our ecosystem's too carefully balanced for that. It's too risky."

"Adina?" Tash turned back as she was hustled to the helicopter by the people in suits, the look in Dejen's eyes frightening her. "Aren't you coming?"

There was nothing I could do now. No amount of pleading was going to save me. I took a shaky breath and used the last of my strength to run and give Tash and Chiku a quick hug. "Of course I'm coming," I smiled weakly. "They don't have room for more than three at a time, that's all. I'll wait here—they'll come back for me when they've dropped you three off."

"I'll wait here with you." Chiku tried to let go of the woman who held her hand, but the woman shook her head and pointed at the humming helicopter.

"We're wasting fuel, we have to get going," she said.

"Go, I'll be along later," I said, stepping back and trying not to cry when the worried faces of my sisters disappeared behind the helicopter's doors.

Dejen was struggling with the two men on the steps who were trying to pull him towards the helicopter. "I'm not going without Adina!" he cried. "Let go of me!"

The man with the medical kit caught my eye through his helmet, and I nodded, distracting Dejen while he slipped a gloved hand into his bag.

"Dejen, listen to me!" I reached out for my best friend, holding his face in my hands. "I need you to be the strong one now. I need you to go to Sanctuary Seven and look after my sisters for me. I need to know they're being taken care of, and you're the only one I can trust to do it."

"I'm not leaving you out in the wilds on your own, Adi!" Dejen said, gripping my arms. "How could you think I would? I love you!"

But just then, the man with the medical bag pressed his syringe to Dejen's neck. Dejen's eyes widened for a second, then his grip on my arms loosened. I could feel him slipping away from me, and I fought the urge to hold on.

I knew if I wanted to save him I had to let him go.

"Take care of Chiku and Tash," I whispered as he fell back against the men in suits. "And take care of yourself. I love you. Always."

"Adi, no…" Dejen eyes glazed over, but I could see the panic welling up behind the closing lids.

I walked away to the top of the steps, my heart screaming at my head not to be so cruel, not to let the others go while I stayed behind. But I didn't have a choice. I'd sacrificed my own biofilter to fix the homing beacon, giving up my chance to make it to the safety of Sanctuary Seven. That was my secret.

I watched the men half carry Dejen to the helicopter, lifting him aboard and pulling the doors closed behind them. They didn't even say goodbye, those people in the biosuits. They just left me behind to rot with the rest of the waste in the African wilds. I tried not to care, but my throat was raw with the effort not to cry, my head aching and my eyes stinging as I watched the helicopter take off and hover for a moment above me.

I fought down the rising panic, searching the plastiglass windows for one last glimpse of Dejen and my sisters before they were taken from me forever. But they were gone in an instant, the helicopter's thrumming blades cutting through the air as it headed away across the sea. My legs collapsed beneath me, and I sat down heavily on the concrete, the fading adrenaline rush leaving me cold and shaking.

I didn't know how long I had left to live, whether I'd succumb to the biopoisons quickly and die in my sleep, or whether I'd linger on and suffer for weeks like Yango. I didn't know what I'd do now—whether I'd just sit here and wait for the end or go and explore the ruined city with the short time I had left on this earth. I didn't know whether I'd be eaten by Nomalies, or whether it was hunger and thirst that would get to me first.

But there was one thing I knew for certain.

The night was closing in, and I was alone in the wilds— the last survivor of Eden Five. I was scared and trembling with cold now that the sun was setting over the wastelands. I had nothing to warm me but the small flicker of triumph glowing in my heart, which was scarred by so much loss. I'd given up everything, but found my redemption out here on the edge of the world. The certainty of the truth was my shield, my blanket, and I'd wrap it around me tight until it became my funeral shroud.

The truth was, I hadn't killed fourteen thousand seven hundred and fifty-six people.

No.

I'd saved the lives of three.

ACKNOWLEDGEMENTS

This is a particularly special novel for me – a YA debut that was many years in the making. Many people have given me support and encouragement along the way, and as always, my mother and brother Martin are top of the list of people I have to thank for helping make my dreams of becoming an author a reality. Friends and family – too numerous to thank individually – have been there for me every step of the way along my writing journey, and I can't thank them enough.

I wish I could list each and every one of my fellow authors who have been such a wonderful source of encouragement over the last five years and more, but that would require a whole new chapter added to this book! Let me say simply that I deeply appreciate their support – both in person and online – and I'm very aware of how much the success of my novels is down to lovely writers who have recommended me for school visits and festivals, bought and reviewed my books, and championed my work online. Huge thanks to them all.

Special thanks go to the team at Neem Tree Press for believing in my books and putting their hearts and souls into the publication process to give each one the best possible start in life. They really have set a very high industry standard for author-publisher working relationships, and I very much appreciate their commitment to supporting not just my individual novels, but my ongoing career as a writer.

I began my writing journey as a reader, but having taught overseas for a number of years, I know that not all children have the opportunity to engage with literature from a young age. I volunteer as Patron of Reading and a trustee with CharChar Literacy, a wonderful education charity which works to train teachers in Malawi in phonics education to ensure that their pupils get the best possible grounding in reading from the first years of primary school. In order to support their work helping the children of Malawi to achieve their reading potential,

20% of the author royalties for this novel will be donated to CharChar Literacy.

ABOUT THE AUTHOR

Victoria Williamson is an award-winning children's author and primary school teacher from Scotland. She has worked for four years as a teacher and a teacher trainer with VSO in Africa. She has also volunteered as a reading tutor with The Book Bus charity in Zambia and is now a Patron of Reading with CharChar Literacy to promote early years phonics teaching in Malawi. Victoria is passionate about creating inclusive worlds in her novels where all children can see themselves reflected.

Discover more books by Victoria Williamson:

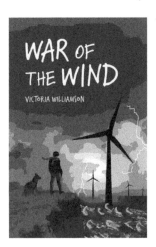

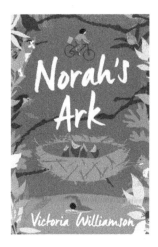